DOUBLE THREAT IN RIPLEY GROVE

DOUBLE THREAT IN RIPLEY GROVE

A RIPLEY GROVE MYSTERY, BOOK 1

SHIRLEY WORLEY

Book and cover design by eBook Prep
www.ebookprep.com

January, 2020
ISBN: 978-1-64457-113-2

ePublishing Works!
644 Shrewsbury Commons Ave
Ste 249
Shrewsbury PA 17361
United States of America

www.epublishingworks.com
Phone: 866-846-5123

ACKNOWLEDGMENTS

I give a round of applause to my friends and supporters. Some were brave enough to read this manuscript in its early stages, while others offered words of encouragement. I dare not mention each person by name, lest I leave someone out. You know who you are.

My sincerest gratitude goes to fellow author, Jeanne Glidewell, for her friendship, inspiration, support and guidance. Along with Jeanne, my husband Bert (who often holds more confidence in my writing abilities than I do), Rachel Heueisen, and Marla Worley were exceptional proofreaders.

Thanks to the past and current members of my critique group: Larry Hightower, Mike Flynn, Judy Swofford, and Jane Perry. I have learned so much from you. Your keen eyes and suggestions make me a better writer.

My deepest appreciation goes to Brian Paules, of ePublishing Works, and Nina Paules, of eBook Prep, for providing this great opportunity and putting their faith in me.

I cannot forget those nearest and dearest to my heart—my family. Thank you for listening to me ramble, answering questions, coming to my aid with computer and technical help, and offering your love and support.

To my husband, Bert, my forever love.

PROLOGUE

It was well after dark when he headed toward home, the traffic practically non-existent, the night peaceful. Despite the calm outside, his pulse hammered against his temples with every heartbeat, and his clenched jaw muscles ached. He slammed a fist on the steering wheel, as though the self-inflicted pain would provide an answer to his problem.

That "problem" happened to be a woman, the kind of woman most men would love to dream about. Not him. To him, she had become his worst nightmare. Like a typical blonde, she had everyone eating out of her hand. But it was all an act. Underneath that sweet façade, she was conniving, calculating and shrewd.

As he passed the familiar office building, a soft light from deep within drew his attention. His eyes widened, surprised to see her black Jeep parked out front.

Maybe it's time to settle this, once and for all.

He expected the look of shock on her face when he entered the office. The element of surprise often gave him the upper hand, but not this time. She wasn't one to back down. The fact that she squared her shoulders, tipped her chin up, and tried her best to intimidate him fed his anger.

They argued, long and hard, until he was out of his mind, out of options, and out of control. In a fit of blind rage, he pulled a knife from his pocket. A terrifying scream echoed in the room. He stepped back as she clutched her chest and crumpled to the floor. The evidence of his deed seeped between her fingers, the horror of it written on her face.

Minutes ticked by as his anger turned to fear, then panic. He paced the floor, wondering what to do next. Her haunting blue eyes followed his every step, her voice rasping out a plea for help. He raked a hand through his hair, certain he couldn't allow his name to cross her lips again. *There's only one thing to do. I have no other choice.* He knelt beside her, the knife gripped tightly in his hand.

The sound of a door swooshed open and footsteps entered the building.

He froze. *What the—*

He held his breath, hoping whoever it was didn't plan on staying. When a desk lamp clicked on, casting a faint light down the dark hallway, he knew that wouldn't be the case. The soft thump of something tossed onto a desk seemed to echo in the stillness—a purse, maybe? A few seconds later, a female voice called out, announcing her presence.

Wait, she could be the answer to my problem. At this point, what's one more dead body? Yeah, this might work. The police will think an argument between the two women got out of hand.

From the sound of the footsteps, she was headed his direction, completely unaware of the grisly scene she would find. He quickly stood, careful not to make a sound. Using the large potted plant by the door to shield him from view, he waited for his next victim to arrive.

ONE

Two Weeks Earlier

I *can't believe Mom's gone. It's just me and Dad now. Not that he cares.*

From the passenger seat of her boyfriend's truck, Cecilia Winslow watched the hearse up ahead make a right turn and lead the procession into the cemetery. Her father, Jack Parker, rode alone in the family car provided by the funeral home. That he never bothered asking her to accompany him spoke volumes about their relationship.

She shouldn't have been surprised by the snub. Jack Parker was her father—legally, but not by birth. He had married her widowed mother and formally adopted CiCi at the age of three. He'd been the only father she'd ever known. Unfortunately, their loving relationship disintegrated during her teen years and became almost non-existent after high school. Avoiding him entirely proved to be impossible but taking back her birth name after her divorce allowed her an emotional degree of separation. Today, she felt that separation more than ever, and it hurt.

Overhead, the sky darkened, and the clouds threatened rain.

The gloom weighed heavy on her grieving heart. A tear trickled down her cheek, followed by another.

Chad Cooper, her thirty-one-year-old boyfriend, reached over and gently squeezed her hand. "You okay, CiCi?"

"I'm fine," she said, giving him a half-hearted smile. "Did I tell you how much I appreciate you being here today?" Having dated the Ripley Grove detective exclusively for the last eight months, she knew getting unscheduled time off was often difficult.

"I'll always be here for you, hon. I only wish there was more I could do." When they arrived at the gravesite, he pulled to the side of the road and shut off the engine.

"I knew this day was coming, but…"

He sighed. "But knowing doesn't make it any less painful."

After the casket had been eased into place, they walked hand-in-hand across the manicured grounds to the funeral tent and took seats on the front row. Her father sat at the opposite end, staring straight ahead, refusing to even look in her direction.

Pastor Young officiated, reading scripture passages and her mother's favorite poem. A hymn and a prayer ended the brief service. Those seated in the first row filed by the casket and then stood nearby to accept condolences from those who had come to pay their final respects.

Lightning crackled in the sky. Seconds later, a clap of thunder rumbled overhead. A slight wind tugged at the tent and gentle rain-drops began to fall. The small crowd dispersed as the April shower pelted the cemetery grounds.

"Stay here," Chad said, putting a gentle hand on her shoulder. "I'm going to pull the truck up close, so you won't have to walk through any puddles." Off he dashed, the rain spotting the jacket of his suit.

CiCi brushed a long strand of wavy, dark blonde hair over her shoulder and turned to say a last goodbye. With tears threatening to spill, she reached out and touched her mother's rose-tinted casket. Her hands trembled as she plucked a keepsake flower from the floral spray.

"I'm going to miss her."

Startled by the rough but familiar voice behind her, she spun around. Standing a bit too close for comfort, her father towered over her with a grief-stricken look on his face. Whether his bloodshot eyes were a result of crying or liquid "pain relief", she didn't know.

"I'll miss her, too," she stammered, surprised he had even spoken to her.

"I bet you will, probably as much as the money she was always throwing at you," he spat. "A car for graduation, money to pay for college. She spoiled you rotten for years."

She took a step back from the spiteful words. "That's a hateful thing to say. I don't expect to benefit from her death if that's what you're worried about. The memories I have are enough."

"Ah, I'm guessing you got a letter about settling her assets. Don't know what made Helen contact a lawyer without telling me, especially since everything she owned belongs to me now."

"The only thing I want is my grandmother's wedding ring. I'm sure you've seen it—a single band with a large diamond and two deep blue sapphires."

He crossed his arms over his chest and sneered with satisfaction. "Like I said, everything belongs to me now. There's no reason for you to meet with the lawyer. It'll just be a waste of your time."

Chad suddenly appeared at her side and cast a questioning glance between the two. He wrapped a protective arm around her shoulder. "Ready to go?"

At the lawyer's office the following Thursday, CiCi had her pick of four leather chairs facing a large mahogany desk. Choosing one at the far end, she perched on the edge of the seat and smoothed a non-existent wrinkle from her slacks. The soft tap, tap, tap of her shoe against the carpet reflected her anxiety.

The door to the office swung open, and a gentleman in his mid-thirties with sandy-colored hair entered the room. She guessed him to be the younger Browning of the Browning, Browning and Culp legal team. Upon a closer look, she recalled seeing him around town, but they'd never had an occasion to meet.

"Good morning, Miss Winslow. I'm Dennis Browning, your mother's attorney. We'll probably be seeing a lot of each other in the coming months, so please, call me Dennis."

She shook his outstretched hand. Though puzzled by the comment, his charming smile and warm brown eyes immediately put her at ease. "Please to meet you, Dennis. My friends call me CiCi."

"Sorry to be late. Saundra, my receptionist, introduced me to your friend in the waiting room." He chuckled and shook his head. "Saundra's determined to see me married before she retires."

"Ah, yes, Megan. We've been close friends since middle school. She offered to tag along for moral support."

"Good friends like that are hard to find." He offered her a cup of coffee, which she declined. After pouring himself a cup, he removed his suit jacket and draped it over the back of his chair before taking a seat. "Shall we get started?"

"Please, because I'm curious as to why I'm here. I assume every-thing my mother owned would now belong to my dad. Have you met with him yet?"

Dennis nodded. "He left here about thirty minutes ago."

"How was he?"

Dennis hesitated. "A bit difficult. Challenging, perhaps."

Though not spelled out in so many words, she knew he meant her dad had been drinking.

"I try not to judge. Everyone grieves the loss of a spouse in their own way. At least he was smart enough to have a friend drive him." He took a sip of coffee and opened a folder on his desk. "Enough about your father. Let's focus on Cecilia Winslow."

A rap sounded on the door and Sandra appeared. "Sorry to interrupt. If you don't have anything pressing for me to do, I thought I'd pop over to the post office and mail those documents you signed earlier."

"That's fine. And would you leave the door open? It's a bit stuffy in here."

"Sure thing. Be back in a jiffy."

"Now, where was I?" Dennis checked the notes in his folder, then pulled a small box covered in blue velvet from a desk drawer and slid it across the desktop.

CiCi's heart jumped with excitement. *Grandma's ring? Please, please, let it be her ring.* She gingerly picked up the box, opened the lid, and let out a small gasp of surprise when she saw the simple diamond pendant on a delicate silver chain. It was the necklace her mother had worn the day she married Cecil Winslow, CiCi's biological father and namesake. Her joy was laced with disappointment. Though thrilled to have her mother's necklace, it was her grandmother's wedding ring she wanted. She smiled nonetheless, grateful to have received such a personal gift. She stood and turned to leave. "Thank you, Mr. Browning."

"Wait. Where are you going?"

"Aren't we finished?"

"Heavens, no. And I suggest you sit, because what I'm about to tell you is certain to come as a shock." Dennis paused, took another drink, and eyed her over the rim of his mug.

With her curiosity sufficiently piqued, she sat.

"Perhaps things will make more sense if I give you a little background first. Agnes and Nathan Zimmer, Helen's parents, accumulated a small fortune over their lifetime. After Nathan's death, your parents sold their home and moved to the farm in order to take care of Agnes during her final years. However, when Agnes died four years ago, her assets passed on to Helen, her only daughter. Helen, and Helen alone, inherited the entire estate."

CiCi frowned. "You must be mistaken. There is no fortune, unless you count the farmhouse and surrounding ninety acres of prime Kansas farmland."

A thump sounded in the hallway, momentarily diverting the attorney's attention away from his client. "Saundra? Did you forget something?" Silence answered his question. He shrugged and continued. "I'm sorry, CiCi, but that's not true. Your mother and her parents were quite well-off."

CiCi's eyes widened and she remained silent, too dumbstruck to speak. After a few seconds, she said, "To say I'm shocked would be an understatement. I honestly don't know what to say. I imagine my father was thrilled with the news."

"Not exactly. Jack received everything he expected to receive after his wife's death. The vehicles, the funds in their joint checking and savings accounts, a small life insurance policy. Everything he expected, but the house and land. Helen also provided him with a monthly allowance of one thousand dollars."

"That's all? How can that be?"

"Shortly before her death, your grandmother amended her will and trust in such a way that Helen had sole use of the estate and could never leave any of the family fortune to Jack, either directly or indirectly. You are now the executor of that estate, and there are similar strings attached," he said. "Helen forbids you to give any of the inherited assets, or monetary value gained from the sale of such, to Jack Parker, or your ex-husband, Richard Davenport. Should you decide not to comply with those stipulations, the assets are to be donated to a designated charity."

"What about the house and land?"

"The farmhouse and surrounding acreage belong to you." Dennis smiled and closed the folder. "Your mother has requested you allow your father to remain in the house for the next two years, free of charge. The arrangement can be re-evaluated after that on a yearly basis, if you so desire. The decision is totally up to you."

"Of course, he can stay. I never expected otherwise," she stammered. From the corner of her eye, she thought she'd seen a shadow in the hallway. When she turned to look, it had disappeared. *I must be imagining things.*

"CiCi, it will be your responsibility to carry out your mother's wishes. The individual bank accounts and other investments are payable on death. But, the farmhouse, acreage and the numerous rental properties are titled in the name of the trust, and you are listed as the only beneficiary. Any items not put into the trust must go through probate, which will take five months, give or take. I'll start by getting the legal notices in the paper. Your mother has paid our firm in advance to help transfer the paperwork, titles, and such into your name and provide any guidance you need."

Rental properties? Investments? What was he talking about? "May I ask how much the estate is worth?"

"Roughly three million dollars, and I would advise you to keep that information under wraps for the time being."

She stared at the attorney, who let the amount roll off his tongue as though he were talking about the price of a gallon of milk. Her mouth opened, but words failed to form. It was a sizable inheritance for someone who hadn't yet turned thirty.

"There are a lot of details to be ironed out. I'll go over them with you one on one, hopefully beginning next week." Dennis drained the remaining coffee in his cup. "I know this has been a lot to process, but do you have any questions?"

The unexpected windfall left her dazed. Dennis picked up a pen and his hand hovered over a legal pad in anticipation of her questions. Suddenly, a frown formed on the attorney's face, and she hesitantly followed his gaze. Her dad stood in the doorway, and from the looks of him, she immediately knew the meeting was about to take a turn for the worse.

TWO

CiCi and Dennis stood after taking in her father's flushed face flushed and the bulging veins in his neck. His eyes were filled with anger, and his large hands clenched into fists.

"Dad! What are you doing here?" she asked.

"Mr. Parker, I'm going to have to ask you to leave," Dennis said firmly.

Her father lumbered into the room. His unkempt hair needed a trim, and his rugged face hadn't seen a razor in days. Standing at six foot two, his sturdy build, plaid button-up shirt, faded jeans, and well-worn boots were reminiscent of Paul Bunyan. Grease stained his calloused hands, a hazard of owning and operating an auto mechanic shop. As usual, he wore the faint smell of liquor the way most men wore aftershave.

CiCi met his cold gaze with more courage than she felt. "Wait, were you in the hallway, listening to our private conversation?"

"Yeah, I listened. What of it?" he snarled. "When I heard Helen left me a thousand dollars a month and someone else owned my house, I knew something wasn't right. That's why I came back. I knew you'd have answers. Looks like you have the answers, my house, *and* my money."

"I'm as surprised as you. I knew nothing about the estate."

"So you say," he growled. "And yet, she left it all to you. If you and your shyster lawyer think I'm going to take this lying down, you're wrong."

CiCi took a step back as Jack's rage boiled to the surface and erupted. He flung a chair across the room as if it were a toy. Lunging forward with the fierceness of a pit bull, he grabbed a fistful of her blouse and slammed her against the wall. Fear rose in her throat like bile. His hate-filled eyes were inches from her face, the smell of booze evident on his breath.

"Your lies and scheming ways turned her against me, you conniving bloodsucker!"

Dennis charged from behind his desk as Jack wrapped a massive hand around her neck.

"Dad, please don't—"

"That farm and money belongs to me. *Me*, not you! I'm going to get it back one way or another. You hear me?"

Anger seeped from his pores. His grip tightened, making it impossible for her to answer. She gasped for air. Black dots began to flash before her eyes as Dennis fought to pry Jack's hands from her neck.

Gary Culp, another attorney with the law firm, burst into the room and joined the fight. Jack's grip loosened, and she crumpled to the floor. The men continued to brawl. Chairs toppled, a lamp fell from the desk, papers fluttered to the floor. Eventually, the two attorneys pinned Jack against the far wall. The commotion brought Megan rushing into the room. She dialed 9-1-1, and then helped CiCi into a nearby chair.

Jack gained a second wind, threw the two men aside, and staggered from the office. Gary followed to make sure Jack left the premises. When Gary returned several minutes later, two police officers were with him. One officer took statements from Dennis and CiCi, while another photographed the injuries to her neck. After they had finished, Saundra, who had returned from her errands, appeared with an ice pack for CiCi's neck and suggested Megan drive her home.

With trembling hands, CiCi dug in her purse and handed Megan the keys. Megan left, but returned far too quickly. She pulled an officer aside and whispered into his ear. He frowned, glanced over at CiCi, and then followed Megan outside. When they returned, Megan tried but failed to hide her irritation.

CiCi straightened. "Megan, what's wrong?"

Megan looked at the officer, then back at CiCi. "Someone slashed the tires on your Jeep."

CiCi cradled her head in her hands. Her mother's illness, death, and funeral had wreaked havoc with her emotions over the last several months. Her dad's assault brought painful memories to the surface, but the vandalism to her vehicle proved to be the tipping point. Overwhelmed, she collapsed into uncontrollable sobs.

CiCi sank into the luxurious leather seating of Dennis' Lexus, leaned her head back, and held an ice pack to her throat. Megan sat stunned in the back seat, while Dennis cast furtive glances in CiCi's direction as he drove. She gave him a weak smile and slipped on a pair of navy sunglasses. If she hadn't known better, she might've thought his swollen lip, torn shirt, and scraped knuckles were the result of a bar fight. "I'm fine. Quit worrying. The worst of it is over," she said, the words sounding flat and distant.

"I'm better equipped to take on a verbal fight in the courtroom than a knock-down-drag-out fight in my office," he admitted. "I'm sorry, CiCi. I should have investigated the moment I heard something in the hallway. I never thought he'd show up like that."

Megan sat forward. "You mean neither of you asked him to come? I saw him storm through the lobby, but assumed he'd been called in to sign some documents."

"No, he wasn't invited," CiCi replied. "Dennis, it wasn't your fault, and I certainly don't hold you responsible. I'm just grateful you and Gary were there."

She shifted the ice pack, then closed her eyes to discourage any further conversation. As they drove across town, the familiar sounds that filtered through the open window told her exactly the route he had chosen. A school bell cut through children's laughter to give a warning that recess was over. She smiled and wondered if Mrs. Allen still taught first grade. The car thumped its way across the railroad tracks and past a noisy road crew. From the smell alone, she knew they were putting down hot asphalt on the street. Twelve bongs resonated from the clock tower as they drove through the town square. Only four more blocks and she would be home.

Dennis parked in front of her residence, the end unit in a small complex of older townhomes at the corner of Pine and Locust. Suite Oasis consisted of three two-story buildings—two faced Pine Street, and one faced Locust. Each building contained four townhouses. Those on Locust were rentals, and those on Pine, where CiCi lived, were owned by the tenants. Ever the gentleman, Dennis got out and escorted her to the door. Megan followed a few steps behind.

CiCi groaned the moment she saw Chad waiting patiently on the porch. After the morning's excitement, she'd completely forgotten they had a lunch date. Fingering her mussed hair into place, she forced her lips into a smile. A walking disaster was not the look she wanted to project.

As Chad took in her mascara-streaked cheeks, scratched neck, and torn blouse, the sexy grin fell from his face. His six-foot frame sprang from the chair and rushed to her side.

"Don't worry. I'm fine," she said, walking into his open arms.

"What happened?" he asked.

"Chad, this is Dennis Browning, my attorney. If you don't mind, I'll let him tell you the *basics* while I get changed." She took off her sunglasses and glanced at Dennis, who nodded with understanding.

Chad took the keys from her trembling hand, unlocked the door, and stepped aside. Entering first, CiCi immediately excused herself and took the stairs to the second floor. She passed through the master bedroom and went straight to the adjoining bathroom, where she swallowed a couple of aspirin and examined her reflection in the mirror. There was little she could do about the bruises starting to form on her neck, or the long scratches. She scrubbed her face, then applied a light dusting of mineral powder and a swipe of lip gloss. As she ran a brush through her tangled hair, there was a light knock on the bedroom door.

"Come in," she called.

Megan entered and leaned against the bathroom doorway, her arms crossed and a frown on her face. "Seriously? You're not going out to lunch after what happened this morning, are you? That'd be crazy! Look at you. You're still shaking," she said, pointing to the brush in CiCi's hand. "What happened in that meeting?"

CiCi took a deep breath, determined to shake off the jittery feeling. She wasn't about to admit how rattled she still felt, and she definitely wasn't going to talk about her dad. "Let's not make a big deal over it. I'm fine. It's over and done." Her voice wavered and gave proof that she harbored a few doubts.

"Do you really think Chad will think it's over? My brother's a detective through and through. He'll look into the matter whether you want him to or not."

CiCi sighed, knowing Megan was probably right. After changing clothes, they went downstairs. Chad and Dennis stood and their muffled conversation stopped the moment the two women entered the room. Chad's eyes were clouded with worry and anger. From the way he watched her every move, it was obvious Dennis had given an accounting of the morning's events.

"Again, I can't tell you how sorry I am," Dennis said as he prepared to leave. "I'll be available should you need any legal counsel. I'll have Saundra set up an appointment with you in the next week or so to discuss matters concerning the estate. Chad, it was a pleasure to meet you." Dennis shook Chad's hand, then turned to Megan. "May I walk you to your vehicle?"

"I'd like that very much," Megan said. The two said their goodbyes and left.

"A hummingbird has nothing on Megan when she flutters those eyelashes." CiCi chuckled and turned. Chad stood so close, she could see the flecks in his deep-set brown eyes—eyes that were full of concern. Brushing her hair over one shoulder, he examined the scratches and bruises on her neck. His extra six inches in height worked to his advantage as his gaze traveled past her collarbone and down to the hint of cleavage showing above the scooped neckline of her T-shirt. Despite his worry, he smiled in appreciation. She held her breath, not wanting to interrupt the moment. He wrapped his arms around her and pulled her close.

Never one to resist a hug, she laid her head against his chest and listened to the steady beat of his heart. He was a good man, a man of integrity who was thoughtful, kind, supportive, and had a good sense of humor. He loved her, and she loved him.

"I'm glad you're okay," he whispered. "Well, mostly okay. From what Dennis told me, things could have turned out a lot worse."

"It could've, but it didn't. Do you mind if I take a rain check on lunch? If you hurry, you should still have time to pick up a sandwich before heading back to work." She took a deep breath and inhaled the masculine scent of his cologne.

"Don't worry about me. Are you sure you don't want to get checked out by a doctor?"

"No, I'll be fine. I'm just going to rest this afternoon."

"How about if I bring dinner by after I get off work? Does that sound good, or do you have other plans?" He smiled, and the dimple she adored made an appearance.

"My evening is free. I might look worse by then, so come at your own risk." She looked into his dreamy brown eyes and sealed the date with a kiss.

After he left, she trudged up the steps that led to the second floor. She paused at the doorway of the spacious master bedroom. Family heirlooms and thrift store treasures filled her sanctuary and gave her a sense of contentment. It was the kind of room dreams were made of.

The black iron headboard and patchwork quilt once belonged to Grandma Agnes and were two of CiCi's most prized possessions. A long antique dresser sat to the right of the door. Beyond that, two double closets flanked a Jack-and-Jill bathroom that opened to a spare bedroom. On the left side of the room, a chair upholstered in flowered chintz sat in front of an old painted desk that held her computer and printer.

She walked over and opened the French doors. From the small balcony, she had an unobstructed view of the grounds, clubhouse, and pool area. A heavily treed area surrounded the manicured lawn. In the distance, a train blew its whistle, long and low, a sound she never tired of hearing. She turned and went back inside. For now, the bed grabbed her attention, as though it were whispering her name.

She pulled her T-shirt over her head and tossed it on the bed. Unbuttoning her slacks, she let them slide to the floor and then climbed under the quilt. A framed picture on the dresser caught her eye. Words failed to express the sadness that followed the recent loss of her mother. Yet, considering her mother's wishes were the catalyst for the day's events, her mind swirled with questions.

How did my mother keep her vast estate a secret? And why did she leave her own husband such a pitiful amount? True, it was her money to do with as she saw fit, but in the grand scheme of things, his allowance was equivalent to leaving a penny tip to a bad waitress. It acknowledged the person, but sent a message. I certainly can't explain why she did it, or change what's been done. Will Dad eventually calm down and accept his wife's decision, or will his anger simmer until he does something he and I will both regret?

Before any answers could form, the soft billowy mattress drew her in deeper and deeper, until she had totally surrendered.

THREE

CiCi slept longer than she intended. She quickly pulled on her favorite blue jeans, the ones that hugged her curves as though they were custom-made. She wasn't fat by any means, but she wasn't rail thin either, due in part to her love affair with anything sweet. In fact, her addiction to sweets was the very reason Chad often called her Sugar. She slipped a navy T-shirt over her head, her feet into an old pair of flats, and swept her long, wavy hair into a loose ponytail. After a few strokes of mascara to emphasize her blue eyes and a quick swipe of lip gloss, she checked the bruises and scratches on her neck in the mirror. They were hard to miss, but there wasn't any way to make them magically disappear.

After stripping the bed and straightening up the bedroom, the doorbell rang. She turned and rushed down the stairs to let Chad in. His arms held two carryout bags and a loaf of Italian bread. She relieved him of the bread and followed him to the kitchen. The aroma of garlic and tomatoes made her mouth water.

"Are you feeling better?" he asked after emptying his arms.

"Much better, although my throat's still sore."

A lock of dark hair fell across his forehead as he angled his head to get a better view of her neck. "That's going to be a whopper of a bruise. In fact, your neck looks a little swollen. Have you been using ice packs like the EMT told you?" He leaned in and gave her a kiss that warmed more than just her lips. An ice pack at that point would have melted within seconds.

"I overslept and didn't get around to using another ice pack."

"Hmm. Well, I hope you're hungry for Italian. I thought spaghetti or fettuccini alfredo might be easy on your throat. I stopped at that little place over on Willow Street." He pulled out several containers from the two sacks and lined them up on the counter.

"How many people are you feeding?"

"I was hoping to be invited back for leftovers." He glanced at her and gave a sly grin.

She chuckled. "Is that your way of telling me not to eat like a pig?"

As she turned to gather the plates, glasses and silverware, Chad removed his Ripley Grove Police Department windbreaker and draped it over a dining room chair. Back in the kitchen, he unclipped his holster and service weapon from his belt and placed them on top of the fridge. He gave her a smile, deepening the dimple in his cheek.

Her heart skipped a beat. The thirty-one-year-old detective was ruggedly handsome. A tan polo pulled slightly across his chest and biceps, hiding the shoulder tattoos she found so attractive. Black slacks hugged his butt and thighs just right and topped a pair of western boots made of smooth black leather. The man loved his western boots and seldom wore anything else on his feet. The clinking sound of ice being poured into drinking glasses brought her back to the present.

They filled their plates buffet style from the counter and then moved to the dining room table, where he poured them each a glass of tea. He plunged a fork into the mound of spaghetti on his plate and mentioned that he hadn't had a chance to eat lunch. Looking at his overflowing plate, she briefly wondered if there would be any leftovers to worry about.

After they devoured a thick slice of tiramisu for dessert, the dishes were stacked in the dishwasher, the leftover food stored away, and the coffee maker started. Chad pulled a small wrapped package from the pocket of his windbreaker and placed it in her hands.

"What's this?"

"Something I ordered last week. I saw them online and thought of you."

She peeled off the paper and opened the small box to find a vintage pair of tortoise shell sunglasses. "Oh, Chad, I love them! They're gorgeous." She gave him an appreciative kiss, then dashed down the hall to check out her reflection in the bathroom mirror. After modeling them for his approval, the glasses were slid into the protective sleeve and carefully tucked into her purse.

She grabbed her unfinished glass of tea and headed toward the living room. Chad followed with a cup of black coffee but stopped in front of an assortment of novelty flash drives that hung on the wall. Years ago, she had purchased an old motel key rack at a flea market, painted it a muted shade of country blue, and added additional hooks to accommodate her growing collection. Some of the flash drives were new and unused, while others held photos from a specific event or trip she had taken. A variety of sunglasses in various colors dangled from wire circles attached to the lower edge of the rack.

"You're running out of room."

"I know, and I have more in my bedroom and two or three on my key rings."

"Is this one new?" He pointed to a flash drive that resembled a poker chip.

"Yeah. A girlfriend in California sent that. She's trying to talk me into going to Vegas with her."

Chad shook his head, then joined her in the living room, where they nestled together on the sofa. The soft music playing on the stereo soothed her nerves, and the strong arms that cradled her lessened the worries from earlier in the day.

He kissed the top of her head and pulled her close. "When Dennis told me what happened, I was furious. What I thought of doing to your dad isn't exactly legal. On the flip side, it made me realize just how much I love you."

"I love you, too." *After being married to Mr. Oh-So-Wrong, and kissing a few toads along the way, how did I get so lucky?* She smiled and her heart swelled with contentment.

"I tried to have a talk with Jack this afternoon. He was too drunk to make any sense. He apparently got into a fight at some bar after leaving the lawyer's office. Do you want me to meet you at the station tomorrow? If you don't press charges, Dennis won't either, out of deference to you, his client. Jack will be issued a warning and released after he sobers up."

Megan was right. He's a cop through and through and isn't going to let this go. She slid out from under his arm and turned to face him. "I know you won't agree with me, but I've decided not to press charges." Chad's jaw muscles tightened and his brown eyes darkened to an inky black. She tipped back the last of her tea, then forged ahead. "Look, he just buried his wife a few days ago, and then received news this morning that would turn anyone's world upside down. I think he simply needs time to adjust."

"That may be, but he had no right to lay a hand on you. Do you want to tell me the news that caused him to react so violently?"

She started to speak, but hesitated. *How do I explain that my mother had a hidden estate and disinherited her own husband? I barely understand it myself.* "I…I'm not ready to talk about it just yet."

"Okay. What about your car? Two slashed tires don't read like a kid's prank to me. Somebody was angry. The responding officer ruled out your dad. I'm beginning to wonder if Richie had something to do with it." He took a sip of coffee. His posture remained relaxed and casual, but his steely gaze tried to pin her down.

She shifted in her seat and frowned. *Yeah—definite cop mode. The detective in him* would *have to draw an immediate connection between my tires and my infamous ex.*

Before their divorce four years ago, she and Richie had been co-owners of RC's Autos, the business being a generous wedding present from his parents. RC's sold gently used luxury cars under the company motto "We Can Give You the Ride of Your Dreams."

She later learned Richie had literally been fulfilling the company motto by giving extra *customer service* in the back seat of every car he sold to an attractive, willing female—and he sold a lot of cars. She smiled at the thought of having taken half of his *assets* in the divorce settlement. Richie may not have been able to hold on to his marriage, but he certainly knew how to hold on to a grudge.

Chad's dislike of Richie ran deep, and with good reason. After his wife had purchased a car from RC's, he learned by mere coincidence that she had received an extended contract on her *customer service plan.* He tried to salvage their marriage until he learned Richie hadn't been Vickie's only maintenance provider. Like CiCi, he filed for divorce and never looked back.

CiCi picked an imaginary piece of lint from her shirt to avoid his stare. "I wouldn't be surprised, but I won't accuse anyone without proof, not even Richie."

"Don't put yourself in harm's way. If you need help, ask. I mean it. I would've come immediately if you had just called."

"It all happened so fast and…afterwards, I wasn't thinking straight. My main focus was to get home, to a place where I feel safe."

"Talking about feeling safe, are you still carrying a handgun in your purse?"

"No. because my new purse isn't as large my old one. For now, I keep the Ruger in my night stand, right next to my Glock."

"Not that it really matters, but is your concealed carry permit still valid?"

"Actually, I've never had one. I always carried a gun when I walked the payroll to the bank every week, but Richie insisted I didn't need a permit. That's why I never applied for one."

Chad snorted and shook his head. "Did that guy *ever* give you a truthful answer? At one time, you could've gotten into some serious trouble for that, but things have changed. Kansas passed a law that now allows residents to carry a concealed firearm without a permit. Can't say I agree with it, but it's the law. How much training have you had?"

"Why the sudden interest in my guns and shooting experience?

If you're worried because of what my father did today, don't be. It's over."

"You sure about that?"

"Other than the funeral and the lawyer's office, I haven't had contact with him for years, and I don't plan to start now."

"Good, because I think your dad has trouble keeping his anger under control."

She didn't comment and deftly turned the conversation to more pleasing topics. They talked a while longer until Chad noticed the time. He rose from the sofa and retrieved his gun and jacket. "I'd better get going. Get some rest tonight and call if you need anything, okay?"

She tucked a few baked goods from her freezer into a to-go sack and walked him to the door. He pulled her to him and kissed her forehead. Then, ever so gently, he brushed a kiss across her cheek. By the time he found his way to her lips, she had goose bumps in all the right places. He pressed her against the doorframe as his passionate kisses grew more intense. His hands slipped under her shirt and caressed her skin as she raked her fingers through his hair and nibbled on his lower lip. Her eyebrows rose when she felt a faint vibration a few inches below her belly button. Chad groaned. She felt the vibration again and smiled. Exasperated, he sighed and pulled the cell phone from his pocket. He looked at the caller ID and shook his head.

"Work?" she asked. When he nodded, she smiled with under-standing and pressed the sack of goodies into his free hand. She watched out the window as he walked to his truck with the phone up to his ear. The void he left behind was nearly tangible.

Their brief, but passionate dalliance proved to be a dangerous and delirious feeling, one that could be traced back to their on-again, off-again romance in high school. Unfortunately, after gradu-ation, they had gone their separate ways. Chad enlisted in the mili-tary, and eventually married Vickie. CiCi, looking for love, eloped with Richie during her second year of college after she found herself pregnant with his child. She miscarried several months later and was devastated beyond words. Richie, not so much.

Despite counseling, the idea lingered that her miscarriage and troubled marriage were a direct result of becoming pregnant before she had a ring on her finger. After the bitter divorce, she vowed never to put herself in that position again. For that reason, she refrained from sexual intimacy outside of marriage, which proved to be a monumental task given her strong attraction to Chad. Chad understood how deeply the miscarriage affected her and vowed to take things slow in order for them to build a solid relationship, one that would last a lifetime.

Over the next couple of days, she worked to get as much done as possible before a new week began. Bills were paid, clothes washed, thank you notes mailed, and groceries purchased. On Sunday, she stayed after the morning service at First Baptist Church to help count donations to the church's yearly Memorial Day picnic to be held at Meadowlark Park. By that evening, she completed the crossword puzzle, read the last five chapters of a cozy mystery, and studied for an upcoming test that would bring her one step closer to becoming a certified real estate appraiser. After a light snack and a quick shower, she slipped into bed.

As she glanced around the room at her secondhand treasures, it was evident she lived and dressed as she had been raised—comfortably, but modestly. Despite owning a thriving business with Richie, they were never what anyone would consider rich. The settlement she received after their divorce proved that. In fact, it was her mother who insisted CiCi have an education to fall back on and paid her college tuition. CiCi often wondered how she managed the cost. Now she knew.

Looking at her mother's picture on the dresser and the blue velvet box beside it, thoughts about her newly acquired inheritance tumbled about in her brain. *As angry as dad is over his portion of the estate, I doubt he will ever hand over Grandma's wedding ring now. Still, it won't hurt to ask.* She reached over and turned off the bedside lamp, hoping to put those thoughts aside for the time being.

FOUR

As CiCi drove through the parking lot early the next morning, Brian, the complex manager, nodded as he raced over the grounds on a zero-turn lawnmower, trying to beat the threatening bank of rain clouds to the west. At the corner unit, Mary waved before climbing into her minivan and heading to work. CiCi returned the wave and drove the four short blocks to visit one of her favorite areas of town.

An old limestone courthouse, a post office, and a library held center stage on the old town square. The three buildings were boxed in on four sides by various businesses. There was a barbershop and hair salon—or gossip barns as some would call them, a small grocery store, several eating establishments, a hardware store, sporting goods store, a gift shop, a florist, and several retail shops. Despite there being a few vacant storefronts, the square had undergone a revitalization. Without a doubt, her favorites were the library and the bakery.

CiCi parked and sprinted into Sadie's Bakery for a dozen turnovers. Nothing chased away the Monday morning blues like Sadie's flaky, fruit-filled pastries.

Back in the Jeep, she headed to work and thought about how

fortunate she was to have landed a position at Five Star Real Estate and Appraisals after her divorce. The small company had a formidable reputation. At first, Rex Hoyt, Floyd Masters, and Bruce Owens—the co-owners who had been friends since high school—thought opening a business in their small hometown would be a huge gamble, but Ripley Grove proved to be the perfect location.

To the west sat Lawrence, a booming college town, and Topeka, the state capital. To the east sat Shawnee Mission, a dense cluster of affluent cities located in Johnson County, the most populous county in the state. Just across the state line sat Kansas City, Missouri, a large bustling metropolis. Their broad service area gave them a boost over the stand-alone appraiser or real estate firms that only operated in one locale.

Steering her Jeep into Five Star's parking lot, CiCi backed into a space on the last row under a shade tree and killed the engine. She took in the low, red brick building and the Christian book store, dental office, and an optometrist that occupied the other suites. Five Star's end unit was too large to be practical, considering most of the employees were out of the office half of the time, but rent in the strip mall was cheap.

She pulled down the visor and looked in the mirror. Despite wearing a collared blouse and chic scarf, the bruises and scratches on her neck were still visible. She took a deep breath, then made her way to the entrance as a light smattering of raindrops fell to the ground.

Tasha, CiCi's best friend and co-worker, greeted her at the door with a warm hug and held the pastry box while CiCi unlocked the entrance. After the confections were paired with a fresh pot of coffee, CiCi went straight to her cubicle. One by one, her co-workers stopped by her desk to thank her for the morning pick-me-up. Their words of sympathy for her mother's death were acknowledged, but the discreet inquiries about her neck were skillfully ignored. Tasha had been the only person CiCi had told about the bruises, and she aimed to keep it that way.

As the day progressed, she fell into a comfortable routine, and the backlog of work that covered her desk grew smaller and smaller.

Most of her work hours were spent doing research, analyzing market data, preparing reports, and running the occasional errand for supplies. She enjoyed the appraisal side of the business, and two years ago started the process to become a licensed appraiser. She often wondered if it was crazy to set her accounting degree on the back burner. Only time would tell.

On Tuesday afternoon, Julie stopped by CiCi's cubicle for a chat. She and Julie had met while taking night classes to earn their accounting degrees. When CiCi struggled with overwhelming grief and depression after her miscarriage, Julie's friendship and support had been a blessing. Unfortunately, they lost touch with each other after graduation. Then, a few months ago, CiCi heard that Julie had been laid off and was working for a local temp agency. At CiCi's suggestion, Five Star hired Julie the following day to cover the accounting position until Norma, the firm's accountant, recovered from a serious car accident.

"Want a cookie? I have an extra," Julie said, knowing they shared a fondness for sweets.

"Thanks. I haven't had lunch yet. Hey, did I see you limping earlier?"

"I tripped over my slippers last night and smashed into a chair." She cringed and rubbed her knee.

"Ouch." CiCi winced. "You'd better keep an eye out for King Leer. He preys on the sick and the injured."

They both snickered. Julie's blonde hair and perfect figure hadn't taken long to attract the salacious attention from Bruce, one of Five Star's owners. The fifty-five-year-old real estate broker and appraiser, a.k.a. King Leer, had hit on every female in the office more than once and his behavior reminded CiCi of a certain car salesman she knew. Floyd and Rex, his partners in the firm, had warned him about his inappropriate behavior. Their admonishments put a halt to his overtures, but occasionally an inappropriate comment would slip out, followed by an apology.

"You have to admit; he is rather handsome. I wouldn't mind seeing if his bite is worse than his bark." Julie waggled her eyebrows and tossed a sly look in CiCi's direction.

I thought we agreed to disagree on the subject of faithfulness. No doubt she's waiting to see if I'll remind her she's married. CiCi replied with a simple smile. "How's your helper working out?" Rex had recently hired a college student to help two days a week in the accounting office.

"Ashley's sharp. She's already caught a couple of small errors."

Both women turned and watched Bruce enter the building with his normal swagger. He headed straight for Tasha's desk. Tasha, who supported the real estate side of the business, handed him a report as he passed. He gave her a wink, said hello to the "girls", then sauntered down the hall and into his office. Tasha rolled her eyes and shook her head.

"I wonder if Bruce is dating anyone," Julie said absently, more to herself than to anyone else. "Did you hear he's thinking of relocating out of state to be near his parents?"

"He mentioned it," CiCi said. "It's still up in the air."

"I imagine his share of the company is worth quite a bit."

"I suppose."

"Being single, I bet he also has a healthy bank account. That reminds me, he and I need to talk before he heads out to do an appraisal. I'll catch you later." She waved, then dashed down the hallway. She fluffed her blonde hair and unbuttoned the top two buttons of her blouse before knocking on the door to Bruce's office. The door opened, and Julie disappeared inside. CiCi raised her eyebrows when the door clicked shut.

On Thursday, CiCi bought a bottle of water from the one of the vending machines and glanced around the breakroom that also served as their conference room. She waved at Izzy, a certified residential appraiser, who sat at a table against the wall, talking on her phone while she ate. CiCi headed to the center of the room and snagged a chair across from Julie. CiCi opened her tote and spread her meager lunch on the table. She nibbled on a tuna salad sandwich and carrot sticks as Julie gingerly ate a ham and cheese sandwich, a bag of chips, a fruit cup, and a huge, decadent brownie. As they ate and talked about summer vacation plans, she couldn't help but notice the black and blue area along Julie's jawline.

"That looks like it hurts," she said, pointing to the bruise. "You said you ran into a door? That's an odd place to get a bruise."

"Stranger things have happened." Julie shrugged and avoided her gaze.

CiCi lowered her voice. "Last month you cut your hand, and a couple days ago you were limping. Now you have a bruise on your face. Are you really that clumsy or did someone—"

"Hey, sometimes I get distracted and careless. You're reading way too much into it."

CiCi placed a gentle hand on Julie's arm. "I'm your friend. I have a right to be concerned. If you ever want to talk, I'm here for you. You know that, right?"

Tears welled in Julie's eyes. She swiped away the moisture with the back of her hand and started to say something, but changed her mind.

"Julie, no one has a right to hit you." CiCi's words were soft, but firm.

Rex entered the breakroom, and his face hardened as he glanced at his watch. After grabbing a cup of coffee, he ambled over to their table. "Taking another extended lunch, Julie?"

"Sorry, I lost track of the time." After Rex turned and left, Julie shrugged. "I better get back to work before he fires me. I'll see you tonight at Stella's." She stood, gathered her empty wrappers, and threw them in the trashcan as she left the room.

CiCi remained seated, worried her intrusion into Julie's personal life had overstepped the boundaries of their friendship. She looked past Julie's vacated chair. Even though Izzy sat two tables away, it became obvious from the way she stared at Julie's retreating figure that she'd been eavesdropping on their conversation.

Izzy swept her purple-tipped bangs away from her eyes and turned her attention to CiCi. "I can't tell you who to be friends with, CiCi, but I wouldn't get too close to that one. She's not as innocent as she lets on. Trust me, she needs more help than you can give. I say what goes around comes around." She popped the last bite of cookie into her mouth and brushed the crumbs from her chest before she stood up and left the room.

The harsh comments and contempt left CiCi puzzled.

———

Every other Thursday night, CiCi and her co-workers met at Stella's Grill for an evening of fun and laughter. Stella's, a favorite local hangout, had a reputation for trendy food, good music, reasonable prices, and friendly service.

A five-foot ball of energy with tightly permed red hair, rainbow-colored eyeglasses, and a smile as wide as her hips wrapped CiCi in a hug the moment she walked in the door. At fifty-three, Stella didn't look a day over sixty. "Good to see you back, hon. So sorry about your mom. She was a good woman."

CiCi returned the hug. "Thanks, Stella. She was."

"Tasha staked a claim to one of the tables in the back. What can I get you to drink?"

"A flavored tea. Don't care what kind—surprise me. And two appetizers for the table. Everything you make is good, so I'll leave the choice up to you."

Stella winked. "A tea and two of my specialties, coming right up."

Spirited conversations were in full swing by the time CiCi arrived at the table. The lights had been dimmed and the sound system belted out a country tune. She took a seat next to Izzy. Julie, the last to arrive, took a seat on the other side of Izzy. Izzy frowned and left to visit the ladies' room. When she returned, she snagged a seat at the opposite side of the round table. CiCi glanced around as Stella delivered their drink orders, wondering if anyone else detected the snub.

While CiCi scrounged in her purse for a tube of lip gloss, Tasha snatched up the car keys. CiCi laughed. "If you're going for a joy ride, don't forget to fill up the tank."

Tasha cackled and her ample bosom quivered. Shiny black ringlets framed her heart-shaped face and the lighting made the expertly applied make-up on her warm brown skin as eye-catching as the glittery purple polish on her nails. She dangled the key ring from a perfectly manicured finger. "I'm just admiring the newest do-hickey on your key ring. I told Ashley about your fascination with novelty flash drives, but I said she'd need to see it to believe it. I think your obsession would rival my shoe addiction any day. Wouldn't Floyd or Rex have a hissy fit if we started using these at work? Girlfriend, Rex would pass a melon if he asked for the Brinker report and I handed him a bunny-shaped thumb drive!"

CiCi pulled out a larger fob that held the keys to her home, Five Star, her safety deposit box, and her mail box. She had never felt comfortable keeping all her keys together on one ring. If her car keys were stolen, she didn't want the thief to have access to her residence, and vice versa. The larger fob also held several animal-shaped flash drives. Several scenarios passed around the group about the kitty and the donkey, and the table erupted with laughter.

CiCi took a sip of raspberry tea and grabbed a spicy Mexican egg roll as soon as the appetizers arrived. They toasted Ashley's end to another successful year at college and presented her with a small gift. Each person had something to add to the evening, whether it was a joke, info about the latest sales at the discount outlet, or a recent movie review. Julie's husband was the first caller to ask the typical "who are you with and when are you leaving" questions. Izzy's husband called next, and the group decided to call it a night.

They said their goodbyes and disbanded for the evening. As CiCi and Julie walked to their cars, Julie groaned when she spotted her husband's truck parked next to her Jeep. The burning end of a cigarette punctuated his hulking silhouette in the driver's seat. His eyes remained on Julie as she walked past his truck and slid behind the wheel of her vehicle.

"Why didn't you come in and join us, Keenan?" CiCi asked as she approached the driver's side of the vehicle. She had first met

Julie's husband after she hired on at Five Star. He occasionally stopped by the office to take Julie out for lunch and appeared genuinely smitten with her. In light of recent events, CiCi wondered if she had made a hasty judgement.

"I'm happy right where I am, just me and my best bud." He lifted a beer can in a mock introduction. "I don't need to listen to a bunch of women yammering. I, ah, I just thought I'd swing by and make sure Jules gets home safe. You never know these days what could happen."

"That's sweet of you, especially with the run of bad luck she's had lately."

"Bad luck? What are you talking about?"

"Haven't you noticed? She was limping a few days ago, and today she has a nasty bruise on her face."

He shrugged and took a drink. "Accidents happen."

"I suppose that might depend on your definition of an accident."

"Mind your own business, or *you* might be the one having an accident." His eyes narrowed as he purposely exhaled a cloud of smoke in her face. With a sneer, he tossed his empty can of beer on the pavement at her feet and then followed his wife's Jeep from the lot. CiCi shook her head and got into her vehicle.

Her thoughts were diverted from Julie's predicament the moment she arrived home and listened to her answering machine. Her dad's slurred voice filled the room, ranting that she was nothing but a bloodsucking leech and she'd be sorry if she didn't figure out a way to give him his rightful share of the estate. The next three messages were more of the same. She deleted the threats and prayed he would regret making the calls when he sobered up.

FIVE

CiCi browsed through her closet Saturday evening like a woman on a mission. She pulled out a green, form-fitting silk sheath with cap sleeves. She wanted to look perfect when she and Chad went to The Angus Steakhouse with Dennis and Megan. The newest restaurant in town sat on a hill overlooking the town square. After reading the glowing reviews posted by a local food critic, she looked forward to ordering a tender filet mignon, and was more than eager to peruse the offerings on their dessert menu.

After Chad gave his name at the reservation desk, the hostess led the foursome to a prime table with a panoramic view. Heads turned as the group made their way through the crowded dining room. The two men were extremely handsome in their fitted black suits. Megan's long black hair cascaded over her shoulders like a waterfall, and her short animal-print dress drew attention to her long, toned legs.

Once seated, CiCi glanced around the room and smiled. The muted lighting, candlelit centerpieces, and soft music added to the ambiance. She placed her hand in Chad's and turned her attention to the window. "What a spectacular view! Look, you can see the new pavilion from here."

Dennis peered over Megan's shoulder. "It's a nice addition to the city. Despite the cloak of anonymity, Ripley Grove is lucky to have such a generous supporter."

CiCi nodded. "Local farmers and crafters rent spaces to sell their produce and homemade items on Saturdays. Megan and I stopped by there this morning after we took a run out to the abandoned train depot and back."

"Are you two training for a marathon?"

Chad chuckled. "CiCi has a wicked sweet tooth and loves to bake. She only runs so she can eat more dessert." The remark earned him a playful poke in his ribs.

"Megan and I run several days a week, and have for a couple of years now. Our runs were put on hold during the last stages of Mom's..." CiCi stopped, her voice choked with emotion. Chad gently squeezed her hand. "I'm sorry. Our jogging habits aren't that interesting, so tell us about yourself, Dennis. How long have you been a lawyer?"

The conversation flowed smoothly as they dined on tender steaks, loaded baked potatoes, salad, and grilled asparagus. Dennis and Chad seemed to know many of the same people, whether they were lawyers, policemen, bondsmen, or judges. Both men marveled they'd never met before. They shared a strong work ethic and were each dedicated to their chosen career.

A chirp sounded in the middle of a lively discussion. CiCi apologized as she slipped her phone from her clutch. Her pulse quickened when she read the name on the caller ID: Jack Parker. She hesitantly lifted the phone to her ear. "Hello?"

Jack immediately launched into a verbal attack. Her eyes widened. After listening to the first few words, she disconnected the call. She'd heard it all before, and it scared her. She released a tension-filled breath and slid the phone back into her purse. When she looked up, all eyes at the table were riveted on her face.

"You're as white as the tablecloth. Is everything all right?" Megan asked.

She sidestepped the question and forced a small smile. "Don't you hate getting a sales call during dinner?" She glanced around the table at her dinner companions. *They're not buying it, but it's better than telling them the truth. My dad's harassment isn't something I want to discuss on a double date.*

"A sales call? How could you tell? You didn't listen for more than a few seconds."

"I guess I'm psychic, or maybe psycho." CiCi laughed half-heartedly at her self-mocking comment. When her phone rang again, she panicked and excused herself from the table to get away from the questioning looks. She hurried to the restroom, where she leaned against a wash basin, closed her eyes, and took a couple of deep, calming breaths. When she opened her eyes and looked in the mirror, Megan's worried face stared back.

"Who keeps calling? If it's that bone-headed ex of yours, let me answer the phone. I'll be glad to give him a piece of my mind."

"It's not Richie, I promise. Everything's fine." *I'd love to confide in her, but she doesn't need to hear about my family's craziness. Besides, she'd probably tell Chad.* "You and Dennis make a striking couple," she said, hoping to change the subject.

"Thanks. We've seen each other several times over the past few days. He definitely has 'significant other' potential. He's smart, has a great personality, a good paying job, and doesn't live with his mother. I don't want to jinx it, but I really like him—a lot."

"In that case, you'd better go back to the table before our waitress slips him her phone number. She seems a little too attentive, if you know what I mean."

"I don't know," Megan said hesitantly. "I don't want to leave you alone."

"Go," CiCi said, giving her a little nudge. "I'll be along in a minute."

Once Megan left, CiCi took out her phone and studied the screen. *Should I call him back? I would in a heartbeat—if I could talk to the dad who used to carry me on his shoulders and call me princess. But that was a long, long time ago. He's only calling because he's interested in one thing—getting his hands on my inheritance. I'm simply a means to an end.* Her emotions and intellect wrestled whether or not to return the call. *Not* won the battle and she shut the phone off.

With a faux smile plastered on her face, she rejoined her dinner companions just as the waiter delivered their desserts. The cheesecake topped with raspberry sauce failed to ease the nervous churning in the pit of her stomach. She ate a few bites and pushed the beautiful rosette of whipped cream aside.

On the drive home, Chad reached over and wrapped his hand around hers. "That dress you're wearing grabbed everyone's attention tonight, especially mine."

"I'm glad you like it." The heat from his touch sent tingles up her arm. She smiled. "You and Dennis seemed to get along well, and Megan couldn't keep her eyes off him."

"Yeah, he's alright, considering he's a lawyer. He seems to be one of the few good ones. Megan could do a lot worse, and has." He paused, tightened his grip on the wheel, and looked over at her. "Overall, I had a great time tonight—at least until you got those phone calls. I wasn't the only one who noticed how distracted you were after that. Megan said you were upset in the ladies' room. What's going on?"

"Nothing." She stared out the passenger window, hoping the late-night shadows would hide her anxiety. *If he learns about the threats, that protective streak of his will shift into overdrive. I can't let that happen. I need to handle this situation myself.*

"Cecilia, you're a terrible liar. You were scared to death every time your phone rang. Did you think I wouldn't notice your hand shaking when you took a drink? You didn't even finish your cheesecake. For someone who lives for dessert, that was a *huge* red flag."

He took a breath and softened his tone. "We promised to build a relationship based on love, trust, and honesty. You can talk to me about anything. You know that, don't you?"

"Yes, I do, but...but I can't—not just yet." She nibbled on her lower lip and studied the passing scenery as his thumb tenderly caressed the back of her hand. Her heart ached and her resolve almost melted.

"Your caller seems persistent. Ignoring the calls didn't have any effect. Someone has you rattled, and I don't like it. Was it your dad?"

"Chad, please, just drop it. I can take care of it."

"Why won't you let me help you?"

"I *can't*. I promise, if I can't resolve the issue, you'll be the first person I ask for help."

He squeezed her hand reassuringly, but the look of concern never left his face.

She met with Dennis the following Monday. His information concerning the estate had been broken down into manageable portions and prioritized by level of importance. After an hour of discussing various subjects, she buried her face in her hands and groaned. "I'm sorry, Dennis, but I can't listen to another word. It's evident you've spent a lot of time preparing for this meeting, but my head is about to explode."

Dennis leaned back in his chair and chuckled. "I forget we don't exactly speak the same language. What if we meet every two weeks? I'll send you home with a packet of material to review. That'll allow you time to process the data and form detailed questions."

CiCi sighed with relief and nodded her approval. "Thank you. I've handled finances and tax forms before, but nothing of this magnitude. The rental properties and all that goes along with that are a total mystery to me."

"Don't worry about it. In fact, I'll ask those who worked with your family's assets in the past to sit in on the meetings that correlate to their field of expertise. Each expert can answer any questions you have and make sure the transfers of assets are done properly."

"I would appreciate that." She paused to add a touch of lip gloss. "It's hard to wrap my mind around having that much money."

"You seem to handle it well. Most people would've spent half of it by now."

"That's not me, and I'm determined not to change my lifestyle. In fact, I haven't even shared the details about my inheritance with Chad yet."

"I think Chad can be trusted with the information, but I would advise against telling anyone else. As you know, your grandparents and mother were very adept at keeping it a secret."

"How did they do it? You know, cope with having so much money. They lived simply and gave no indication of being wealthy."

Dennis stopped and gave her question some thought. "From my interactions with them, they were a lot like you. They were humble people, content with what they had. That's not to say that they simply hoarded the money without any regard for others. You'll learn about that over the coming weeks."

"What do you mean?"

"Well, for instance, who do you think donated the money to build the new pavilion, or supplied the funds to help revitalize the town square?"

CiCi's eyes widened. "I had no idea."

"Your family has been a valuable asset to this community in more ways than one, and yet never wanted any recognition. In fact, anonymity was a stipulation when they donated. It will be up to you to decide if you want to continue your family's legacy."

"Dennis, did Mom tell you *why* she left my dad so little of the estate?"

"No, and I didn't ask. She was an intelligent woman. I'm sure she had a good reason."

As he combined the various documents into a neat stack on his desk, CiCi briefed him on the recent phone calls from her father. Dennis immediately stopped and leaned back in his chair. With a stern look on his face, he listened intently.

"I had a suspicion about those calls you received the other night during dinner," he admitted. "I assume you've talked to Chad about this."

"No, I haven't. I don't want to involve him unless absolutely necessary. I was hoping you might be able to do something, since you're aware of his complaint."

Dennis rapped his pencil on the desktop while considering her request. "I'll call, or make a visit if need be. That may be all that's necessary to get him to stop. If he continues, you'll need to get the police involved."

CiCi winced at the thought. "Let's hope it doesn't come to that."

SIX

On Wednesday morning, CiCi made a wide turn through Five Star's parking lot and backed into her favorite spot in the last row. As she stepped from the vehicle, she noticed Julie parked about a dozen slots over, talking on her phone. CiCi walked across the empty spaces that separated them and pushed down the twinge of envy that struck whenever she looked at Julie's black Jeep, which had all the bells and whistles anyone could possibly want.

Julie, finished with her phone conversation, got out of her vehicle and reached across the driver's seat for a sweater and lunch tote. When she turned around, she gasped, startled to find someone standing behind her. "CiCi, you scared me to death!"

CiCi frowned when she spotted the purple bruises that curled around Julie's upper arms. "Julie, what the—are you okay?"

"It's nothing." Cursing under her breath, Julie rushed to put her sweater on.

"You call those bruises nothing? Seriously? Did Keenan do that to you?"

"In case you've forgotten, every couple has spats now and then," Julie snapped.

"He may be your husband, but that doesn't give him the right to hurt you. No one deserves to be treated like that." CiCi fought to control the tightness in her chest as she watched Julie struggle to come up with a plausible excuse.

"I shouldn't have harped about his fishing trip last night. For the life of me, I don't understand why he quit a good paying job to become a handyman. How can he think he *earned* a vacation when he barely brings home a paycheck?"

"I thought his new business venture was doing well."

"Hardly. He's not getting much work, and his check barely pays for the tools he's purchased, which is what started the argument. I should've stopped the moment I saw he'd been drinking, but I didn't. It's my own fault."

"You're going to blame yourself? Are you kidding me?" CiCi's anger grew as Julie turned and swiftly walked across the lot. CiCi caught up with her and grabbed her elbow to slow her down. "Stop! Just stop for a minute and let's talk."

Julie spun and jerked her arm away, causing CiCi to stumble, fall against a parked car, and then to the ground. She scrambled to her feet and brushed herself off. Julie glared and pointed a finger in CiCi's face. "I know you mean well, but you need to back off."

"If you want to be angry at someone, be angry with your husband, not me. I just want to help. Why don't you stay at my place until things cool off?"

"Thanks, but I'll be fine. Besides, he leaves tomorrow for his *vacation*. I'm thinking a little space will do us both some good."

Norma limped into their midst wearing a rigid, knee-high orthopedic boot on one leg, and a cast on her left hand and forearm. Not an easy task for someone in their mid-fifties with such injuries. Norma had held the firm's only accounting position for years and excelled at working with numbers—with people, not so much. As evidenced by the sour expression on her face, having a prettier and much younger woman like Julie temporarily filling her job hadn't set well.

"Norma!" CiCi stuttered. "I'm surprised you're back to work so soon."

"I convinced Rex I could answer the phones and manage the

front desk. Someone needs to keep an eye on things when he's gone." CiCi bit back a retort and opened the door. As Norma hobbled through the entrance, she left them with a final thought. "If you two stand out there arguing all day, you'll be late."

Julie pulled a lime green iPod from her purse, dangled it between her slender fingers, and gave CiCi a mischievous look. "In the meantime, I have my own way of getting a little payback. Keenan loves this thing, and will be looking high and low for it to take on his trip."

"That's a dangerous game to play."

"I don't plan to play the game much longer. If you really want to help, don't mention the bruises on my arms to the rest of the staff. They don't need to be all in my business. I know you can understand that," she sarcastically, "or you would've told the truth about those bruises you had on your neck last week."

CiCi stood with her mouth agape, unable to defend herself. Julie turned and stormed inside. They avoided each other for the remainder of the day.

———

Shortly before lunch on Thursday, Julie stopped by CiCi's cubicle and sheepishly held a novelty flash drive shaped like a bumble bee. "Friends?" Julie asked.

"Friends." CiCi smiled and accepted the peace offering. "Aw, it's so cute."

"I'm sorry I went crazy on you yesterday," Julie said. "Between work and home, I've been a little stressed. I guess it's hard to admit Keenan gets a little rough when he's drinking. I appreciate your offer of a place to stay, and I'll keep it in mind."

CiCi reached over and gave Julie's hand a reassuring squeeze. "My door's always open."

Julie leaned in. "Can I ask you something that would stay just between the two of us?"

CiCi followed Julie's gaze as it darted nervously around the room. Izzy was on the phone, Tasha stood at the copy machine, and

Norma sat working a crossword puzzle at the front desk. From the sound of it, Ashley and Floyd were in the lunchroom trying to shake something loose in the vending machine. CiCi nodded.

"You used to be an owner and accountant at RC's Autos, didn't you?"

"Yes. I did the books and Richie did the customers, neither of which is a big secret around town." CiCi gave a little chuckle and shook her head.

Julie lowered her voice to a whisper. "There are a couple entries in the ledger I have questions about. I asked Bruce about it last week, but he brushed me off and hasn't gotten back with me. Would you mind taking a look without alerting Norma?"

How can I refuse? If I do, she may not ask for my help the next time Keenan gets out of control—and there will be a next time. "Sure, not a problem."

Julie slid CiCi a black metal tampon wallet roughly the size of an inch-thick stack of index cards. The words "Scourge of the Month" were inscribed in bold red letters on the top of the hinged lid. "There's hard copy of an account folded up inside. Let me know if something jumps out at you. And don't worry, I don't need the case back right away. It's a spare."

CiCi smiled and pulled a similar metal case that read "PMS Princess" from her purse. They both chuckled.

"Are you free tonight? We could meet at Stella's after work, my treat. That'll give me time to look for other questionable entries and back up the files to a flash drive," Julie whispered, "in case you need more information."

"Be forewarned, I may not have a chance to study the copy before tonight."

"That's okay. Bring it and I'll show you what caught my attention. If you think it warrants a second look, I'll give you the flash drive to take home. Remember, not a word to anyone. Norma will have my head if she finds out."

"That's for sure. Do what you can, but don't take any chances."

"Are you sure you don't mind?"

"Of course not, and trust me—my lips are sealed." CiCi pulled an imaginary zipper across her lips. When a shadow fell across her desk, she swiveled her chair around and saw Norma lurking just outside her cubicle. *Uh-oh. How long has she been standing there, and how much did she hear?* CiCi glanced at Julie, glad she had the foresight to hide the hard copy in the tampon case. If Norma happened to see the transfer, she would simply assume Julie was helping an unprepared friend during her time of the month.

"Julie, dear, CiCi will never get caught up if you girls chat all afternoon." Norma spoke with a honeyed smile, but the tone of her voice produced a sharp sting.

"Did you call the bank yet about that discrepancy, Julie?" Rex joined the group and scowled at Julie, who remained silent. "I didn't think so. Call them again. I'll expect to hear what they have to say before the day is over." He turned and headed to his office, with Norma on his heels.

CiCi shook her head. "I don't know why he's always on your case like that."

"Trust me, karma is going to bite him in the butt one of these days."

CiCi glanced up a few minutes before quitting time and saw Julie emerge from Rex's private office. With a sly grin on her face, she disappeared into the accounting office across the hall. *Wonder what that's about? It's not often anyone other than Norma walks away wearing a smile after dealing with Rex. He's the prickliest of the three co-owners, and the hardest to please. Maybe he apologized for his earlier behavior.*

CiCi grabbed her purse and hurried down the corridor. She rapped twice on the doorjamb to Julie's office. Julie stood with her back to the door, nodding her head while flipping through folders in a file cabinet. CiCi reached out and tapped her shoulder. Julie shrieked.

"You've got to quit doing that!" she gasped. She removed the earbuds, wrapped the cord around the iPod, and tossed both into the center drawer of the desk.

"Sorry. I'm leaving, but I'll meet you at Stella's around seven." CiCi cut off a response with a wave when she noticed Rex exit his office. Not wanting to be saddled with a last-minute project, she scurried down the hall and said good-night to Norma and Ashley on her way out. As usual, Ashley smiled and Norma grunted.

Much to Julie's dismay, Rex entered the accounting office shortly after CiCi left. The man was the epitome of organization and neatness. Those admirable traits were evident by his meticulous grooming habits and attire. On the flip side, his elitist and condescending attitude made it difficult for him to carry on a conversation with any of the employees other than Norma.

"I'm surprised you're still here," he said.

"Actually, I'm just about to leave. By the way, have you given any thought to that insurance matter we discussed earlier?"

He gave her a silent, steely look before replying. "Yes, I have, but the price seems high."

"That's the cost of doing business, Rex. Sometimes you just have to bite the bullet, as they say. Maybe you should ask Bruce or Floyd for their opinion."

"That's not necessary," he snapped. "I'll handle it myself."

"That's up to you. You're the boss."

"Can you stay after work to discuss the details?"

"Sorry. I'm meeting CiCi tonight at Stella's. Maybe tomorrow? That'll give you time to think about the pros and cons." She smirked. "There is a deadline, you know." In the short time she'd been employed at Five Star, she discovered Rex despised making quick decisions, especially when it involved money.

"I guess that'll have to do," he replied, clearly annoyed. "I need time to consider my options. There should be room for negotiation."

"As I see it, the options are limited and there's no room for negotiation, especially when you think about what's at risk."

Bruce and Floyd entered the room and joined Rex at her desk.

She sighed, anxious to leave for the day. Floyd grabbed a key chain lying next to the computer mouse and twirled it on his finger. "Hey, is this yours?"

"Hardly. I purchased that for my husband's nephew. He loves farm animals."

Floyd took a seat in the empty chair next to her desk, humming the theme from *The Godfather* as he double-checked a bill for office supplies. Satisfied, he signed the bottom and then handed it to Julie. Bruce reached over Floyd's shoulder and passed her an invoice that needed to be logged and sent out.

The men wished her a good evening as they left. Julie tossed the pig-shaped flash drive into her purse, shut down the computer, shut the file drawers, and grabbed her lunch tote. As she headed to the exit, she glanced across the room. Rex and Norma appeared to be in the middle of a serious discussion. He stopped momentarily when he caught Julie watching. She smiled and bid them both a good evening. He ignored her and turned back to his conversation with Norma.

CiCi waved to catch Julie's attention as she entered Stella's a little after seven.

"Sorry I'm late. Has the waitress been by?"

CiCi shook her head as an arm reached out and placed two menus on the table. They browsed the specials, then placed their order. CiCi chose a hand-breaded tenderloin sandwich with fries, while Julie selected a turkey club sandwich with slaw. After the waitress left, a few friends stopped by their table to chat. Once they were finally alone, CiCi offered Julie an apology. "Sorry, I haven't looked at the copy you gave me."

"You left the office in such a rush, I didn't have time to tell you I found a solution to the problem. I don't know why it never occurred to me before, but after looking at it from a different angle, the pieces started falling into place," Julie said with a glint in her eye.

"You're like me—you like to tackle things on your own before involving anyone else."

"That's exactly it. But I do have a problem. I need to double-check a couple of figures before I tackle payroll tomorrow. Think I could borrow your key to Five Star so I can take care of it tonight? I don't want Rex to think I can't handle the job, or he'll be sure to give a bad report to the temp agency."

"I don't know. I've never loaned my key to anyone. I'm going in to work early in the morning, probably around five o'clock. Why don't you meet me then?"

"There's no way I'd be able to get up that early. Look, I promise I won't tell a soul, and I can leave the key for you in the planter outside the front door. I wouldn't ask if it wasn't important."

CiCi sighed heavily as she took the key from her key ring. "Okay, but don't make me regret doing this. Promise you'll leave the key in the planter?"

"Promise. I'll know tomorrow if I have assessed the situation correctly. I copied everything to a flash drive as a safeguard. I'll let you know..." Before Julie could finish, the waitress arrived with their food. All work conversation ceased until after they had eaten.

As CiCi finished the last of the sweet potato fries, an uneasy sensation crept up her spine. She tried to shake it off, but couldn't. Scanning the room, she spotted King Leer sitting at the bar, looking in their direction. He made eye contact and nodded. Within minutes, he headed toward their table and asked to join them.

"Can I buy you ladies dessert? I can't stay long. I have a party to attend and don't want to miss the entertainment." He wiggled his eyebrows.

"I'd love dessert," Julie purred, "but only if you'll stick around to help me eat it."

He glanced at his watch. "I think that can be arranged. Order whatever you like and I'll be right back. CiCi, would you like anything?"

"No, thanks. I'll be leaving soon."

While Bruce went back to the bar to grab his jacket, CiCi leaned over and whispered, "Remember. Not a word to Bruce about the key."

"Promise."

"Watch my purse while I run to the restroom." CiCi left her keys and purse on the table and headed for the restroom. She returned to find the aroma of warm cinnamon and apples scenting the air. Julie seductively took a bite of the apple pie a la mode. Bruce couldn't seem to tear his eyes away from her lips. He returned her smile, picked up his fork, and sampled the heavenly treat.

She certainly has his attention. I feel as though I'm watching Eve entice Adam with the forbidden fruit. I suppose this is how it all began.

After a bit of small talk between the three of them, CiCi decided to call it a night. She paid her tab and gathered her things. "I'll see you both next week."

"Next week?" Bruce said, clearly confused.

"Remember? I am taking a day of vacation. A few friends and I are headed to the Ozarks for a weekend getaway. Don't worry. I'll have the Hinckley report finished and ready for your approval before the sun rises. I plan to be on the road before rush hour traffic begins."

They both wished her a safe trip and a good time. She reached the exit and turned one last time to wave goodbye. With his arm casually draped across the back of Julie's seat, he pulled something small and shiny from his pocket and pressed it into her hand. From the look on her face, it pleased her. He leaned over and whispered in her ear, causing her to laugh.

Julie, Julie, why are you playing with fire? Keenan may be out of town, but what if he hears about you flirting with Bruce? You know what he's capable of when he's angry.

She didn't like seeing this side of her friend, but from previous discussions, she knew their views on fidelity were miles apart. She opened the door and stepped out onto the sidewalk, shaking off her troubled thoughts. There were other things to worry about, like the upcoming test for her appraisal class. With any luck, she could log an hour of study time before the night ended.

SEVEN

CiCi opened one eye and squinted at the alarm clock. One o'clock. She hadn't been able to sleep no matter how many times she fluffed the pillow. Exasperated, she decided to face the inevitable and head to work. Once her reports were out of the way, she could always come back home to grab a nap before leaving on her mini-vacation. She stifled a yawn, rolled out of bed, and slipped on a simple T-shirt and khaki shorts.

When she pulled into Five Star's parking lot twenty minutes later, it surprised her to see a black Jeep parked near the door. *Hmm. Either Julie had more problems with the accounts than she anticipated, or Bruce diverted her attention elsewhere last night, causing her to work later than expected.* CiCi parked beside Julie's vehicle and thought back to the many times she had stayed late to work undisturbed on a stubborn problem.

The crisp morning air felt deliciously cool on her bare skin as she walked to the door. Through the slatted blinds, a faint glow came from the hallway. After checking the potted plant for the key and not finding one, she rapped on the glass and then wiggled the handle to get Julie's attention, only to find the door unlocked. *Well, that's not good. Julie must have forgotten to lock up when she arrived.*

She entered, locked the door, and went directly to her cubicle, one of eight workstations behind Norma's new "throne", which was front and center in the lobby. She glanced around as the PC booted up and the two large monitors flickered to life. *Why didn't Julie turn on the overhead lights?* She switched on a task light, which gave a soft glow to her cubby, and then tossed her purse on the desk. It landed with a thud, sending a burst of air across the desk. Loose sheets of paper fluttered in the air around the cubicle and she grabbed as many as she could before they hit the floor. She pulled her sunglasses and a book from her purse in search of a breath mint, but failed to find one. Downing the last few sips of orange juice, she tossed the empty bottle in the trashcan. Without the rival noises of humming computers, ringing phones, and clacking keyboards, the sound seemed to increase by tenfold. A muffled sound from the accounting office caught her attention.

"Hey, Julie," she called. "It's CiCi. Did you start a pot of coffee?" She stepped from the cubicle and walked towards the well-lit accounting office. Seeing another errant slip of folded paper on the floor, she slipped it into the back pocket of her shorts. As she entered the room, the six-foot tall dracaena plant brushed her right shoulder. She stopped and her jaw dropped. To her left, the drawers in Julie's desk hung open. A small vase of flowers lay on its side and water covered the desk littered with reports. Shattered glass from a framed photo sprinkled the carpet like confetti.

"Julie?" A soft moan made the hair at the nape of her neck stand on end. The click of the light switch and the rustle of dracaena leaves caused her to whip around, but not before the room plunged into darkness. Her heart dropped to the pit of her stomach, and her eyes strained to identify the shadowy figure of a man that stepped from behind the plant.

Adrenaline coursed through her veins when his arm rose to strike. She reeled back and narrowly escaped the blow. His next attempt came so close, the displaced air ruffled her hair. She shoved an empty chair between them. He lunged again. She dodged and fell against the desk. When her hand landed on a metal three-hole punch, she swung the makeshift weapon with all her might. It clanked against something in his hand, and the impact knocked both items to the floor. Pushing her fear aside, she landed a swift kick between his legs. He faltered and staggered from the room. Seconds later, the exit door at the end of the hall slammed shut.

She rushed over, locked the door to the accounting office, and flipped on the lights. The thumping of her heart echoed in her ears and her body trembled. A large pocketknife lay at her feet, its blade covered with blood. Her stomach lurched, and she slumped against the door as the room swayed around her.

Panic set in when she realized her cell phone was in her purse at her desk. Glancing around the room, she noticed a cordless handset on the floor near Julie's desk and grabbed it. Her hands shook, making it difficult to tap the three digits that would summon help.

"9-1-1, what's your emergency?" the operator asked.

"I've been attacked! I need help!" she said, then rattled off her name and location.

"If you are not in immediate danger, stay where you are. Officers are en route."

"I don't think he's still in the building, but I'm not positive." She glanced around the room. Her heart seized when she spotted a foot peeking out from behind the desk. She inched forward. An involuntary scream erupted from her throat.

"Oh, dear God! My co-worker's been stabbed!"

She set the phone aside, grabbed a scarf draped over the back of a nearby chair, and applied pressure to Julie's wounds. Julie tried to speak, and CiCi struggled to make sense of the distorted syllables. "Hang on, Julie. Help is coming."

A whisper of movement caught her attention. Fear took over. She picked up the phone, but it slipped from her fingers. She wiped her hands across the front of her shirt and tried again. With the phone to her ear, she whispered, "I think he's coming back!"

"Ma'am, are you in a safe place?"

"Maybe. I'm in a locked room. Please hurry."

"Stay there until help arrives. Should be any minute now."

What if he kicks the door in? CiCi instinctively grabbed the pocketknife from the floor and clutched it until her knuckles turned white. She stood and pressed her back against the wall, ready to spring into action if need be. Seconds later, the empty vase on the desktop rolled and smashed to the floor. Her shoulders sagged with relief.

"Sorry, false alarm," she told the operator. "Wait, I hear sirens."

"Ma'am, stay on the line until the officers are on the premises, okay?"

Emboldened by the close proximity of help, she hesitantly poked her head out of the office, checking the area to see if their attacker had returned. She darted to the entrance and unlocked the front door. Two patrol cars screeched to a stop outside. As she flipped on the overhead lights, an officer burst through the entrance.

"Police! Drop the weapon and put your hands up! Now!" He pointed a firearm at her chest and repeated the command. Another gun-wielding officer joined the first. Together, their loud demands reverberated in the room. The first officer stepped closer and ordered her again to drop the weapon. Until that moment, she hadn't realized she held a firm grip on the bloodied knife. She released the weapon and stepped back with her hands in the air.

"You...you don't understand. I'm the one who called 9-1-1. My co-worker needs medical attention. She's in the second room, down the hall on your left. Please, help her."

He kicked the pocketknife aside, patted her down, and put her in handcuffs while the second officer rushed down the hall.

After speaking with the dispatcher for several minutes, Officer Guzman removed the handcuffs and led her outside. Leaning against the patrol car, she watched the EMTs dash inside with their lifesaving equipment. With her eyes fixated on Five Star's entrance, she answered the officer's questions. A third patrolman arrived and began to string crime scene tape in a wide arch around the entrance and both vehicles. She glanced again at the entrance. *They should have brought Julie out by now and taken her to the hospital.* After several minutes of little to no activity, she pushed away from the car and started toward the building.

Guzman pulled her back with a firm grip. "Where do you think you're going?"

"I need to check on her. Why are they taking so long?" She tried to free herself from his hold, but he was bigger and stronger and refused to let go.

"Ma'am, she's in good hands. If you want to help, you can cooperate by going to the station to give a statement about what happened. Let the emergency personnel take care of your friend. Right now, you'll only get in the way."

Her eyes zeroed in on the entrance of the building, willing them to rush Julie to the hospital. "You're probably right."

"Good. Take a seat in my car. Another officer is on the way. She'll escort you downtown."

"I can drive. I just need to go inside and get my purse."

"Sorry." He shook his head. "Your purse and vehicle are part of the crime scene."

As she climbed into the back seat of his patrol car, an unmarked police car pulled into the lot and parked. The officers outside immediately took notice. Detective Mark Sullivan, Chad's co-worker and best friend, emerged from the vehicle. Officer Guzman shut her door and walked over to confer with the detective. As Guzman talked, Mark's head snapped up and looked in her direction. He nodded to Guzman, then both men disappeared inside.

Officer Guzman returned without her handbag. "Detective Sullivan will bring your purse to the station when he's finished here. He'll be the one to take your statement. Can we get the keys to your car? It'll make it a lot easier."

"Yes, whatever helps. It's the smaller of the two key rings. Are the EMTs still working on Julie? Is that why they haven't come out yet?"

He solemnly looked back at the building, then cleared his throat and directed his attention to CiCi. "Here's your ride," he said, as female officer pulled alongside his patrol car.

CiCi moved from one vehicle to the other and was driven to the Ripley Grove Police Station, where the female officer took photos of her bloody clothes and any injuries to her body.

"Your clothes are evidence. I need your shirt and shoes. Don't need your shorts since there's no blood on them." She handed CiCi a plaid, button-down shirt. "Here's a spare shirt I found in Detective Cooper's office. I doubt he'll mind that I gave it to you."

Dazed, CiCi complied. The officer placed her T-shirt and shoes in evidence bags. After her fingerprints were taken and fingernails scrapped, she washed the blood from her hands and used the restroom. Having an officer wait outside the bathroom unnerved her. She finished quickly and was led down the hall to a small dreary room, furnished with a table, a couple of metal chairs, and a box of tissues. The starkness of the room surprised her. She cringed when the door slammed shut behind her. She took a seat and waited. And waited. And waited.

Outside the room, footsteps raced down the hallway, followed by a frantic, muffled discussion. The heavy door made it impossible to make out the conversation. Several minutes later, Chad entered the room. She immediately threw herself into his arms and burst into tears.

With a worried look on his face, he asked, "Are you okay?" He held her close and whispered calming words in her ear.

"I...I think so," she stammered.

He coaxed her trembling body back into the chair and draped his RGPD windbreaker around her shoulders. He knelt in front of her and gently brushed the hair away from her tear-stained face with a shaky hand. The tightness fell from his face when he realized she hadn't been hurt in the attack. "Guzman told me you were okay, but I had to see for myself before I go back to the crime scene."

She choked back a sob. "Chad, it was so terrifying."

"I know, Sugar, but you're safe now," he said, holding tight to her hands.

"When are they going to take my statement? If someone doesn't come soon, I'm leaving. I need to check on Julie."

His gaze dipped slightly before meeting hers. "I'm sorry, hon. She died at the scene, shortly after the EMTs arrived."

CiCi collapsed into sobs as the gravity of his words sank in.

When the phone at his hip buzzed, he glanced at the screen.

"CiCi, I know this is difficult, but Detective Sullivan is going to need a statement from you. He'll be along once the crime scene is under control." His phone buzzed again. He sighed. "I'm sorry, hon. I've got to go." He kissed her hard, then left the room.

She knew he had a job to do, but his absence left her numb and yearning for the comfort of his touch.

EIGHT

An hour later, a rap on the door caught CiCi's attention. Her head jerked up from the table as Detective Mark Sullivan walked into the room. He carried a carafe and two glasses. Taking a seat, he filled a glass and pushed it across the table. She hadn't realized until that moment how thirsty she was.

Mark's stern face revealed little emotion. The crow's feet that framed his brown eyes were probably a job-related hazard from squinting so much during harsh interrogations. His nose had been broken a time or two, but added character to an otherwise handsome face. His dark brown hair had grayed at the temples, which seemed a bit premature for someone who had recently turned thirty-six. He watched her empty the glass, then pulled a pen and notebook from his shirt pocket.

"I'm very sorry about your friend."

"Thank you. Did you find her killer?"

"Not yet."

"Then why aren't you out looking for him?"

"In order to do that, I need to know what happened this morning." He wasted no words. His voice was sharp and to the point.

"Start from when you left your house; stop when our officers arrived at the scene."

CiCi recounted her morning, moment by moment. Tears flowed as she described the gruesome scene in Julie's office. He held out the box of tissues and waited while she regained control. He asked questions, pausing only to take notes. A knock sounded at the door and an officer entered, holding a purse. Instinctively, CiCi reached for it, but the detective grabbed it first and held it out of her reach.

"May I examine the contents of your purse?"

"If it's really necessary." She sighed with resignation. There wasn't a woman alive who enjoyed watching a man paw through her purse.

"It is." He emptied the soft shoulder bag and spread the contents across the table. His thick fingers examined each item before tossing it back into the bag. One item about the size of a retro cigarette case piqued his curiosity. As he read the words "PMS Princess" inscribed on the outside, the corners of his mouth twitched.

Her face flushed with heat. *I'm glad I left Julie's tampon case in my desk at home. What would he think if he found two tampon cases in my purse?*

Without saying a word, he cleared his throat and moved on to a tube of lip gloss. One eyebrow lifted as he dangled a large key ring from his pinkie. It held several keys and various flash drives disguised as farm animals. "I thought we took the keys to your Jeep."

"You did. I have two key rings. Those are the keys to work, and my house, mailbox and bank box. Well, minus the work key, which I loaned to Julie."

He shook his head and tossed the key ring into her purse.

She straightened in her seat. "Wait. Where are my sunglasses— the ones Chad bought me? They were on my desk."

He nodded and gave the handbag back to its owner. "Which is now part of a crime scene. You'll get them back in due time. Now, let's get back to business," he said. A buzzer sounded. He unclipped the phone from his belt and glanced at the screen. "Sullivan," he grunted into the phone. He frowned and responded with single syllable answers. He disconnected, closed the notebook, and clipped the pen to his shirt pocket. It appeared the interview had come to a halt. He stood up and headed to the door. CiCi also stood, more than anxious to leave.

"Sit," he ordered. "I'll send someone to finish up. I don't want you talking to the media about what happened this morning, understand? And don't leave town."

CiCi nodded and slumped back into the uncomfortable metal chair. After he left, she withdrew her cell phone from her purse and called Tasha, who readily agreed to wait outside the police station and provide a ride home.

Detective Logan entered the room ten minutes later, drinking a can of pop and licking the remains of a candy bar from his fingertips. His overall personality differed drastically from that of his coworker. After fumbling through the few remaining questions that Detective Sullivan had left, he produced a chocolate-smudged search warrant for her car, answered what appeared to be a personal phone call, and then waved her away. CiCi slung the purse over her shoulder, scurried from the room, and never looked back.

Water coursed down CiCi's face and mingled with her tears as the spray from the showerhead cascaded over her body. The warm water turned cold, a clear indication she'd been in the shower far too long. She dressed and went downstairs, where Tasha made her a cup of hot tea. CiCi curled up on the sofa and wrapped her hands around the warm mug. Tasha sat in the recliner and listened in horror as CiCi described the gruesome discovery.

"I don't understand. How did Julie get into the building?" Tasha asked.

Tears of guilt and shame leaked from CiCi's red-rimmed eyes. "I let her borrow my key. She needed to double-check something and didn't want Rex harping at her again."

"Hey, it's not your fault. She asked for a favor, and you tried to help, like you always do. You had no way of knowing she would go to work in the middle of the night. Sounds to me as if someone must've forced their way in when she unlocked the door."

"Maybe. But if I hadn't given her the key, she wouldn't have been there."

CiCi's home phone rang non-stop as news of the murder spread in the small community. The two women fielded calls until CiCi hit her limit and unplugged the landline. As dinnertime approached, she gave Tasha an appreciative hug and insisted she go home. After locking the door and closing the blinds, CiCi sat on the sofa and flipped through a magazine. She tossed it aside and turned on the stereo to break the silence. Antsy and looking for a project to calm her nerves and keep her mind occupied, she headed to the kitchen.

She pulled out the cookbook that once belonged to her grandmother and gathered the ingredients to make cookies. Baking had become more than a hobby in her life—it became a necessity. The methodical process of measuring and mixing proved to be therapeutic in times of stress. After hours of therapy, ten dozen cookies, two dozen brownies, and four loaves of banana bread were wrapped and stacked in the freezer.

She stretched out on the sofa, but sleep remained elusive. Her nerves were on edge and her emotions too raw to rest. She aimlessly paced the floor until exhaustion set in. Midnight had come and gone when a light knock sounded at the door. Peering through the peephole, Chad's face came into view. She unlocked the door and was immediately pulled into his arms.

"I saw the light on and thought you might be up," he said. "How are you doing?"

"Okay, I guess. Can't sleep. I feel as tired as you look. You hungry?"

"Starved."

"Tell me you caught the guy who killed her."

"Not yet."

In the kitchen, he grabbed a glass from the cabinet and opened the freezer compartment to get ice. His eyes went wide. He stared for several seconds, taking it all in, then turned and gave her a knowing look. She shrugged, then fixed him something to eat.

Neither of them spoke as he devoured a thick ham and cheese sandwich and chips. After he refilled his tea, they gravitated to the living room sofa. His presence normally calmed her when nothing else could, but with a murder on her mind, she wanted answers.

"What happened, Chad? Was it a botched robbery?"

"I don't know, honey." He pulled her close and tucked her under his arm. "When dispatch called and said there'd been a woman stabbed at Five Star, I nearly lost my mind. I don't know what I'd do if something happened to you." He gently pushed a strand of hair away from her eye. "Our dispatcher praised your control under the situation. I listened to the recording. You did a great job considering the circumstances."

"I certainly didn't feel in control. What happens now?"

"Mark will want to talk with you again." He paused before saying, "As a precaution, I'd suggest you take an attorney along."

Her head snapped up. "Why would I need an attorney? I tried to help Julie the best I knew how. I don't know CPR and I'm not trained in first aid."

"Mark will need to determine if you are a witness, or a prime suspect."

"A suspect? That's absurd! I didn't kill her. The guy who attacked me killed her!"

He lifted a hand to stop her protests. "You don't need to convince me, but I'm not in charge. Since you were found alone with the victim and had the murder weapon in your hand, you're a suspect until the evidence proves otherwise. Mark is the lead investigator on this case, and nothing will keep him from the truth."

"That's not comforting, because I don't think your best friend likes me."

"He's probably sick of hearing me talk about you. Once he gets to know you better, he'll love you as much as I do. At the moment, he's exactly the person you want heading this investigation. He's a top-notch detective. But I'll warn you, don't expect much in the way of preferential treatment."

"What about my car?"

Chad shook his head. "Part of the crime scene."

She carried his glass to the kitchen, the worrisome phrases swirling in her head. *Attorney. Investigation. Prime suspect. Murder weapon.* Lost in thought, she stashed the flour and sugar containers in the freezer. She stared blankly at the dirty bowls and bakeware on the counter, then began filling the sink with cold water.

He reached around her and shut the water off. "You're not thinking clearly. What you need is some sleep. This can wait until tomorrow." After planting a kiss on the top of her head, he led her to the staircase and nudged her up the stairs.

She stopped on the second step and turned. "Lock up when you leave, okay?"

"I'll lock up, but leaving? Not gonna happen. I don't want you staying alone tonight. I'll camp out on the sofa. If you need me, I'll be here. If you don't, no harm done." He looked into her eyes and placed a finger over lips that were ready to protest. "Don't. What you saw today would take an emotional toll on anyone, even a seasoned cop."

She shrugged. "I'm too tired to argue. You might as well sleep in the spare bedroom. It'll be more comfortable than the sofa."

She fell into a fitful sleep. The frightful look on Julie's face, the red stains that covered her blouse, and the shouts from the police officers played over and over in her mind. A dark, massive figure chased CiCi with a knife, swinging and slashing. Terrified, she struggled to escape, to free herself from the blackness. Her heart pounded in her chest. A piercing scream cut through the stillness. She bolted to a sitting position and gasped for air.

Chad burst into the room and wrapped his arms around her until the tremors subsided. Once her breathing returned to normal, he eased her back on the bed, pulled her grandmother's quilt over her, and held her tight until she drifted off to sleep.

NINE

The aroma of coffee and bacon wafting up from the kitchen had to be the best alarm clock ever invented. When CiCi's sluggish brain suddenly remembered Chad had stayed the night, she scrambled out of bed and showered before heading downstairs.

"Good morning." She entered the kitchen with her nose in the air. "Mmm, smells good."

"Hey. Feeling better?" He stood at the stove and stirred a skillet of scrambled eggs. Two plates on the counter held slices of buttered toast and crispy strips of bacon.

"Somewhat. Sorry I woke you last night." She leaned up and gave him a soft kiss. She wrapped her arms around his waist and laid her head against his broad chest, the memories from the day before heavy on her mind. "I'm glad you stayed. The nightmares were terrifying. I needed you more than I thought."

He rested his chin on top of her head and gave her a gentle squeeze. "I couldn't leave you alone after what you went through yesterday. Of course, I'll be happy to lock you in my arms more often just to hear you say you need me."

"If that's your idea of protective custody, I like it." She glanced up and smiled halfheartedly. She poured herself a glass of juice and

Chad a cup of coffee while he plated the eggs. They ate at the breakfast bar and glanced at the morning paper. The headlines and accompanying photo put Five Star and the murder front and center. Not wanting to be reminded of the ordeal, she turned the paper over.

"I'll be heading to work as soon as I finish eating," Chad said. "You going to be okay?"

"I'll be fine."

"I expect to have another long day. By the way, I took two messages while you were in the shower. The first call was from Mark."

She stiffened and set her fork down. She pushed aside the half-finished plate of food, her forehead creased with worry. "Did he say what he wanted?"

"He wants to see you in his office around two this afternoon. After I hung up, Dennis called."

She nodded. "I left him a message late last night."

"When I informed him of your appointment with Mark, he said he'll be here at one o'clock and drive you to the station, unless he hears otherwise. Don't look so worried. Dennis will take good care of you."

After a goodbye kiss that nearly made his leaving worthwhile, he grabbed two pieces of bacon and headed out the door. She cleaned up their breakfast plates, as well as the mountain of dirty dishes she'd left from the baking marathon the night before, and then paid a couple of bills online. Her mind continually wandered to Mark's request to see her at the police station. Just thinking of the meeting left her stomach in knots and unable to eat lunch.

At the station, she and Dennis were led to a stark gray room with a one-way mirror. She took a seat beside Dennis at the table. Shortly thereafter, Mark Sullivan entered the room with a manila folder tucked under one arm. He shut the door, dropped the folder onto the table, and sat in the only vacant seat across from them. His eyes were bloodshot and his clothes were rumpled.

"Miss Winslow. Mr. Browning." He gave slight nod.

She frowned at his formal greeting, especially in light of their casual friendship through Chad. "Mark," she said.

"Considering why we're here, Detective Sullivan seems more appropriate. First, let me again offer my sympathy on the loss of your friend."

"Thank you."

"Now, let's begin. I need to read you your rights. Be aware that everything you say will be recorded." His clipped words and comment made her acutely aware of where things stood.

Unintentionally, her gaze traveled to the surveillance camera mounted near the ceiling. The electronic device made her uneasy. She looked to Dennis for guidance and assurance.

"Is that necessary?" Dennis asked. "Are you charging her with a crime?"

"No, it's simply a precaution. I can't guarantee what her answers might reveal today, and I don't want any loopholes to deal with later. Surely you can understand that." After he finished reciting the Miranda warning, he asked, "Do you understand your rights as explained and are you willing to answer my questions?"

She nodded. "I do. I have nothing to hide."

"First, I need you to review the statement you gave yesterday."

Her eyes misted as she read the document, her mind reliving the horrible scene with each word. She cleared her throat to keep her emotions in check, nodded her approval, and then passed the papers back across the table.

"No discrepancies? Good."

CiCi answered numerous questions about her relationship with Julie, her other co-workers, and her employers. His inquiries about her education, past employment experience, and current job responsibilities seemed a waste of time.

"How did you and your co-workers get along with Mrs. Reynolds? Any issues?"

"Not really. Everyone liked her. Rex gave her a hard time from day one, but that's just Rex. He's hard to please and can be difficult at times."

"Let's talk about Thursday night. You met Mrs. Reynolds at, let's see…" He stopped to check his notes. "Here it is…Stella's Grill. I understand this wasn't one of your typical Thursday night gatherings. Why didn't any of your other co-workers tag along?"

"Julie had a question about something at work and wanted my input."

"What else did you talk about?"

"Nothing much." She closed her eyes for a few seconds, deep in thought. "We chatted with a few friends. Talked about a book we'd both read and a new recipe I wanted to try. She told me about some great buys she found at an antique mall."

"Did you leave together?"

"No. Bruce Owens joined us and bought Julie dessert. She and Bruce were still sitting at the table when I left."

"Did she say if she intended to go straight home afterward?"

"She didn't say, but I'm guessing she didn't."

"What makes you say that?"

"Julie had on the same clothes Friday morning that she wore on Thursday. If she'd gone home, she would've changed into something more comfortable."

"Was she planning to meet someone later that evening?"

She cast a furtive glance at Dennis. He leaned in and she whispered in his ear. He nodded and responded in a hushed tone, his lips hidden behind a cupped hand.

"It's possible. From past conversations, 'forsaking all others' wasn't a part of her marriage vows, if you know what I mean. With her husband out of town, I don't think it would be out of the question for her to hook up with someone," CiCi replied.

"When Mrs. Reynolds talked about seeing other men, did she mention any names?"

"Never."

"Do you know how she gained entry to the building. According to the owners of Five Star, Julie didn't have a key."

CiCi's lower lip trembled as she fought back tears. "I loaned her my key so she could double-check some work. If I hadn't done that, she'd probably still be alive."

"Huh. You mentioned that Mrs. Reynolds repeated the word 'key' several times. Do you have any idea what she meant by that?"

"No. I assumed she was referring to the key I'd given her." Her fingers twisted the tissue in her hands and her foot tapped against the cement floor. Suddenly, she stilled. "Keenan. I thought she said 'key', but she might've been trying to say her husband's name. Does he know about Julie?"

"We haven't located him yet. Do you know where he is?"

"No. I understand he left Thursday afternoon to go on a fishing trip with some of his buddies. Ask Ivan, Izzy's husband. They're best friends."

"According to a few of your co-workers, you and Mrs. Reynolds were viewed as acting secretive at work."

Dennis interrupted before CiCi could answer. "Detective, there's nothing criminal about whispering or having secrets at work."

"Then she won't mind answering the question." Sullivan tapped his pen on the tablet. His gaze never wavered from CiCi's face as he waited. Dennis motioned for her to continue.

CiCi sighed. "Julie came across something she didn't understand. Because of my past bookkeeping experience, she asked if I'd take a look. By the time we met at Stella's, Julie said she'd found a solution to the problem, making my help unnecessary."

"Why didn't she ask Norma? Wasn't that her job?"

"Norma wasn't keen on being replaced after her car accident, even temporarily, and Julie didn't want to give the impression she couldn't handle the job. She worried Norma might influence Rex when it came time for a job evaluation. That's why we agreed to meet at Stella's. Julie had spoken to Bruce about the problem days earlier, but he never got back with her. Maybe that's what they stayed to discuss after I left Stella's."

"But you have doubts about that, don't you?" The detective flipped to a new page in the notebook. "According to your employers, you were more than qualified to handle Norma's job. It must've been hard to see someone from outside the company fill the vacancy. Were you angry Five Star hired Julie for the position?"

"It was *I* who suggested Floyd contact the temp agency to hire Julie. She and I had taken college classes together. Although we didn't travel in the same circles, she helped me through a very rough patch in my life. I wanted to return the favor."

"Why didn't you just fill the position until Norma returned to full duty?"

"My mother's condition had worsened by then and I spent less time at work than usual. Besides, I found I prefer researching for the appraisers over accounting."

"So, you just going to let all that education go to waste?"

"I have other ways to keep my skills sharp. I help in the accounting office at work when they get swamped or take vacation, which isn't often, and I also volunteer my services to a couple of small charitable organizations once or twice a month."

Dennis frowned. "Where are you going with this?"

"Well, Mr. Browning, I'm trying to determine if your client harbored any resentment after being passed over for Norma's job. Pent up animosity is a dangerous thing and might be a motive for the altercation Miss Winslow had with Mrs. Reynolds in the parking lot a couple of days prior to her murder."

Dennis straightened and glared at his client. "Detective," he said sharply, "I need a few minutes alone with Miss Winslow. And turn that audio/video off when you leave."

The detective grabbed his notes and left the room. CiCi tried to swallow, but her throat turned as dry as a slice of burnt toast.

"How in the hell could you forget to tell me something like that?" Dennis snapped. He glanced at her pale face and sighed, immediately regretting his outburst. "Okay, let's both take a deep breath. Now, word for word, tell me what was said during that argument."

A few minutes later, Detective Sullivan came back into the room carrying an envelope. He took a seat and focused a steely gaze on her face. As he rolled up the sleeves of his shirt, his voice took on a decidedly different tone. "Let's take up where we left off. What were you two arguing about? A witness says Mrs. Reynolds threw a punch and knocked you down."

"That's a lie!" CiCi tapped her foot nervously against the floor. Dennis laid a firm hand on her knee and subtly shook his head.

"Okay then, tell me your version."

CiCi started from the beginning, describing Julie's numerous "accidents" and Keenan's veiled threats in Stella's parking lot. By the time she told of her and Julie's argument in Five Star's parking lot, her voice wavered under the strain.

"I caught her by surprise that morning and saw deep bruises on her arms. She and Keenan fought the night before about him taking a fishing trip they couldn't afford. When she took the blame for her injuries, I lost it. I confronted her because I know how it feels to be…"

She inhaled sharply, surprised the words had slipped from her tongue. Her gaze lowered to the shredded tissue in her hands. *Compose yourself. Take it slow and easy. Stick to the present and what actually happened. Don't reveal more than he needs to know. It's none of his business.*

She cleared her throat and then continued. "I wanted her to stay at my place, away from that abusive jerk. When she refused, we argued. I ran after her and grabbed her arm. She jerked away and I fell. It was purely unintentional."

He fingered the envelope on the table before he looked up and asked, "Tell me again how the blood got on your shirt that morning."

"I've already told you. I was talking to the dispatcher, but had to put the phone down to put pressure on Julie's wounds. When I picked it up again, my hand was covered in…" She paused to swallow, wishing she could erase the image from her mind. "After the phone slipped through my fingers, I wiped my hands on my shirt."

He pulled a photo from the envelope and slid the picture of a pocketknife across the table. CiCi stifled a gag as her eyes fixated on the blade covered with blood—Julie's blood. She pushed the photo aside and looked away.

"Have you seen that pocketknife before, Miss Winslow?"

She steeled herself and looked again. "Other than Friday morning, no, I haven't. We keep a similar knife in the supply room, but that," she said, pointing to the photo, "isn't it. The blade is longer and the design on the handle is different."

"You're observant," he said, nodding with approval. "Were you mad enough to continue that argument on Friday morning?"

Dennis stood at the onset of the blatant accusation. "That's enough, Detective! She's your witness, not a suspect. If you have evidence to prove otherwise, charge her. If not, get your act together, or we're leaving." He advised CiCi not to answer, but his words fell on deaf ears.

"What are you saying?" Her voice crackled with disbelief and anger. Tears threatened to overflow as she jumped from her chair and pushed her attorney aside. Sullivan rose from his seat when she charged around the table. She angrily jabbed a finger in his chest, increasing the pressure with each statement. "Are you accusing me of murder? I would never hurt Julie! Never. I tried to help, but I failed. I failed, and now she's dead."

Dennis pulled her back into the chair, where she sobbed openly. He handed her a handkerchief, then whispered in her ear. She nodded. Her hands trembled as she dabbed away the tears and blew her nose.

"You haven't been accused of anything," Sullivan snarled, "at least not yet. It was a simple question. So far, all I have is your account of what *supposedly* happened and a murder weapon with only one set of identifiable fingerprints on it—*yours*."

"I have a perfectly good explanation why my fingerprints are on the knife. I thought the attacker was coming back, so I picked it up. I was the last person to use it—no, no…not *use* it, I meant *touch* it." Her gaze darted to the surveillance camera.

"Not another word, CiCi," Dennis commanded. "She's been more than cooperative, Detective Sullivan. Are we done?"

"Not quite. I have a few questions *about* Miss Winslow."

"Miss Winslow's personal life is not the focus of this case."

"We'll see about that."

TEN

CiCi tensed at Detective Sullivan's last comment.

"Let's talk about you, Miss Winslow. Do you have enemies, someone who wants to cause you harm?"

She looked at Mark, and their eyes locked. He had hit a nerve, and they both knew it. She glanced at the twisted handkerchief in her hands and shook her head. "Concentrate on finding Julie's killer and leave my problems out of it."

Sullivan ignored her comment and continued his line of questioning. "What if the killer actually came looking for *you*, Miss Winslow? Think about it. You and Julie both have blonde hair, drive black Jeeps, and work at the same place. Maybe *she* died instead of *you*. Perhaps her murder was a tragic case of mistaken identity."

CiCi jerked back as though she'd been slapped. Her heart raced, and panic filled her chest like a balloon. *Is that possible? Was Julie simply in the wrong place at the wrong time? Was I the intended victim, the one who was supposed to die?*

She closed her eyes against the new revelation that placed her front and center in the murder case. Dennis leaned in and quietly urged her to answer. She shook her head and refused to cooperate.

"I'll let you in on a little secret, Miss Winslow. I've read the two police reports taken not too long ago at Mr. Browning's office. I'd consider your dad a viable threat, wouldn't you?"

"If you read the reports, why ask? My family problems have nothing to do with Julie's murder. They are two different animals."

"Maybe, maybe not. My job is to look at all the possibilities. Let me rephrase my earlier question. Did your father show up that morning to finish what he started at the lawyer's office?" He stood and leaned over her chair. He lowered his voice, but the power and authority behind it were unmistakable. "Did Jack Parker attack you after he stabbed your friend to death?"

Her body seemed to crumble under the weight of his words. Her watery gaze held his until a bygone image of a pocketknife slashing her thigh flashed through her mind. Her fingers absently traced along the scar. She blinked several times, and then looked away. "This…this couldn't have anything to do with my dad," she stammered.

"I think you're having doubts. Are you sure the killer and your father aren't the same person?"

She lowered her head and closed her eyes to shut out the world. The room remained silent, the stillness broken only by the loud growling of her stomach. Still, the detective hovered and waited for an answer—an answer she could scarcely put into words.

Detective Sullivan softened his tone. "Okay, so give me one good reason why you think it *wasn't* your dad. Just one."

Seconds ticked by. Then, in a voice softer than a whisper, she answered. "Because I remember all too well what my dad's anger feels like in the dark."

Shock flickered across Sullivan's face, then quickly disappeared. His jaw clenched and his eyes turned hard. "Would you repeat that, Miss Winslow, a little louder, please?" he asked.

Her attorney tilted his head and leaned close in order to hear, but she declined with a shake of her head. The detective pulled back and glanced at the one-way mirror. He ran a hand across his face, then turned and took a seat. He watched and waited for her to make the next move.

She inhaled deeply before finding the courage to speak again.

"Everything happened so fast. The darkness distorted my perception, but the guy didn't seem as tall or as big as my dad."

"What do you mean 'as big'?" The hard, sharp edge in his voice had vanished.

"You know, not as big around. Kind of like you and Chad. You're close to the same height and build, but you're a tad thicker in the body." She grimaced the moment the words left her mouth. *Insulting him is not the smartest thing to do.*

Detective Sullivan flipped the notebook closed and slid the pen into his shirt pocket. "That'll be all for today. Remember, don't leave town, and don't talk to the media. As soon as we are finished processing your car, we'll let you know. I'm sure we'll be talking again." In a surprising move, he pulled a candy bar from his pants pocket and slid it across the table. "Here, take this. I hear you've got a big sweet tooth. It'll tide you over until you can get something decent to eat."

Detective Sullivan showed the attorney and his client the way out before walking down the hall and into the room where Officer Frank Guzman and Detectives Al Logan and Chad Cooper had been watching the interview. He reminded the men not to discuss the interview with anyone and then gave a nod to indicate Logan and Guzman were dismissed. Guzman patted Chad on the shoulder as he passed. After the door closed, Sullivan heaved a sigh and slumped into a chair next to Chad.

"I know that was tough to watch, but I had to treat her like anyone else. Of course, had she been anyone else, I probably would have pushed harder. Or at least, arrested her for assaulting an officer of the law."

"You don't know how difficult it was to keep from busting the door down, scooping her up in my arms, and taking her out of there."

Mark studied the pained look on Chad's face, not with the eyes of a seasoned detective, but with the heart of a friend. "You've fallen hard for her, haven't you?

The corners of Chad's mouth lifted and he nodded. "More than you know."

Mark rubbed a beefy hand over his face. "We all know she didn't do it. It's a shame we don't have any usable prints on the pocketknife except hers. None of her co-workers mentioned the bruises or problems at home, so at least she gave us a few new leads to follow."

Mark directed a pointed look at Chad. "I plan to check on Jack's whereabouts that night. I want *you* to stay away from him. Understood?"

Chad nodded in frustration and raked a hand through his hair. "I barely heard her answer at one point, but what I did catch…"

"That may be something you'll want to follow up on in the future. If it were me, I'd leave it be for now." Mark's yawn brought his advice to a halt. He shook his head, stood up, and stretched. "Tomorrow we'll piece together what we have, do some follow-up interviews, and see if we can locate the owner of that bloody footprint we found behind that big leafy plant at the crime scene. I suspect that's where the killer hid when CiCi came down the hallway. In the meantime, I've got a car posted outside the victim's home in case the husband shows up. When he does, I'll give you a call."

He stopped in the doorway on his way out. With a bemused expression on his face, he turned and patted his midsection. "Call me next time you go to the gym. According to your girlfriend, I need to spend more time working out."

As CiCi walked with Dennis out to his car, her body trembled with the emotional after-effects of her police interview. Once she settled into the passenger seat, Dennis pulled a sweatshirt from the back seat and draped it across her shoulders.

"Take a breath, CiCi," he said. "You did fine."

She gave him an incredulous look as she broke off a chunk of candy bar and popped it into her mouth. "You're kidding, right? He thinks I killed her! Did you miss the part about my fingerprints on the knife and my shouting match with the victim in the parking lot? I'll probably be arrested as soon as I get home."

"You have nothing to worry about. Detective Sullivan is smart enough to know that an innocent suspect is a good source of information. He was goading you. His job is to push people to the edge. People often say or remember things when they're under pressure. There's no evidence against you or he would've charged you with murder on the spot."

"I hope you're right."

He started the engine and let the car idle. Strumming his fingers on the steering wheel, he stared out the window, as though deep in thought. He turned with a stern expression and faced her. "Detective Sullivan made an excellent observation, CiCi. As your attorney, I want you to be honest with me. *Was* it your father who attacked you and murdered Julie Reynolds?"

"No. At least, I don't think so. As I said, it was dark and it happened so fast." CiCi leaned her head back against the seat and closed her eyes. "I understand why he would link my assault to the murder, but I think he's jumping to the wrong conclusion. I know my father better than anyone, and I'm almost certain he wasn't the man I tangled with."

"Okay. That's good enough for me, at least until the detective proves otherwise. If he wants to interview you again, call me. I'll refer you to someone who's more familiar with criminal law than I am. I don't want you to be tricked into making a confession, although I can't imagine you'd fall for that, considering how stubborn you are." Dennis shook his head as he pulled away from the curb.

Fifteen minutes later, she and Dennis stood in line at the Speckled Pig. Dennis pulled out his wallet. At the urging of her lawyer, CiCi placed an order. Before she knew what had happened, her pulled pork sandwich and a chocolate shake had all but disappeared.

ELEVEN

C iCi found a bleary-eyed Chad in her kitchen the next morning, sipping coffee and eating a slice of cinnamon raisin toast. His work attire indicated he would not be attending church with her, or taking her to an afternoon movie, or washing his truck. After a morning kiss, she turned to the fridge for a glass of orange juice.

"I didn't hear you come in last night. It must've been late."

"It was. I tried not to wake you. I assume you slept well, if the snoring I heard was any indication."

"I don't snore!"

"It was either you or a train rumbling through your bedroom." He grinned and finished the last of his coffee. He clipped his gun and badge on his belt, then kissed her goodbye.

CiCi glanced at the clock, and then dashed up the stairs to shower and change. An hour later, she slipped into her usual pew at First Baptist. Tasha slid over to make room. Several people turned and caught CiCi's eye with a sympathetic nod, a friendly wave, or an encouraging smile. A thin veil of whispers floated across the sanctuary and drew CiCi's attention to her right. Two older women had their heads together, nodding and murmuring behind cupped hands, glancing CiCi's way. When she smiled back, they quickly looked away. *Are they talking about me, or am I being paranoid?*

"Chad working?" Tasha whispered when she noticed CiCi had come alone.

CiCi nodded and opened her hymnal as the robed choir took their places on the raised platform behind the pulpit. After two hymns, a congregational prayer, a vocal solo, and the collection of tithes and offerings, Pastor Young began his sermon. The scripture reading was like a soothing balm to her troubled mind. At the conclusion of the service, she chatted with a few friends, then bid Tasha goodbye and headed home.

After eating lunch and tidying up the house, she swept the patio and filled the bird feeder hanging from the porch's overhang. Back inside, she read the Sunday paper, finished the crossword puzzle, and then surfed the internet. She called Julie's home, but no one answered. Bored, she shut down the computer and looked around. There was little else to do other than laundry. She wrinkled her nose at the thought. Fresh air and a change of scenery sounded like the perfect antidote.

She raced upstairs, slipped on her running clothes, and tied her hair back. After a series of stretches to warm her muscles, she grabbed a cheap pair of red sunglasses and headed out the door. A gentle breeze caressed her face as she ran in the opposite direction of her usual path. The guilt she felt over giving Julie a key that ultimately led to her death dogged CiCi's every step.

Twenty minutes later, she found herself at the entrance to Meadowlark Park. Slowing to a walk, she followed the path that circled the outer edge of the field. Halfway around the park, she stopped to drink from the water fountain, and then moved to a grassy area. A few cool down stretches and deep cleansing breaths later, her mind and body felt rejuvenated. She glanced around. The sweet sounds of life were everywhere. Families picnicked on blankets spread on the grass, children giggled as they played, dogs raced after Frisbees, and a coach shouted instructions to the uniformed players on the field.

Her gaze came to rest on a familiar face. She took off her

sunglasses before pulling the neck of her T-shirt up to wipe the perspiration from her face. With her glasses back in place, she made her way across the grass and stopped beside the picnic table where Izzy sat with her nose in a book. Izzy never looked up. "Hey, Izzy. This seat taken?"

"CiCi! What? No, please, take a load off. I'm just catching up on my reading while the kids play. Beth has soccer practice and Billy is skateboarding. I'm hoping they'll burn off some energy before they drive me crazy."

"How's TJ?"

"Doing great. He and his Scout troop went camping this week-end. He should be home later this afternoon." Izzy's eyes were dull and the dark circles indicated a lack of sleep. A faint red mark and scratches peeked out from the neckline of her top. Izzy self-consciously covered the area when she caught CiCi looking.

"What happened to your neck? Ivan give you a hickey?"

"Yeah, but not where you can see it," she chuckled.

When Izzy sidestepped the question, CiCi dropped the subject. She knew Billy had behavioral issues, and Izzy's pride would never let her admit her son sometimes got out of control.

"It must be draining to keep up with the kids' school work, appointments, and extracurricular activities," CiCi said.

"It'll get worse when school's out for the summer. After TJ's dad and I divorced, I nearly went crazy trying to cope with every-thing by myself. I never want to be single again, especially now with three kids. I'm lucky to have married Ivan. He's such a great dad."

"I'm guessing Five Star will be closed for a few days. That should give you some 'me time' before school ends."

"I guess, but I can't say I care to take time off at Julie's expense."

"I know what you mean. I keep thinking I'll wake up and find it's all been a bad dream. Speaking of bad dreams, have the detec-tives talked to you yet?"

Izzy nodded. "Detective Logan has spoken to me a couple of times now." Izzy snickered when CiCi rolled her eyes. "Yeah, I had the same impression. He's about as sharp as a marble." Her gaze wandered the grounds to check on her kids. "I can't imagine walking in and finding her like that. How are you holding up?"

"Okay, I suppose. The last few days have been a blur, but every day is better than the last. It feels good to get out of the house and away from the phone. It kills...uh, bothers me to think the police consider me a prime suspect."

Izzy's eyes widened. "Seriously? They'd have to be plain stupid to believe you could do something like that."

"I know, right? The lead detective blasted me with questions until I cried. I never want to go through that again. You knew Julie better than I did. Were you able to think of anyone who might have wanted to hurt her?"

"No," she said, a little too quickly. "Well, except for maybe her husband. That man's a real piece of work."

"Yeah, except for him. For better or worse, Julie must have loved him a lot. I imagine he'll be devastated when he hears the news." CiCi wiped a smudge from her sunglasses. "I would imagine Ivan's upset, too. Didn't he and Julie attend high school together?"

Izzy glanced over again to check on Beth and Billy. "He and Julie graduated the same year and were very close, so naturally he's upset. We used to get together all the time, but you know how it is. People change." Izzy fell quiet, as though trapped in bygone memories.

"By the way, where is Ivan?" CiCi craned her neck and looked around the park.

"He had to go in to work. Such is the life of a self-employed electrician. When he gets a call, he goes—doesn't matter if it's a Sunday, or three in the morning."

"I'm surprised he didn't go fishing with Keenan this weekend," CiCi said.

"He planned to, but...things didn't work out."

"Hey, mind if I ask a personal question? I noticed some tension between you and Julie recently. Did it have something to do with work?"

"Sort of," she answered. "My referral landed Julie a prime job last year. Then out of the blue, she shows up at Five Star as a temp.

I asked around and heard she left the company because of an affair with a top executive. After I stuck my neck out for her, she goes and does something like that. Naturally, I was pissed. We got into an argument over it and she told me to butt out. She even went to Ivan's office and tried to turn him against me. Ivan was livid and told her to leave. Like I said, people change."

"As much as I liked Julie, I could never agree with her view of marriage. She called me old-fashioned and conservative, and I thanked her for the compliment."

"Good for you."

"Did you mention her affair to the detective?"

"No. The affair, *if* it's true, is bound to surface when the police check with her previous employers. I don't need Detective Logan darkening my door again, especially over a rumor."

Beth ran up, threw her arms around her mother's neck, and begged to go for ice cream. Izzy beamed with maternal love as she returned the hug. CiCi smiled and glanced away, hoping to hide the pain of not having a child of her own to love. For whatever reason, she never became pregnant again after her miscarriage, and it wasn't for a lack of her and Richie trying. CiCi's heart ached with envy as she watched them leave.

Chad's sister blew through CiCi's front door late that afternoon like a Kansas tornado, apologizing for not rushing back from the Ozarks sooner. "How are you coping, CiCi? Honestly."

"Now that the initial shock has worn off, I'm doing okay."

"When you didn't show up at the resort, I assumed you'd changed your mind," Megan explained. "I shut my phone off the moment I arrived, and didn't read Chad's text until I checked out. Your phone was busy every time I called. I was freaking out. I finally got ahold of Chad and he caught me up to speed. Talking about speed, I'm lucky I didn't get a ticket on the way home."

CiCi answered Megan's questions as they sat in the living room sipping tall glasses of iced tea. As CiCi described the event, the more upset she became.

"Let's talk about something else," Megan suggested. She gave a hilarious recap of their friends' shenanigans and a detailed review of the resort. Ultimately, the vacation destination earned a three-star rating from the group. Megan tried to convince CiCi she hadn't missed a thing, but CiCi argued that even a one-star resort beat a murder any day.

The phone rang frequently, proof that morbid curiosity was alive and well. Friends, co-workers, and even a local reporter called, each trying to glean a juicy tidbit of information. Later that evening, Chad stopped by after a long day at work. According to him, the investigation had turned up several new leads, but he stopped short of revealing anything specific.

CiCi heaved a sigh when the phone rang again. Snuggled in Chad's arms, she let the answering machine kick in. They listened as a voice drifted through the room.

"CiCi, Floyd here. Just calling to let you know Five Star will remain closed this week, and the office will get a professional cleaning before anyone returns to work. Everyone will receive their normal salary without dipping into vacation hours. I hope you're doing okay. If you need anything, or have questions, give me a call." There was a long pause. "And CiCi? We'll need to talk later about that key you loaned Julie. In the meantime, pick up an extra key the next time you're at the office."

Her machine beeped as it logged the message. The phone rang again and CiCi frowned. "I'll bet Floyd's had second thoughts about letting me have another key."

The angry voice on the recorder spewed venomous accusations and threats. Megan's face paled. "CiCi, is...is that your *dad?*" she asked.

Chad stiffened. CiCi shot out of his arms and across the room to stop the recorder, but he reached out and pulled her back. After the message stopped, he gripped her shoulders and turned her to face him. "It's him, isn't it? Don't deny it. I know that voice," he said sternly. "Is that the 'wrong number' you received the night we went out to dinner?"

"Yes, although I doubt that he even remembers he called."

"CiCi, you said you'd take care of it, but—"

"I *did* take care of it, Chad. I talked to Dennis, mostly because he understands why my dad is so mad at me. He promised he would handle it."

"Well, whatever he did, it isn't working. How often has Jack called?"

CiCi sighed. "He left similar messages after the meeting at the lawyer's office, and then again the night of our double date. I should have mentioned them, but I wanted to handle the situation myself. I thought Dennis could make him stop, but I guess I was wrong."

Chad's eyes turned stormy. The muscles in his jaw worked overtime and the cop mentality emerged. "Damn it, Cecilia! You need to file—"

"No! I'm not filing anything. When he realizes his scare tactics don't work, he'll eventually leave me alone."

"These threats sound serious, and they certainly bolster Mark's theory that you may have been the intended target."

"Well, I'm almost positive Mark's wrong," she said firmly.

"*Almost positive*? That's not good enough for me, especially if you're in danger." Chad released her and walked across the room. "I won't stand by and let him hurt you. I let you handle it, just like you wanted. Now, it's my turn." He tapped a few buttons on his cell phone. After hitting the play button on her answering machine, he recorded and saved the message to his phone.

She frowned. "Is that really necessary?"

"I know how to do my job, Cecilia." He returned the phone to his belt clip before his hard gaze fell on CiCi. "Do you want to explain what he has against you? It must have something to do with your mother's will if Dennis is involved."

Chad's cell phone buzzed. He glanced at the screen and marched outside to take the call away from listening ears. By the time he returned, his mood had softened.

"I'm sorry." He pulled her into his arms. "It's just...Jack's so unpredictable. After what happened at the lawyer's office, I'm worried he might follow through on those threats. I made a call, and an officer will pay him a visit this afternoon. If he shows up here, don't hesitate to call 9-1-1. Understand? I have to go check on another lead."

She turned her head, offering only her cheek and silence when he leaned in for a kiss. The look on his face sparked a thread of guilt. *That was petty of me. He's only trying to help.*

Chad stiffened. "I'm not backing down on this, CiCi. We'll talk later." As he walked to the door, he looped his arm through his sister's and pulled her outside.

CiCi peered out the window. Chad leaned against the bed of the truck with his arms folded his arms across his broad chest. He shook his head as he talked and nodded towards the house. Megan fired back and poked a finger in his chest. The back and forth exchange went on for several minutes. He pulled his phone from his belt and glanced at the screen. Giving his little sis a hug, he jumped into his truck and sped from the parking lot.

CiCi threw up her hands in frustration when Megan re-entered the kitchen. "That brother of yours can be infuriating at times."

"Don't I know it. I've had to deal with that protective streak of his for years." Megan took a can of pop from the fridge. After she pulled the tab and took a drink, she looked at CiCi. "But honestly, CiCi? How did you expect him to react after hearing that phone message? Especially after what happened at the lawyer's office. I can't figure out why you won't let him help you."

"I have my reasons." *Chad's an experienced detective. If he learns about the inheritance, one question will lead to another, and I'm not willing to go down that road. At least, not just yet.* "If it were anything else I would, but this stuff with my dad…it's complicated." She nibbled on her bottom lip and stared off into the distance. "Maybe if I call Dad back, I can put a stop to this nonsense. Besides, I've been wanting to ask if he's found my grandmother's wedding ring."

"Oh, no you don't. That's a very bad idea. Let Chad handle your dad."

"Chad shouldn't have to take on my problems. He has enough to deal with at work."

"Face it, CiCi, if something affects you, it affects him. Chad would protect you with his life if need be. You could never say that about Richie."

"True. You don't think Chad would do anything that would jeopardize his job, do you?"

"Like go crazy and beat up your dad?" Megan shook her head and took another drink. "I've never known him to step over the line, or lose his head. He loves his job too much—*almost* as much as he loves you."

"What else did he have to say in the parking lot?"

"He told me if things don't work out between me and Dennis, he would hook me up with Detective Logan," she said with a wink.

"And here I thought your brother loved you." CiCi laughed and immediately felt the tension in her chest ease its grip.

"I have an idea. Why don't I text Chad and tell him I'll stay over tonight? It'll be fun, like a slumber party," Megan said. After CiCi nodded her approval, Megan smiled. "Good. I haven't gone home yet, and my suitcases are still in the car."

Megan left, retrieved a small overnight bag from her vehicle, and carried it upstairs. When she returned, she wore pajamas and a big smile. "Let's get this show on the road. I'll make popcorn while you change, then we'll pick out a couple of movies."

TWELVE

"Morning, Detective Cooper." Detective Sullivan glanced at his watch. "Twenty minutes. Your fastest time yet." Mark's mental state was all business, as evidenced by the greeting.

"Didn't want to keep you waiting." Chad smiled and handed his co-worker a hot cup of coffee from a nearby convenience store. "This'll have to do, since there aren't any coffee shops open at one in the morning. I figure anything's better than the day-old sludge in the breakroom. What's happened so far?"

"Keenan Reynolds has been told of his wife's murder and Mirandized. He asked for a few moments alone. I took him in a cup of yesterday's coffee. Instead of going straight home after his fishing trip, he apparently stopped at Tipsy's and had a few beers. He insists he's sober enough to answer questions. So far, he's declined to have a lawyer present."

"Need me to back you up?"

"No. The Chief wants you to take a back seat until CiCi is officially cleared. You can monitor the interview from the other room." He glanced around. "Where the hell is Logan? He said he needed to take a leak. That was thirty minutes ago."

The two detectives separated. Chad slipped into the adjoining room to watch through the one-way mirror. Sullivan waited another minute for Logan to show up, then gave up and entered the interview room alone. Keenan sat at the table with his head cradled between his hands. He reeked of booze, body odor, and fish bait, in that order. Even sitting, Keenan was a tall man. Sullivan tossed a folder on the table and took a seat. Detective Logan shuffled into the room a few seconds later. Sullivan shook his head as Logan stuffed the last bite of a doughnut into his mouth and positioned himself at the back of the room against the wall.

"Mr. Reynolds, I know this is a difficult time for you, but we have a few more questions. You understand this conversation is being recorded, correct?"

Keenan nodded. "Yeah."

"Tell me about the last time you saw your wife." Sullivan leaned back in his chair. He hadn't had much sleep in the last three days, but he knew without a doubt he looked and felt better than Keenan.

"I met her around nine, uh, Thursday night in the parking lot at Five Star. I was out picking up supplies for my trip and thought I'd say good-bye before I left town for the weekend."

"Why she was working so late?"

He shrugged. "Something to do with payroll. I was supposed to leave earlier in the day, so she didn't expect to see me."

"What did you two talk about?"

"Nothing much. I told her I'd be back whenever I got back. She said okay." He shook his head and stared off into space. "Actually, Jules—"

"Jules? Are you referring to your wife?" Detective Logan asked.

"Yeah, I call her Jules. She said a lot more than that. She was pissed—pissed about me going on the trip. She said I didn't work enough hours to earn a vacation, but I didn't care. I needed to get out of town. Being self-employed is more stressful than I thought."

"Did you go inside Five Star to talk?" Logan pushed away from the wall and casually took a seat at the end of the table.

Keenan cocked his head and looked briefly at Sullivan, then Logan. "Nope."

The slight hesitation didn't escape Sullivan's attention. "Were there any other cars in the parking lot?"

"No, but someone pulled out at the other end of the lot as I pulled in."

"Could you tell who it was, or what kind of car?"

Keenan frowned and shook his head. "Sorry."

"Did she leave the premises when you did?"

After clearing his throat, he said, "Nah. She, uh, went inside when I pulled out of the lot.

Sullivan sat forward and pushed a legal pad and pen across the table. "Mr. Reynolds, I want the name of everyone you saw between eight o'clock Thursday night and two o'clock Friday morning. Also, write down what route you took to your destination."

"What? You asking me for an alibi?" The stony look on Sullivan's face spoke volumes. Keenan did as he was told. When he finished, he shoved the information across the table. "My buddies didn't show until Friday morning about ten o'clock. We fished all weekend, but didn't catch a thing."

"Mr. Reynolds, what size of shoe do you wear?"

"You've got to be kidding me. My wife has been murdered, and you're asking what size shoe I wear? Unbelievable." Keenan looked at Sullivan with disgust and sighed. "Twelve."

Sullivan's gaze rested on Keenan's hands and then moved to the open collar of his shirt. "How did you get the scraped knuckles and the scratches on your neck?"

"Seriously? You don't go traipsing through brush, chop kindling, or gut fish without getting a few cuts and scrapes."

"That may be true, but your wife scratched someone that night." He slid a picture of the bloody pocketknife from the folder. "Recognize this?"

Keenan leaned forward and took a close look at the picture. The muscles in his jaw turned rigid. "My dad gave me a knife like that for my eighteenth birthday. Is…is that what she was killed with?"

Sullivan ignored the question. "When's the last time you saw your knife?"

Keenan stiffened. His eyes flamed with anger as his gaze

bounced between the two detectives. He pointed an accusing finger at Detective Sullivan. "I see what you're doing! You're not going to pin this on me! I would *never* do that to her! I loved her."

"When's the last time you saw your knife, Mr. Reynolds."

With a cocky smirk, Keenan said, "I want a lawyer."

Two hours later, attorney Gene Volker arrived and demanded time to consult with his client before questioning resumed. When Sullivan and Logan returned to the room, Volker sat talking to Keenan. Their low murmurings came to a halt as the detectives took a seat.

"Detective Sullivan, are you charging my client with murder?"

"Mr. Reynolds admitted to owning a knife similar to the murder weapon. I simply asked the whereabouts of that knife. Any assumptions he drew from that are not of my doing."

"It would be in my client's best interest if we continued after he has had some rest."

"Let's get on with it!" Keenan shouted over his attorney's protests.

Sullivan complied. "Mrs. Reynolds had bruises on her arms. I understand they were put there by you."

"You must've been talking to that nosy gal at her work. She needs to mind her own damn business. She tried to turn Jules against me, but Jules loved me too much to listen to her."

"The medical examiner also noted several scars and old fractures during the autopsy. Do you have a reasonable explanation for those injuries?"

"Mr. Reynolds, don't answer that," Volker commanded.

"I merely want Mr. Reynolds to enlighten me how his wife acquired so many injuries. Did she suffer from a medical condition that caused her to lose her balance and fall? Were they into S&M, trying to spice up their sex life? Or, did a few of their arguments get out of hand? I'm guessing it might've been the latter."

Keenan crossed his arms over his broad chest. "Every married couple has arguments that get out of hand, but that doesn't mean I killed her. We've had our ups and downs, but Jules never complained."

"Is that so. Did your wife plan to take a trip while you were out of town?"

Keenan's eyes narrowed and his nostrils flared. "What the hell are you talking about?"

"You'll be getting your wife's Jeep and personal effects back in a few days, so I might as well tell you what we found." Sullivan tried to hide the pleasure he took from revealing the next bit of information. "The back of her vehicle contained several suitcases. I'd say she was planning on leaving town. Maybe instead of complaining, she decided to do something about it."

Keenan's shock morphed into denial, and eventually gave way to full-blown rage. He slammed both fists on the table and stood with such force, his chair overturned and slammed to the floor. Volker scrambled out of the way as both detectives barreled forward and pinned Keenan against the wall. The door to the room flew open. A burly officer with a stun gun stood ready to enter the fray.

"Calm down," Detective Sullivan growled. "Don't make this harder than it needs to be, or you'll find yourself in a cell. Now, when we let go, you sit your ass in the chair and keep it there. Understand?"

Keenan nodded. After releasing their grip, the two detectives stepped back. Keenan turned. His eyes darted about the room as he calculated the looming odds against him. In defiance, he slammed the chair upright and sat down. Sullivan and Logan resumed their earlier positions. The backup officer remained inside the doorway, his hand resting on his weapon, until Sullivan dismissed him. The officer nodded and closed the door behind him.

Volker immediately jumped to his client's defense. "He's upset and still under the influence. It's traumatic enough to arrive home and find his wife dead and the police lying in wait. To be viewed as a murder suspect would push anyone over the edge."

Sullivan removed a document from the folder and pushed it across the table to the lawyer. "Here's the search warrant for his home, financial records, cell phones, and vehicles. My team has already begun."

Keenan cursed and banged a fist on the table, but the hatred and outrage he directed toward Sullivan had no effect.

"I think we're done here, detective," Volker said.

"That'll be all, at least for now. We'll be in touch."

Volker started for the exit. Keenan followed close behind. As he walked out the door, he shouted a few explicit suggestions about what the detectives could do in their spare time.

Sullivan dismissed Logan, then slipped into the adjoining room. Chad shook his head. "His shoe size isn't a match, but pretty darn close. It might be his knife, but hell, do you know any guy around here who doesn't carry a pocketknife? That brand is about as common as you can get. And if she did scratch him, it doesn't prove murder, even if the DNA matches."

Sullivan nodded in agreement. "I'll have Logan contact every name on the list Keenan gave us and check to see if he stopped for groceries or gas."

"There's no doubt he stopped for beer on the way. Personally, I think the only fishing he did was when he fished a beer out of his cooler."

"Yeah, and who knows what else may turn up?" Sullivan looked at his watch. "I'm beat. I'm going home to catch a couple hours of sleep. You might want to go home and do the same."

"Good idea."

THIRTEEN

Around ten o'clock Monday morning, after CiCi had taken a casserole from the freezer to thaw for dinner, the phone rang. "Hello?"

"CiCi? This is Maxine, from A Hand-Up. I hope I didn't catch you at a bad time, but I wanted to touch base with you about Saturday." A Hand-Up was a local charitable organization that helped those struggling to make ends meet, and Saturdays were always busy.

"Not to worry. I'll be there at my usual time, Maxine. In fact, I'm looking forward to it." CiCi donated her accounting expertise a few hours a month, and afterward helped Maxine and her staff hand out food, clothing, and words of encouragement to families in need. A local teen made balloon animals, much to the delight of the children.

"That's why I called. I've read about what happened at your place of employment, and also heard a few rumors. The whole matter is quite disturbing. Perhaps it would be best if you took a little time off. I'm sure we can manage until things blow over."

"But, why? I…I'm certainly not a killer if that's what you're worried about."

"Of course, you're not," she purred, "but we need to consider the comfort level of the families and children who come here. You understand, don't you, dear? I'll call you next month. With any luck, the matter will be resolved by then. Take care. Bye-bye."

I wonder how many other people around town think I'm guilty of murder? It wasn't a pleasant thought.

The sound of the doorbell startled her back to the present. She went to the door and relieved Tasha of a carryout tray holding two large cappuccinos. "Let's take these to the living room and get comfy."

They settled on the couch, sipped their drinks, and discussed the troubling events at Five Star. When CiCi brought up the topic of Maxine's phone call, Tasha shook her head. "Girl, until now, I've never heard of anyone being forced to take a leave of absence from a volunteer job."

"To insinuate I might be guilty of murder is just wrong," CiCi said as she set her half-finished drink on the end table.

"Don't worry. Knowing Maxine, she probably started the rumors herself. She'll be begging you to come back when she gets in a bind. You're the most experienced volunteer she has when it comes to straightening out their books."

"Speaking of needing my expertise, that reminds me of some-thing." CiCi then mentioned Julie's plea for help with an account and the flash drive she promised to make, but failed to deliver. "I need that flash drive to view the problem as a whole, because I looked at the copy Julie gave me and didn't see an issue with the report."

"Do you think Julie stopped by home before she showed up at Stella's? Maybe she left it there."

CiCi quieted, as though deep in thought. "I need to drop off the suit I wore to Mom's funeral at the dry cleaners, and return a baking dish to Mrs. Harmon. Since we'll be out and about, it wouldn't hurt to make a quick stop by Julie's house to ask."

"You know, one of these days your curiosity is going to get you into trouble."

"Think about it. What if that flash drive has a connection to

Julie's murder? I know it's a long shot, but if I discover anything that will help move the investigation along and clear my name, I'm all for it. Do you have any idea how I feel when people whisper behind my back at church or suddenly turn and head in the opposite direction when I walk down a grocery aisle? Not good. Besides, Julie was a huge support after my miscarriage. How did I repay her? I give her a key to a building where she gets murdered."

"What happened at Five Star is not your fault, CiCi."

"Tell that to my heart."

After dropping off the suit at the cleaners, they drove to the home of Mrs. Harmon and caught her just as she stepped outside with her little black dog. Tasha stayed in the car while CiCi returned the empty dish. "I came to return your dish and thank you for the delicious meal you brought over after Mom's funeral. It was so thoughtful of you."

Mrs. Harmon, an energetic woman in her late fifties, took the dish with a smile and set it on the floor inside the front door. "I'm glad you liked it, and you're timing is perfect. Inky and I are headed out for a brisk stroll. We walk several times around the block every morning and every evening." Inky pulled at her leash and barked repeatedly at CiCi. "Yes, we do," she cooed, turning her full attention to the black ball of fur. "Is mama's girl ready to go for a walk? Yes, she is."

"Well, I'll let you get to it, and thanks again for the meal."

CiCi and Tasha then drove to the Reynolds' house to offer condolences and deliver the casserole CiCi had taken from the freezer earlier that morning. The food she received after her mother's funeral had been a comfort and she thought it only fitting to offer that same courtesy to another grieving soul. She had to admit, after knowing how Keenan had treated his wife, she was curious to see how Julie's murder affected him.

As Tasha pulled in front of the house, CiCi gazed at the boat parked askew in the driveway and asked, "Do you think anyone's home?"

"I don't know. I don't see Keenan's truck."

"Julie's Jeep is fairly new and Keenan's truck and boat aren't more than a couple of years old. How do you suppose they afford such expensive vehicles? Julie said Keenan's new business venture was struggling."

Tasha shrugged as she shifted the car into park and turned off the engine. The two women got out and made their way to the front door, where Tasha rang the doorbell.

Keenan answered, and leaned unsteadily against the doorframe with a beer in his hand, looking as though he had just returned from his fishing trip. His sunburned face and bed-head hair were nearly the same color. His clothes were rumpled and soiled, with what she didn't want to know. His bloodshot eyes filled with contempt when he spotted her. He removed a pair of green earbuds from his ears. "Well, if it isn't Miss Goody Two Shoes and her side-kick. Sorry, I'm not taking visitors. There's been a death in the family."

CiCi momentarily lost her voice, but quickly recovered. "We're sorry for your loss. Tasha and I came to offer our condolences. We brought you an enchilada and rice casserole." She held out the casserole, only to have it refused.

"Don't need your kind of help. You've done enough. I bet you're the one who told the police all kinds of lies about me. Now they suspect me of killing my own wife." He studied her face as he took a swig of beer. "You don't seem surprised. Now, why doesn't that shock me?"

"For your information, they suspect me also. I answered the detective's questions as truthfully as I could. I want Julie's killer brought to justice." Her gaze slid over to Tasha, only to find her friend had taken a step back.

Keenan pulled himself upright and stepped outside. His height alone was intimidating, and a drop of fear trickled down CiCi's spine. "But you *think* I killed her, don't you? Well, I didn't. I loved her, even though we had our share of problems. Believe me, Jules was a different person at home than what you saw at work."

"Speaking of work, Julie copied some work information to a flash drive. I know it's not the most appropriate time to ask, but I wonder if she might have left it here. I really need it." Now that the only breadwinner in the household had died, CiCi decided to step outside the box. "I'd be willing to pay if you find it."

The mention of money caught his attention. "The police left right before you showed up," he said. "They searched the house. Even took my truck. I read over the list of stuff they took, but I don't remember seeing one. If I come across it, how much you talking about?"

Oh, yeah, he's drowning in grief. "We can haggle over a price when you find it. Julie intended to give it to me Thursday night at Stella's but must've forgotten."

"Stella's? I met up with her at work. Told me she had to work on the payroll."

CiCi's eyes widened. "You saw her Thursday night at Five Star?"

"What the hell was she doing with you at Stella's?" His voice rose and his eyes shot daggers at CiCi. He stepped forward, forcing both women to take two steps back.

"We..." CiCi gulped and cleared her throat. "We met to talk about work, but ended up chatting about other stuff over dinner. You know...girl talk."

"Was she complaining that I need to get a real job? I may not have brought home the dough, but that didn't stop her from buying designer clothes, or going out to eat at fancy restaurants every week with Leslie, or filling her closet with pricey shoes." His eyes glanced from Tasha's face to her purple and red platform sandals. "I bet you had something to do with that."

"Hey! Don't be giving my shoes the evil eye."

"Honestly, Keenan, she never mentioned a word about your job situation that night." CiCi wondered if he caught the qualifier, because *that night* was one of the few nights Julie hadn't mention his lack of a steady paycheck.

"Then what? Was she bellyaching again that I mistreated her?" Keenan spat on the sidewalk, then pointed a finger in CiCi's face. "Was she moving in with you? Huh? Is that why she packed up her stuff? You and your foolish ideas are the reason she's dead. If she'd been home where she belonged, she'd still be alive. Get off my property, both of you, and leave me alone!" Keenan leaned forward, both hands balled into fists.

As Tasha and CiCi stepped back out of his reach, CiCi stumbled and the casserole slipped from her hands. The contents fell in the grass nearby, and the container landed in a small bush. Her arms circled in the air as she tried to keep her balance. She lost the battle, fell against Tasha, and they both ended up on the ground. When CiCi tried to right herself, she slipped, and her butt landed smack dab in the middle of the enchilada casserole. She winced at the mushy feeling under her derriere and gritted her teeth when Keenan doubled over with laughter.

"I couldn't have asked for a better end to your visit." Keenan turned and went inside. The door slammed shut with a deafening thud.

CiCi stood and stepped over to retrieve the empty container. Two mutts from next door nearly ran her over trying to get a free lunch. With part of an enchilada clinging to the back of her pants, she felt lucky one of the dogs hadn't tried to take a bite out of her behind.

Questions spilled from Tasha's lips as they walked to the car. "What was that all about? What did he mean about Julie packing up? Was she was moving out?"

"I haven't a clue. Maybe this Leslie person knows. I don't recall Julie mentioning her name, but they must be close if they went out to eat every week."

CiCi traded Tasha the empty dish for a white kitchen trash bag kept in the trunk for emergencies. If having your butt covered in enchilada casserole didn't qualify as an emergency, CiCi didn't know what did. While Tasha tucked the casserole dish in an empty cardboard box, CiCi opened both car doors on the passenger side and stood between them. Tasha came around and held out an extra bag to block CiCi from public view.

CiCi tore open the bottom of the trash bag, slid the bag over her head and down to her waist, and tightened the drawstring. She simultaneously shimmied out of her slacks and pulled down the open end of the trash bag to cover her near nakedness. Tasha dropped the soiled garment into the spare trash bag, while CiCi jumped into the passenger seat and buckled up.

"What do you suppose the police found inside their house?" Tasha asked as she climbed into the driver's seat. Together, they sat and stared at the dogs chowing down on the free meal.

"Don't have any idea. Well, what should we do now?" CiCi laughed when Tasha's stomach rumbled. "I'm guessing we need to stop somewhere for lunch."

"You *do* remember you're wearing a trash bag for a skirt, don't you? The pink hearts on your bikini panties show right through the bag. Of course, if the person taking our order gets a peek at that, we might get to eat for free."

FOURTEEN

"You wanted to see me?" The nervousness in CiCi's voice was unmistakable as she stood at the entrance to Detective Sullivan's office late Tuesday morning.

"Yes, yes," he said. "Come in and have a seat."

She gave Mark a wary smile as he circled around the desk and gave her a firm handshake. Though he reeked of confidence, of one used to being in control, he appeared far less intimidating than he had during her interview.

He smiled, then settled into the large swivel chair behind his desk. "Considering I almost pushed you over the edge during our last meeting, I felt it only fitting to deliver the good news face-to-face. We have eliminated you as a prime suspect in the murder of Julie Reynolds."

She closed her eyes for a few seconds and savored the moment. Her shoulders relaxed and the tension in her body seemed to melt away.

"I apologize for being so rough on you the other day, but that's my job, to dig out the truth when horrible things happen to people. However, you're our only witness, so if you remember anything else, we want to hear about it. I'm sure you would feel more comfortable talking with Chad, but keep my number handy in case you can't get in touch with him."

"Detective, can you tell me what changed your mind, besides the fact that I didn't do it?"

"Come on, CiCi, drop the formality. You can't hold it against me because I was doing my job. Chad would've done the same thing if the situation was reversed."

"You're right," she sighed. "I'm sorry. Julie's murder has been so upsetting."

"I understand, and I'm sorry for what you're going through. I can't tell you everything, but I'll tell you this much. From the angle of her wounds, the attacker was at least six-feet tall, which supports your recollection. Also, we found a receipt in your purse showing you purchased a bottle of juice at the corner convenience store before you went to the office. That's something you forgot to mention. We reviewed their surveillance tapes. There were no visible signs of blood on your clothes. I won't get into the technical aspects, but the medical examiner said Mrs. Reynolds received her first injury before you arrived."

"What about my fingerprints on the knife?"

"Yeah, about that…the only other print on the handle was too smudged to identify. The crime scene techs picked up numerous prints around the room. Yours, of course, as well as Ashley's, Izzy's, the three owners, and a couple of unidentified prints we're still trying to find a match for."

He leaned forward, braced his elbows on the desk, and paused, as though unsure whether or not to continue. "The autopsy revealed Mrs. Reynolds had numerous injuries consistent with abuse. I applaud you for trying to help her. It was a courageous thing to do. Not many people are willing to get involved with domestic issues. In a way, you tried to save her life twice."

"I tried, but my help came too late," she replied. Her eyes misted at the thought.

Mark leaned forward and handed her a tissue. His voice was full of compassion and he spoke without judgment or pity. "I can't reveal the specifics, but something you said had an impact on her and it appeared she was ready to make some changes in her life. I hope that brings you a little bit of comfort. You did the best you could. You tried to help, and I think I know why. If there's something you—"

"No, there's nothing more to say." Her heart raced and heat flamed across her cheeks. She looked at him briefly, then dropped her gaze to the purse on her lap.

"On another note, I interviewed your dad yesterday. His alibi for the time of the murder checked out, although his witness seems questionable."

"I'm telling you, I don't think he was the person who attacked me that morning."

He leaned back, clasped his hands behind his head, and gave her a pointed look. "So you say. After listening to the message Chad recorded from your answering machine, I'm not willing to take that possibility off the table. Chad tells me you refuse to file for a restraining order."

"There's no need. Outside of our encounter at the lawyer's office, I've barely spoken to my dad in the last ten years. I don't expect that to change. Those phone calls were most likely made when he was drunk. In time, this will all blow over."

"I know that's what you want to believe, but Chad and I are not convinced. Regardless," he said firmly, "we're going to keep an eye on him. In the meantime, I'd suggest you keep your distance, just to be on the safe side." He stood, opened a drawer, and pulled out a small padded bag. "By the way, we've finished processing your vehicle."

"Finally." After she signed the release form, Mark handed her the evidence bag containing her car keys, escorted her down the hall to Chad's office, then said goodbye. Chad held a phone to his ear as he sat behind a desk heaped with paperwork. He raised a finger to show he needed another minute. When he finished, he came around the desk and brushed a kiss across her cheek.

"I hope it puts your mind at ease, knowing your name's been cleared," Chad said, stepping back and leaning against his desk.

"It does."

"By the way, your car's a mess and fingerprint dust is every-where. I called Shiner's to see if they have an opening. They can pick up your Jeep at the evidence garage and have it washed and detailed by closing time on Thursday. Would you like me to make the appointment, or would you prefer to *take care of it yourself?*" The tone of his voice and the emotion behind the simple question hinted to their war of wills on Sunday evening.

Aware of the veiled reference, she stared into his eyes and answered without reservation. "Having Shiner's wash and detail the Jeep is an excellent idea. Would you mind making the appointment, please?"

"Not a problem," he replied, nodding his compliance to her wishes.

"Thanks for asking." Her words were respectful, but pointed.

His eyes narrowed slightly and a smile tugged at the corners of his mouth. "I try not to cross the line—*unless* I feel it's necessary."

Silence filled the room as she digested his words.

He stood and pulled his truck keys from his pocket. "If you need a vehicle, you can use mine. I can always hitch a ride to work with Mark."

The offer surprised her, especially knowing how protective he was over his new set of wheels. New was a relative term because the recently purchased four-wheel drive truck was two years old. He loved his truck more than CiCi loved her Jeep, if that were possible.

"Thanks, but I can get by without driving your big tank," she said, handing him the evidence bag containing the keys to her Jeep.

"Let me know if you change your mind." He tossed the bag into a desk drawer.

"Thanks, but I'll be fine. Megan and I are going to lunch. Want to join us?"

He smiled and shook his head. "Thanks, but I'd better eat at my desk and make a dent in that mound of paperwork. Maybe another time."

Stella led CiCi and Megan to a booth by the window. As they perused the menu, whispering at a nearby table made the hair on CiCi's arm stand on end. She glanced over the top of her menu. The couple murmured to each other and looked her way. They quickly focused on their meal when they caught CiCi's glare. "What is it with people judging me without knowing what really happened?"

"Don't let them get under your skin. Gossip is the only entertainment some people have."

Over lunch, CiCi listened as Megan chatted about her upcoming vacation. She and several physical therapy colleagues spent a week every year taking full advantage of Florida's sunny beaches by day and the hip nightclubs at night. Megan had compiled a list of items she needed before her trip and talked CiCi into going shopping with her on Thursday.

"First, I thought we might have breakfast at…"

Although CiCi nodded at the appropriate times but couldn't get her mind off Julie's murder. There were questions that begged to be answered. She knew the when, where, and the how, but *who* wanted Julie dead and *why*? Several possible suspects and motives ran through her mind. She pulled out a pen and wrote a name on a napkin.

"…and I saw the sexiest bikini at Buford's…"

Julie's husband held the top spot on her list. *Keenan is abusive and has a physique much like the attacker's. Had he somehow seen Julie and Bruce getting cozy at Stella's? Maybe not. He seemed surprised when I mentioned Julie and I met at Stella's, though his reaction could've been an act. Perhaps he discovered Julie planned to leave him. With his short fuse and mean disposition, any number of scenarios could have provoked a heated argument that turned deadly.*

"…Under Cover is having a lingerie sale we can't miss…"

She awarded Bruce a spot on her suspect list. *He and Julie seemed pretty chummy at Stella's. Did they end up talking about the financial issue that troubled Julie? If so, the two could've met at Five Star later that evening in order for Bruce to verify the problem and approve any further action. After all, he was the boss.*

"…of course, I'll need new shoes to match the…"

Could there be something sketchy in the accounts Bruce wanted to keep hidden? Unlikely, but possible. Could he have killed Julie out of anger if she led him on, then rebuffed his sexual advances? Again, anything was possible.

CiCi nodded and absentmindedly smiled as she considered her two suspects. She scratched a line through Keenan's name. If everything she had read in books or seen on TV were true, a victim's spouse would be the first person to come under suspicion. Keenan had already proven himself to be volatile, leaving her no doubt he would come under Mark and Chad's intense scrutiny. Bruce was another matter. He was directly connected to Five Star, CiCi's home turf, a place she was fiercely loyal to and protective of. Knowing Bruce had pushed aside Julie's concerns about the accounting problem, she determined the accounting records would be the most logical place to start.

Julie had mentioned she copied everything to a flash drive as a safeguard. *As a safeguard…against what? With Five Star closed for the week, the absence of co-workers would allow me plenty of uninterrupted time to look through Julie's computer files. With any luck, I might also find that flash drive.*

"…and then I thought you could model your new thong and dance topless around the town square with a rose between your teeth."

"Yeah, that sounds great," CiCi murmured.

"CiCi!" Megan's sharp tone startled CiCi out of her trance. "You haven't heard a word I've said for the last ten minutes! I'd be willing to bet that whatever you're writing down has nothing to do with our shopping trip. Where'd you go?" Megan crossed her arms over her chest and eyed her lunch companion.

"Sorry. My thoughts keep dragging me back to work."

"Work…or the murder?"

CiCi shrugged and stuffed the napkin into her purse. During dessert, she devised a plan to check out the accounting records to see if they held a clue to Julie's murder. She asked Megan for a lift over to Skyview Plaza on Megan's way back to work. Always the skeptic, Megan expressed doubts about CiCi's intentions to shop in the pricey shopping district.

"Hey, I need a distraction to pull my mind in a different direction. Besides," CiCi teased, "aren't you the one always telling me I need to expand my horizons and give my thrift store mentality a break?"

"I suppose. I'm just concerned for you, CiCi. You've had a lot to deal with lately—your mother's death, then the craziness going on with your dad, and now this murder. I'm beginning to wonder if you're under more stress than you realize."

"You worry too much."

"That's what friends are for."

FIFTEEN

CiCi stepped from Megan's car and into a boutique. A blue camisole adorned with tiny beads caught her attention, but she winced at the amount on the price tag. *I know it's crazy not to splurge on something so pretty now that I have a huge inheritance at my disposal, but somehow it doesn't feel right. Maybe in time.*

She lingered long enough to make certain Megan hadn't circled back around, then exited the store and headed for her intended destination. The beautiful day made the four block walk enjoyable. As she approached Five Star, she remembered she no longer had a key to the building. She breathed a sigh of relief when she noticed the biohazard van in the parking lot. The presence of a cleaning staff meant she had a way of getting inside.

Most of the crime scene tape had been removed from the front door, save for the tiny remnants that fluttered in the breeze like crepe paper streamers. Holding her head high, she entered with an air of authority. The specialized cleaning crew never questioned her presence. The workers were busy removing the stubborn fingerprint residue, which made her all the more thankful Chad suggested having her Jeep washed and detailed.

She scanned the work area beyond Norma's throne. Papers were neatly stacked on desktops as though everyone had stepped out for lunch and would return at any moment. Her eyes widened in surprise when she reached her cubicle. Although free of the fine black powder, papers littered the desk, and the drawers of the desk and file cabinet were open and in disarray. She took a seat and let her mind drift back to Friday. The mental image of her cubicle that fatal morning clashed with the mess in front of her. *Who searched my workspace? The cleaning crew? Doubtful. The police? Maybe. At least the sunglasses Chad bought me are still here.*

She made her way down the hallway. Her pulse quickened and her hands began to sweat. Vivid scenes from the previous week flashed through her mind. Standing in the doorway to Julie's office, she noticed the stained carpet had been replaced with tile, and the walls painted a fresh, neutral color. The mingled aroma of paint, disinfectant, and industrial strength deodorizer made her slightly nauseous. Though the furniture had been arranged in a new config-uration, she couldn't stop her gaze from traveling to the spot where she had found Julie.

Her feet seemed rooted in place. She took a deep breath and forced herself to enter the room. She sat behind Julie's desk and switched on the computer's tower and monitor. While waiting for the logon screen to appear, she carefully rummaged through the center drawer. She set aside a couple of flash drives found among the jumble of paper clips, rubber bands, pencils, pens, and sticky notes. After a thorough search of the desk and file cabinet, it occurred to her she never came across the green iPod Julie had tossed in the drawer. *Interesting.*

When the monitor blinked, her fingers flew across the keyboard as she typed in the password. "Access Denied" flashed across the screen. *How can that be? Maybe I hit a wrong key. Caps lock off? Yes.* Her second and third attempts were both denied. Not one to be deterred by an unexpected turn of events, she scooped up the flash drives and took them to her cubicle. Checking each one on her computer, none appeared to contain the information printed on the hard copy

Julie had given to her. Disheartened, she returned them to Julie's desk drawer.

She slipped into Floyd's office and scanned the room for the company laptop that would give her access to the financial programs she needed. Other than taking one of the extra keys to the building he kept on hand, her search came up empty. Thinking back to her conversation with Izzy about Julie's abrupt departure from her last job, CiCi's next move came on a whim. She searched through Floyd's files for Julie's job application. She made a mental note of Julie's previous employers and tucked the application back into place. She then moved down the hall to search the other two offices for the laptop.

The cleaning crew had left by the time she emerged empty-handed from Rex's office. She glanced at her watch and realized time had gotten away from her. She and Dennis were to meet at the bank soon. Yet, here she was, on the other side of town without a car. She rang his office, explained her lack of transportation and he agreed to pick her up at a nearby café, which happened to be in his line of travel to the bank. Eager to see if her grandmother's wedding ring had been tucked away safe and sound in her mother's safe deposit box, she gathered her purse and favorite sunglasses and hurried from the building.

Bruce stood just outside the entrance, casting an admiring glance back at his shiny new convertible while he snuffed out a cigarette in the freestanding ashtray. His free hand gripped a laptop case. His eyes widened with surprise when he saw her. "CiCi, I didn't expect to see you here. How are you holding up, hon?"

Better than you. With rumpled hair and sunken eyes, he appeared bedraggled and sleep-deprived—a very uncharacteristic look for King Leer. "I'm doing okay, all things considered."

"I don't see your Jeep in the lot. Do the police still have your car?" He shifted his six-foot frame to block the sun from shining in her eyes.

"They released my car this morning, but it's at Shiner's getting cleaned up. It'll be a couple of days before I get it back."

"By the way, what *are* you doing here? I thought we gave

everyone the week off. What's so important to bring you back to a crime scene?"

"I, uh, was shopping not far from here and thought I'd walk over to pick up the sunglasses I left on my desk last week." *Might be best if I don't mention Floyd said I could pick up another key to the building.* She smiled, pulled the vintage shades from her purse, and slipped them on. "How about you? Have you been working from home?" She pointed to the laptop case and fought the urge to snatch it from his hand.

"No. Floyd had it and I offered to bring it back to the office on my way home."

"If you like, I'd be happy to cover Julie's job until other arrangements are made. I can take the laptop and make sure things stay current." Bruce cast a suspicious look her way and then glanced around, making her more aware than ever they were alone.

"Things are up in the air right now. It seems Julie changed the password to the accounting program without permission, and none of us can access the system."

CiCi feigned shock at the news and hoped the perspiration on her forehead didn't belie her outward calmness. "Really? How could she do that, and why?"

"Who knows?" he said, opening the entrance door.

"That's pretty bold for a temp."

"Bold? That's one word for it. You wouldn't happen to know her password, would you?"

"Sorry, I don't."

"Rex knows someone who can unlock and reset it, but it'll be a few days before he can get to it. When I get the new password, I'll text it to you. As for covering Julie's job, that's still under discussion. Rex wants Norma back, but I don't think she's ready." He paused and glanced around. "Someone from the police department should be along any minute to return items they took that aren't connected to the murder. When he leaves, I have a house to show this afternoon. It's not too far from your place. I can drop you off at home on the way, if you like."

Police Department? CiCi's heart raced as she wiped the perspiration from her face. Certain Chad wouldn't approve if he knew she'd been looking for a clue that would point to Julie's killer, she decided to make an exit before the police officer, or a certain detective, arrived. "Thanks for the offer, but I think I'll walk."

"Okay, but there's something you and I need to discuss. Let's get out of this sun." With a hand on her back, he tried to steer her inside.

She resisted. "Sorry, Bruce, but I can't. I have an appointment with my lawyer this afternoon. Before I go, I'm curious about something. Did Julie explain exactly what sort of problem she had with the accounts?"

He stilled. His face turned an unhealthy shade of red, and she was positive it had nothing to do with the sun. "How did you know about that?"

"She asked for my help when she didn't get a response from you. She gave me an account to look over and planned to give me the rest on a flash drive that night at Stella's."

The firm set of his jaw and the icy glare indicated he wasn't pleased. "You know you're not to take that sort of information from the premises," he snapped, moving around her and essentially blocking her exit. "And the police said *you're* the one who loaned Julie the key to the building. Who gave you permission to do that?"

"I tried to help a friend who wanted to go above and beyond to do a good job. Loaning her that key was a huge mistake on my part. I know that now. It's something I'll regret for the rest of my life." She lashed out at him, but quickly got herself under control. "Speaking of keys, while you were at Stella's, did she hint at her plans for the rest of the evening? From the way you two were looking at each other after I left, I doubt you were discussing work."

A puzzled look crossed his face. "What are you talking about?"

"As I turned to wave goodbye, I saw you slip something into her hand. I'm going to take a wild guess and say it was a key."

"If you must know, the key I gave her belonged to my new car. She said she'd been thinking about buying a convertible. I hopped in the passenger seat and let her take it for a quick spin around the block. I dropped her off at her car, and then left to go to the party I told you about."

"How could she afford a convertible?"

"Didn't ask."

"Did you meet up with her later that night?"

"No. If we had, we would've…" He paused, and the sly grin on his face quickly vanished. "Wait a minute. Are you asking if I have an alibi for the night she was murdered?"

Yes, I am. "Of course not. I'm just wondering where Julie went between the time she left Stella's and the time I found her at Five Star." Though his posture remained intimidating, she stood her ground. Of course, there was no room to take a step back even if she wanted to.

"I have no idea. Like I said, I went to a party. Ask the police if you don't believe me. Surely they would have brought me in for more questioning if they found fault with my alibi or consider me a suspect."

"You're right. I'm glad you cleared that up for me." *Although, I still wonder why you didn't discuss the accounting issue with her. Are you hiding something?* "Now, if you don't mind, I need to go."

She darted around him and made the walk to the café in less than fifteen minutes. While sipping tea and waiting for Dennis to arrive, she called the investment firm listed on Julie's employment application and asked to speak with Julie's former boss.

"Julie reported to Diana Erickson. She's out of town this week. Let me forward your call to Leslie Montgomery, another executive in the same department."

Leslie Montgomery? CiCi's stomach flip-flopped. This certainly had to be Julie's dinner companion.

"Hello, Montgomery speaking. How may I help you?" The deep voice that filtered across the line sounded smooth and sophisticated.

"I'm…I'm sorry, I need to speak with Leslie."

A chuckle rippled over the connection. "That's me. Lesley Montgomery, Lesley spelled with an e-y. I prefer to go by Les. Now, who am I speaking with and how may I help you?"

"My name is Cecilia Winslow and I'd like to ask a few questions about Julie Reynolds." She didn't receive a response for several seconds. "Hello? Are you there?"

"Mind your own business."

His tone sent a shiver up CiCi's spine. Before she could reply, the line went dead, leaving her to wonder if Lesley's name should be added to the list of suspects.

SIXTEEN

After dinner, CiCi sorted her dirty clothes, hoping to get a load washed before Tasha arrived. When she came to the khaki shorts she'd worn the morning of Julie's murder, her stomach knotted. She checked each pocket, mostly out of habit. Her curiosity piqued as her fingers pulled out the wayward sheet she had picked up from the floor outside Julie's office.

Unfolding the piece of paper, she recognized the logo of the HideAway Inn, a local run-down establishment known as the "no-tell motel." The hand-written receipt listed I. Hughes as the guest. *Wait—as in Izzy Hughes, one of Five Star's appraisers?*

She shook her head and scanned the receipt. The bill listed the date of occupancy for a time when Izzy had supposedly traveled out of town to meet with a client. CiCi was certain of the date because she had to finish several of Izzy's reports that were due during her absence. As CiCi studied the receipt, she realized the last four digits of the credit card were 8458—identical to those embossed on the company credit card CiCi often used to purchase supplies for the office.

Wow. Had Izzy fraudulently used the company card for her own personal pleasure and submitted the receipt as a travel expense? If Julie questioned the expense, she may have threatened to share that information with the owners. In that case, Izzy would certainly lose her job and ruin her reputation. Finding another job would be difficult, if not impossible, and she would be forced to tell her husband about her rendezvous at the motel.

CiCi's mind quickly took the scenario another step further. *Who had Izzy met at the motel? How could she justify her actions, yet look down her nose and make snide comments about Julie's lack of morals? Izzy swore she never wanted to be single again, but if Ivan learned of an affair, she may not have a say in the matter.*

An hour later, over a plate of brownies fresh from the oven, CiCi told Tasha of her follow-up call to A Hand-Up. "I explained to Maxine that it's ridiculous to think my presence would make anyone uncomfortable, but she refused to listen." CiCi set her half-finished drink on the end table. "Speaking of uncomfortable, did you notice Izzy and Julie seemed at odds lately?"

Tasha nodded. The crop of tight black curls that framed her brown face bounced like tiny springs. "I came up on the tail end of something at the copy machine two weeks ago. Izzy hissed something and pointed a finger in Julie's face. She stopped the minute I walked up. I assumed she was scolding Julie for leaving the paper tray in the copier empty. You know how that drove Izzy nuts."

"When Julie took a seat at Stella's, Izzy got up and left. When she came back, she sat as far away from Julie as she could without sitting at the next table."

"I noticed, but didn't want to say anything."

"I have another theory on why they were at odds." CiCi pulled the motel receipt from her pocket and handed it to Tasha. Tasha's eyes grew wide when CiCi explained the significance of the date and credit card number. Though unsubstantiated, they agreed the receipt opened the door to a whole list of other possibilities, none of them good.

"You could be on to something."

CiCi took back the receipt. "I wish I knew for certain if this is part of what had Julie upset enough to ask for my help. I don't want to confront Izzy without solid proof of wrongdoing, so here's what I'm thinking…"

Tasha listened and shook her head. "That's a harebrained idea if I ever heard one. You do know there's such a thing as customer privacy, don't you? They're not going to tell us a thing."

"Well, I happen to know the owner plays poker on Tuesday evenings at my ex-father-in-law's house, and has for years. His elderly parents cover for him at the front desk. They might not be as prickly about privacy issues as their son. Other than ask Izzy directly, it's the easiest way to find out if she misused company funds. If Julie questioned the expense receipt for the motel, she held Izzy's livelihood and marriage in the palm of her hand. That, my friend, would explain Izzy's hateful attitude toward Julie, and be a solid motive for murder."

"Admit it, girlfriend. You want to know who Izzy hooked up with."

"Look me in the eye and tell me you aren't the least bit curious."

"I'm a whole lot of curious." Tasha grinned. "Maybe she met with that guy named Lesley."

"What kind of mother names their son Lesley?"

"The kind of mother that would name their boy Sue?"

"Anyway, why would Izzy fool around when she has so much to lose? There's got to be something we're missing." CiCi grabbed the receipt and tucked it into her purse. As she started for the door, she stopped and went back to the kitchen. She hastily sealed a few brownies in plastic wrap and placed them in a small paper bag. "I've got grandma covered. If grandpa is on the desk, you can captivate him with your stunning smile." Pausing, she grinned and dropped her gaze to Tasha's low-cut T-shirt. "Or if necessary, dazzle him with your, um, big *personality*."

They drove along the outskirts of Ripley Grove until they reached the HideAway Inn. A woman, who appeared to be in her eighties, sat behind the front desk, her attention riveted on the little TV under the check-in counter. She struggled to her feet, straightened her pink warm-up suit, and greeted CiCi and Tasha as they approached. CiCi smiled in return as she read the name printed on the woman's makeshift badge.

"Good evening, Gertrude," CiCi said. "I need your help with a little problem."

"I'm good at solving problems. Work the crossword puzzle every day."

"My problem is a little more complicated than that, so I hope you're up to the challenge. To show my appreciation, I've brought a small batch of homemade brownies." CiCi placed the paper sack on the counter.

Gertrude ran a tongue over her bright red lips. "I like a challenge, but I *love* brownies, especially homemade. Tell Gertie what you need, darling."

"I work for a local appraisal company," CiCi said, holding out her company badge, "and an employee recently rented a room for a client. The document submitted to our accountant doesn't meet company standards. As you can see, the last four digits on the receipt match those on my company credit card. I was hoping you might supply a more detailed copy so we can process the claim for reimbursement." CiCi handed over the receipt and the company credit card. With her fingers crossed behind her back, she gave Tasha a sly smile.

Gertrude opened the reading glasses hanging from the beaded chain around her neck and perched them on her thin nose. Her lips moved as her eyes moved across the receipt. CiCi resisted the urge to reach out and steady the woman's gnarled hands.

"Oh, yes, the credit card system went down and I wrote out two receipts by hand that night. A receipt is not something many of our customers ask for, if you know what I mean," Gertrude said, peering over the rim of her glasses. "I remember him. Ivan is an unusual name, especially for someone so good-looking."

CiCi and Tasha glanced at each other at the mention of *Ivan* Hughes. Stunned, neither woman uttered a word.

"Must've come from one helluva of a business meeting that night, because he was pretty snockered when he and his client arrived," Gertrude said as she handed the receipt back to CiCi. "Then there was the fight. Bet he didn't tell you about that. Early the next morning, Ivan and the woman got into a nasty argument in the parking lot. After she stormed off, he came into the office. Apparently, he had second thoughts about putting the charges on the credit card. He asked me to reverse the charges, and paid the bill with cash. He thought he'd thrown that receipt away, and he searched every wastebasket in the lobby trying to find it. Never did, to my recollection. Well, let me get you that copy to prove we reversed the charges."

After Gertrude walked away, Tasha whispered, "That shoots your theory to shreds."

"Not necessarily. If Ivan *did* pay with a company credit card, that means Izzy must've checked in with him. Maybe Gertrude will remember her."

"I thought Izzy met with a client out of town."

Gertrude came back with a sheet of paper in her hand. "Oh, dear," she said.

"Is there a problem?" CiCi asked.

"You could say that. My eyesight's not what it used to be and I apparently mistook the threes for eights when I copied down the credit card number. His card ends with 3453, not 8458, so the original charges never even went through. Forgot all about that."

"So, Ivan Hughes was here, but he couldn't have used our company credit card because the numbers don't match."

"Looks that way. Good news is, my son bought me a new pair of glasses." Gertrude eyed the sack on the counter. "Sorry for the confusion."

"You've been very helpful, Gertrude. Would you be able to identify the woman who argued with Ivan if I showed you a photo?"

"Oh, dear, I don't know. I pretty much kept my eyes on him, if you know what I mean." Gertrude's conspiratorial wink looked more like a small seizure.

CiCi scrolled through the pictures on her phone, certain that Izzy's purple-tipped bangs would jog Gertrude's memory. CiCi pulled up the one of Julie, Keenan, Izzy and Ivan, arms thrown around one another, posing for the camera at Floyd's birthday party a few weeks earlier. CiCi held out the phone. "Would this help?"

"Yes, that's her." Gertrude smiled and patted her blue-tinted hair as she reminisced. "I know it's hard to believe, but I had long blonde hair like hers once upon a time."

CiCi struggled to maintain composure as she tucked the phone back into her purse. She thanked Gertrude and handed the sack across the counter.

Gertrude's eyes sparkled as she opened the sack and took a whiff and pulled out a brownie. She literally moaned after the first bite. "Diamonds may be a girl's best friend," she said, "but nothing beats a homemade brownie."

Tasha turned to CiCi as they walked to the car. "Well, there goes your theory Izzy misused company funds and had an affair. Wow. My mind is reeling."

"I wouldn't put an affair past Julie, but with Ivan? I'm as shocked as you, especially since Keenan and Ivan are best buds. Do you think Izzy knew?"

"I don't know, but if she did, would she be mad enough to kill?"

"It's hard to say what a person will do under stress. She loves Ivan. I can't see her giving him up without a fight, especially with three kids to take care of. Even so, Izzy couldn't have stabbed Julie. I definitely didn't fight with a woman that morning."

"It wouldn't be unheard of for a wife to hire someone to do the job, but how would Izzy know Julie would be at Five Star?"

"Haven't figured that part out yet. I don't want to believe it, but I'd better put Izzy's name on my list of suspects simply because she has a motive. And we can't forget Keenan. If he got wind of Julie messing around with his best friend, I hate to imagine how he would react."

They sat in silence for several minutes and stared through the lobby window at the older woman behind the desk. Gertrude's information shed a whole new light on the situation.

"I know one thing for sure," CiCi said. "If the HideAway Inn wants to keep the 'no-tell motel' motto, they'd better get Gertrude off the front desk."

SEVENTEEN

CiCi responded to a knock at the door just before lunch on Wednesday and found Chad and Mark on her doorstep. Their body language indicated the unannounced visit wasn't a social call. Entering the house, their cop faces and sunglasses remained firmly in place. They each chose a barstool at the breakfast bar and watched in silence as she poured two glasses of iced tea. The drinks, as well as the plate of freshly baked oatmeal raisin cookies she placed on the counter, were blatantly ignored. Their sunglasses came off, and Chad gave her a chilling glare. Her insides quivered, but not in a good way.

"I heard something disturbing today from a patrolman that made a delivery to Five Star yesterday," Mark said, breaking the heavy silence. "The officer arrived early and found the parking lot empty. He parked in the far corner of the lot to write up a report while he waited for Mr. Owens to show up. A woman left the building just as Owens finished his cigarette. From the officer's observation, their discussion appeared polite until Owens tried to steer her back inside. Things got heated. She dodged around him and left on foot. The woman had wavy, light brown hair and wore an animal print shirt over tan pants. Sounds identical to what you wore to the station yesterday morning."

"In case you haven't noticed, my hair is dark blonde."

"Don't play games with me, CiCi," Mark barked. "Dark blonde, light brown, it's all the same to me. What were you doing over there?"

The combined bulk of the men's bodies reminded her of a stone wall. Their faces were as hard as the Kansas clay soil and their steely gazes made her heart race.

"If you must know, after I went shopping at Skyview Plaza, I decided to stop by work to pick up my favorite sunglasses. They were a gift from Chad. I'd be very upset if they were lost or stolen." She smiled at Chad ever so sweetly, but he never returned the smile. "The crime scene tape had been removed, so I hardly think my stop warrants an official visit."

"How did you get there? Chad says your Jeep is in the shop." Persistence and intimidation were two of Mark's well-honed skills. His eyes never left her face.

"Megan dropped me off after lunch." She squirmed under his scrutiny as she wiped down the countertop. "I thought shopping might take my mind off things. After I got my sunglasses, Dennis picked me up at a nearby café, we stopped at the bank, and then he drove me home. Cookie?" she asked, hoping to create a diversion. Again, her treats were ignored.

Chad crossed his arms over his chest and picked up where Mark left off. "I see two things wrong with your story. One, you could have waited to pick up those sunglasses when you returned to work, because you have plenty of others you could've worn." He tipped his head toward the rack on the wall that held at least six pairs of sunglasses. "Two, I've never known you to shop at Skyview Plaza. You're a thrift shopper at heart and their prices are way out of your comfort zone."

"Maybe I like to be adventurous. It never hurts to try something new."

"Is that so?" The corners of Chad's mouth lifted slightly and one eyebrow raised.

She turned and rinsed the dishrag, hoping he wouldn't notice the flush of her cheeks. "Speaking of Bruce, did his alibi for the night of Julie's murder check out?"

Chad answered her question with a stony silence, but Mark said, "And that's your business because...?"

A simple yes or no would be nice. I'd better keep Bruce on my suspect list, at least until I find that flash drive to prove he's not hiding something. "Just wondering."

"How'd you get in?" Mark asked. "I thought we had your key to the building in our possession."

"The cleaning crew, and Floyd gave me permission to take one of the spare keys."

"Huh."

"Um, when I picked up my sunglasses, I noticed someone had rifled through my desk and file cabinet." Her voice cracked with nervousness under Mark's unrelenting stare.

"The crime scene crew went over your cubicle with a fine-tooth comb. Last I checked, they left everything in good order," Mark said.

"Well, it's wasn't in good order yesterday. And Julie tossed Keenan's green iPod in her desk drawer when I left work Thursday night, and now it's gone. When I paid Keenan a visit on Monday, he'd been listening to music on a green iPod. If I were you, I'd want to know when he got it back."

Chad stiffened and leaned forward. "What were you doing at the Reynolds' house?"

"Tasha and I took over a casserole and offered our condolences."

"CiCi, I don't want you anywhere near Keenan." Chad's voice was steady, but firm. "You, of all people, know what he's like."

"Fine." She didn't have to be told twice to stay away from that red-headed hothead. "Are you done playing twenty questions?" She assumed the inquisition was over, but Mark's body language said otherwise.

"Earlier this morning," Mark said, "we went to Julie's previous place of employment. According to the woman at the front desk,

118

she fielded a call yesterday afternoon from a woman asking to speak with Julie's former boss. We have our suspicions as to who that woman might be. Is there something you want to tell us?"

"Okay, so I called. It's not a crime. Maybe I wanted to make sure Julie's former co-workers knew about her death."

"I don't know what you're up to, but I doubt that was the reason for your call."

"You won't be mad when I tell you what I found out," she said smugly.

Mark and Chad exchanged glances, but remained silent, waiting for her to continue.

"I think I spoke with a person Julie met for dinner every week, according to Keenan. I expected to talk with a woman named Leslie, but Lesley, spelled with an e-y, turned out to be a man who goes by the name Les Montgomery. The moment I mentioned Julie's name, he hung up on me."

"And?" Mark asked.

She gasped. "You knew? But, how?"

"The 'how' is not your concern," Mark said. "Remember when we asked you to help look into Julie's murder?"

She frowned. "Um, no."

"That's right, we *didn't*. We know how to do our job, and we don't need your help. Stay out of this investigation. Do I make myself clear?"

Frustrated, she pursed her lips together and tossed the dishrag into the sink.

"CiCi, do I make myself clear?" The muscles in his jaw clenched and unclenched.

"Yes, Mark, you've made yourself clear. But I need to do *something*. Julie was my friend, and she wouldn't have been murdered if I hadn't given her the key to Five Star."

"You don't know that."

"Neither do you," she said, planting her hands on her hips. "And in case you've forgotten, I'm still on Five Star's payroll and have a right to be there as much as anyone. Technically, I didn't do anything wrong. As I see it, I can talk to anyone I please."

Mark pointed a meaty finger at her. "That may be true, but you're a researcher, not an investigator. Quit poking your nose where it doesn't belong."

Mark and Chad put their sunglasses on, stood, and walked to the door without saying goodbye. CiCi followed. As soon as Mark crossed the threshold, she grabbed Chad's arm and held him back. He turned, puzzled by her sudden move.

"Have you got a minute?" She peeked around him, checking to see if Mark lingered within hearing distance. "I didn't say anything earlier because I knew Mark would explode. It's about Ivan. It doesn't matter how I found out, but there's something you need to know." She nibbled on her lower lip. "Or maybe not. Maybe I'm making something out of nothing."

"Tell me, and let me be the judge." He crossed his arms over his chest and listened to a brief recap of her and Tasha's trip to the motel. When she finished, he shook his head and repeated Mark's warning. After a quick peck on her cheek, he turned and walked away with a determined stride.

"You get things squared away, lover-boy?" Mark leaned against the car and smirked.

"Jealous?"

"Darn right. Who wouldn't want a woman who likes to be adventurous and try new things?"

"And *that*'s what you took away from that entire conversation?"

"That, and your girl's up to something. She all but confessed to snooping around in Julie's desk. I'm guessing she went looking for something to do with the murder." He slid into the driver's seat and glanced back at the townhome to find her watching from the doorway.

Chad, sitting in the passenger seat, shook his head. "Admit it, if she hadn't been nosing around, we'd have never known an iPod went missing from Julie's desk. If she's correct, that means Keenan lied about going into the building that night."

"Yeah, I know. Looks like we have yet another reason to talk with Keenan."

"I don't like her poking around anymore than you do, but you'll want to hear what she said after you left." He sighed, then relayed the conversation word for word. Mark exploded, as CiCi predicted. After he calmed down, Chad offered an observation. "She expected that reaction from you. I think you scare her."

Mark grinned. "I hope so, for her own good."

EIGHTEEN

T hat afternoon, CiCi slid into the passenger side of Tasha's car and buckled the seat belt. They rode in silence, each lost in their own thoughts. CiCi stared out the window at the passing scenery, feeling apprehensive about attending Julie's funeral.

"Tasha, am I doing the right thing by going to the funeral? People are bound to talk and some will wonder if I am a heartless killer. I don't want my presence to be disruptive or cause Julie's family any more pain."

"You're doing the right thing. Anyone who knows you, knows you're innocent. Her death was *not* your fault."

"Poor Julie. Her name and reputation are sure to be tarnished as the police delve into every area of her life. Without a doubt, Keenan and her family will learn things about her they never imagined. Lesley, Ivan, and who knows what other dark secrets will be exposed. In some respect, I'm guilty for uncovering some of those secrets. I never expected that to happen, but it couldn't be helped. I want her killer found and charged."

"I'm sure Chad and Mark are working hard to do just that."

After she and Tasha signed the guest book, they stepped into a room over-flowing with people. The receiving line snaked around the perimeter of the room and inched forward one step at a time. When they reached Julie's mother, the grieving woman wrapped her arms around CiCi and offered heartfelt thanks for attempting to save her daughter's life. CiCi choked back a sob of relief and dabbed at tears that blurred her vision. Keenan, next in line, turned his back and refused to acknowledge their presence.

Fragrant flowers were abundant on either side of the simple white casket. Uplifting music played softly in the background. Keenan took a seat in the front row alongside his family and stared at the open casket. CiCi and Tasha found empty seats several rows behind the family. Ivan whispered his condolences to Keenan and gave a tearful hug as he passed by. Izzy slid in next to CiCi as the service started and Ivan took the seat beside his wife. CiCi held tight to Tasha's hand and fought back tears as the pastor spoke of a beautiful life cut short. Sniffles and muffled sobs echoed around the room.

CiCi turned slightly and surveyed the throng of somber faces during the final hymn. Rex, Bruce, and Floyd and his wife sat on the opposite side of the room. At the back, Chad and Mark studied the crowd. She caught Chad's eye and he smiled. *I'm going to interpret that to mean my snooping has been forgiven.*

After the service concluded, the immediate family left for the private graveside burial. CiCi waited off to one side while Tasha chatted with a friend. Nearby, Ivan stood talking with friends. She felt relieved, because she had no desire to strike up a conversation with him. Looking around, she was startled to see Gertrude heading her way.

"Gertrude, I'm surprised to see you here."

"I brought my friend, Ethel, because she doesn't drive anymore. Years ago, she lived next door to the deceased. Didn't realize she was the women we talked about when you came by the motel. Thanks again for the wonderful brownies. They were delicious."

"You're welcome."

"I'm sorry if my poor eyesight caused you to waste time

checking out Ivan's receipt. Oh, Ethel's waving. I guess she's ready to go. It was nice to see you again. Bye-bye."

After Gertrude left, Ivan turned and fixed a steely gaze on CiCi. His eyes darted around the thinning crowd, his brow creased with worry. He stepped over, grabbed her elbow, and led her to a quiet corner. "So, you know. How did you find out?" he hissed. "Did Julie tell you?"

"I found your motel receipt on the floor near Julie's office the morning of the murder."

Confusion flickered across his face for the briefest second before panic set in. "What? How did it end up there?"

"I don't know. You tell me."

"I have no idea," he whispered. "I thought I had thrown it away at the motel."

"I'm not condoning what you did, not that you would care anyway, but why on earth would you pay with a credit card? You're lucky Gertrude copied down the wrong numbers."

"In case you haven't heard, common sense flies out the window when you're drunk." He cast a nervous glance about the room. "Look, I drank too much that night. The next thing I remember is waking up next to Julie in a motel room. It wasn't planned—at least not on my part."

"What are you saying? That Julie plied you with alcohol and lured you to the motel?"

"That's exactly what I'm saying. Julie and I were engaged once, long before I met Izzy. Julie told me no matter how many husbands or lovers she's had since, she's never loved anyone but me. I told her she was out of her mind, that I'd never leave Izzy and the kids."

Engaged? Izzy never mentioned that little tidbit when we talked at the park. "What did you argue about in the parking lot?"

"What *didn't* we argue about? Her delusional fantasy that we could be together again? Her attempts to break up my marriage? I was so mad, I could've…"

"Could've what—killed her?" CiCi whispered, but her words packed a punch. Ivan's mouth formed a tight line as he struggled to maintain composure.

"I may have lost a friend that day, but I don't intend to lose Izzy or my family over it. I never saw Julie again after she left the motel. Now that she's dead, I see no reason to bring it up. I had nothing to do with her murder, and that kind of info would cause the police to consider me a suspect. What did you do with that receipt?"

"It's back at my house. The police will find out eventually. If you're not guilty, it would look a lot better if you told them yourself, on your own terms."

"No. No way. I'll take my chances." His panicked gaze darted about the room, then fixed back on her face. His hand latched on to her wrist. "I want that receipt."

"Let go, or I'll make a scene." CiCi matched his glare as his demand hung in the air between them. They broke eye contact at the sound of approaching footsteps. Ivan stepped back and released his grip.

"There you are, honey. I've been looking for you." Izzy appeared at Ivan's side and murmured an apology for her intrusion. She brushed her bangs to the side and pulled him over to a group of mutual acquaintances.

CiCi searched the room until she found Tasha. Together they stepped outside to the small courtyard, where they continued to mingle.

"CiCi, look near the entrance," Tasha whispered. "Mark and Chad are having a chat with Ivan and Izzy. Ivan doesn't look too happy."

CiCi turned and caught a glimpse of Ivan's face, who looked far from congenial. He glanced around the lingering crowd with a mixture of anger, fear, and embarrassment. He caught CiCi's eye and gave her a menacing look.

Murmurings and speculation fluttered across the crowd as Ivan and Izzy got into their vehicle and followed the undercover police car from the parking lot. The information they gleaned from various conversations that afternoon after Ivan and Izzy's abrupt departure dominated Tasha and CiCi's conversation on the drive home.

"I've seen Chad and Mark in action," CiCi said, "and I wouldn't want to be in Ivan's shoes when they question him. I only hope Ivan doesn't reveal the motel receipt is in my possession. I forgot to mention that to Chad. He and Mark will blow a gasket if they find out."

NINETEEN

CiCi slid into the passenger seat of Megan's car the next morning, slipped on her favorite sunglasses, and fastened the seatbelt.

"Hey, nice sunglasses," Megan said. "They look great on you. Are they new?"

"Yes, Chad bought them for me." She gave her friend a half-hearted smile. "I know I said I would, but I'm not really in the mood to go shopping. Besides, I have a three o'clock appointment at the library to take my final appraisal test."

"Nonsense. We have plenty of time, and a little retail therapy is exactly what you need."

"If you say so, but don't expect me to fall victim to your spend-thrift ways, Miss Cooper. I'm not the shopping diva you are."

Megan laughed. "I may not be as thrifty as you, but I love a good sale as much as anyone. I saw two patients early this morning, so I'm free the rest of the day. My flight doesn't leave until Saturday, but I have a long list of things I need before I start packing."

"Where to first?"

"To prove I'm not a snob, I thought we'd start our shopping

spree on the town square. After lunch, we can head over to Skyview Plaza."

"The town square isn't far. Why don't we walk?"

"Nothing doing. I plan to buy a lot, and I'm not a pack mule."

They found a parking space, then began their journey around the square. The shop owners were delighted to see CiCi's familiar face, and many called out as she passed by.

Marge stuck her head out of her consignment shop. "CiCi, got a couple of nice furniture pieces coming in tomorrow."

"CiCi, my triple berry cobbler just came out of the oven. It's a new recipe, and I think you'll love it," Sadie promised from the doorway of her bakery.

"Fresh batch of songbird feed came in this morning. Want me to save a bag back for you, CiCi?" asked Art as he swept the sidewalk in front of his hardware store.

She responded to each and smiled at the friendliness of her town. Though several big box stores had cropped up on the west side of town, she vowed to remain a loyal customer to these mom and pop stores on the square. To her, they were the true heart and soul of Ripley Grove.

By the time noon rolled around, they were both ready to take a load off their aching feet. They ate at Peggy Sue's Diner, then walked across the street to sample a scoop of Sadie's cobbler. Sadie didn't lie; it tasted delicious.

At Skyview Plaza, they visited several stores, where Megan bought the remaining items on her list, and then some.

"If I didn't know better, I'd think you're never coming back. Impressed as I am with your eye for a sale, are you sure you need all this stuff?"

"I've budgeted all year for this trip and buying new clothes to wear on vacation is half the fun. Besides, some of us only see each other once a year and I want to look nice. Ooh, CiCi, look at that balconette bra. It's to die for," Megan said as she ogled Under Cover's window display. "We've hit the jackpot. They're having a huge sale."

Megan rushed inside and began filling a basket with goodies.

CiCi followed and browsed the aisles. She never intended to make a purchase, but when an embroidered demi bra caught her eye, she couldn't resist. The sale prices were too tempting. She updated her wardrobe with sports bras, lacy bras, T-shirt bras, bikini panties, shorty summer sleep sets, and a barely-there nightie. Her modest outer attire belied her penchant for ultra-feminine lingerie.

CiCi laughed as they carried their bounty to the car. "You're a bad influence on me, Megan Cooper."

"Your purchases weren't entirely my fault. Those prices were too good to pass up. Besides, lingerie is something I know you'd never buy at a thrift store."

"So true."

"I bet Chad would love to see you model your purchases." Megan wiggled her eyebrows.

After stopping at the bank for traveling cash, Megan called it a day and dropped CiCi off at home. CiCi put her purchases away and then took a catnap. She wanted a clear mind before heading to the library to take the last test that would put her one step closer to becoming a licensed appraiser. Over the last thirty months, every test following the completion of an online class had to be proctored, which meant the exam had to be timed and monitored by a designated person on the library staff.

Sitting at one of the library's computers, she logged in, took a deep breath, and nodded to the librarian. Two hours and forty minutes later, she clicked on the submit link, finishing a full twenty minutes ahead of the allotted time. She left the building with a smile on her face, fully confident she had done well on the exam.

That evening, CiCi and Chad met up with a group of his friends at the bowling alley. The lanes were crowded, the lights flashed in disco mode, and the music blared. Though all of Chad's friends wore blue jeans, T-shirts, and ball caps, they still looked like cops. As Chad and a few of the guys went to the snack bar for refreshments, CiCi watched as they laughed, slapped each other on the back, and heckled one another like brothers. Camaraderie seemed to be the perfect word to express their relationship.

"Your friends are a lot of fun to be around," she remarked on the drive home. "I had a great time, but I wish I had bowled better. I must've been your team's designated handicap for the evening." They both laughed as thunder rumbled overhead. A storm had moved into the area and rain pelted the windshield.

"It takes practice. We'll go again sometime, just you and me. By the way, most of the guys are jealous."

"Jealous? Of what?"

"You. Me. They think you're way too beautiful for the likes of me." He glanced over as she shook her head in disbelief. "Mark also told them how smart you are."

"Mark said that?"

"Don't misinterpret what I'm saying, because we still don't want you snooping around, but you gave us a couple of good leads yesterday. Mark won't admit it, but he was impressed how you pieced together the bits of information. Me, too."

She smiled at the compliment. "Thanks. Mark and I may have gotten off on the wrong foot, but the more time I spend around him, the more I like him. Anyway, I had fun tonight and look forward to going again."

Chad tightened his grip on the wheel to maintain control as the wind buffeted the truck. They rode in silence until CiCi could no longer hold her tongue.

"I saw Ivan and Izzy follow you and Mark from the funeral home yesterday. What was that about?" He turned to look at her. From his expression, her question had caught him off guard.

"We had questions for Ivan. I think you can guess why."

"Unfortunately, I can. I'm not excusing Ivan's actions, but I'd bet he wasn't the only person Julie slept with. I feel sorry for Izzy."

"Yeah. Most people hate to speak ill of the dead, but that didn't apply to Izzy yesterday."

"Can you blame her? First, she gave Julie a glowing job referral, which she screwed up by having an affair with one of the executives. Then Izzy finds out Julie seduced Ivan with the intention of

130

breaking up their marriage. That's cold. Do you think Izzy and Ivan are somehow involved with Julie's murder?"

"It's too early to say. What prompted you to go to the motel in the first place?"

CiCi gnawed on her lower lip and stared out the window. A bolt of lightning flashed across the angry sky. She took a deep breath and explained how she found the motel receipt, first at Five Star, then later while doing laundry. She ended the account with her brief conversation with Ivan after the funeral. She glanced over at Chad, who had remained quiet during her recap. A flash of lightning highlighted the hard lines of his face.

"I know you're not happy I questioned Gertrude," she said, "but hear me out. The main purpose for going to the motel was to find out if Izzy had misused company funds. I had no idea that receipt would reveal a connection between Ivan and Julie. The only thing I can't figure out is how that receipt came to be on the floor at work."

"You don't need to figure anything out. Leave that to me. I wish you'd told me earlier about the receipt."

"Sorry. I should have mentioned it."

He reached over and gave her hand a gentle squeeze.

"Chad, Ivan loves Izzy. He was terrified Izzy would find out, but I don't think he would kill Julie to keep her quiet. Besides, he's nowhere near the size of the man who attacked me."

"In this instance, size doesn't matter. What if he saw someone else there that night, or a car nearby, or heard Julie take another call? Every clue is vital." He gave her a stern look and said emphatically, "I'm going to need that receipt."

"I know. It's upstairs in my desk drawer."

Lightning flashed and a thundering boom shook the truck. Rain hammered against the windshield and the wipers barely made a difference. Chad leaned forward and strained to see through the downpour. "Did you ever see Ivan go into Julie's office?"

"I've never seen him at Five Star. Why?"

"Curious. Considering the nature of his relationship with Julie, we're checking his prints to see if they'll match one of the unidentified sets from the crime scene." He frowned and shook his head. "I don't want you snooping around again. Didn't Mark and I make that clear?"

"Yes, but in my defense, that inquiry at the motel was made before your warning."

"That's the only thing in your favor. I need to call Mark and let him know the latest. You'll be lucky if he doesn't come over to give you a good tongue-lashing."

She cringed. "Certainly you can talk him out of doing that."

Chad snorted. "Sugar, I have as much control over Mark as I have over you."

Lightening lit up the sky overhead as the neighborhood plunged into darkness.

"Looks like the power's out in your complex. I'll drop you off at the door." When he came to a stop, he reached across and opened the glove compartment. "Take my flashlight and watch your step. I'll be in after I bring Mark up to speed."

She jumped from the truck and ran to the cover of the front porch as Chad drove off in search of an empty parking spot. A train whistle echoed through the night air and a flash of lightning split the sky as she unlocked the door and stepped into the pitch-black foyer.

TWENTY

The flashlight flickered and died as soon as she stepped inside. She gave it three shakes—nothing. Tripping over something in the foyer, she fumbled her way to the kitchen to find a candle and matches. Lightning flashed through the aluminum blinds and illuminated upended furniture and piles of debris. A feeling of déjà vu washed over her as she processed the scene in her mind. Fear rippled through her chest as she slowly backed away.

Out of the blackness, a strong arm snaked around her midsection and pinned her arms against her body. A gloved hand muffled her terrified screams. She struggled as he half-carried, half-pushed her deeper into the living space. Outside, the sound of approaching footsteps slapped against the wet pavement. The intruder swore under his breath and threw her to the dining room floor. Instinctively, she stretched a hand forward to break the fall. Sharp, searing pains radiated up her arm and rendered her speechless. Something wet trickled down her arm.

Unsure of where the attacker had gone, she hunkered against the wall and bit back sobs. The entry door to the townhouse squeaked open and Chad's silhouette appeared. She called out a warning as he made his way down the darkened hall. Behind him, a shadowy figure darted from the half bath and rushed toward the door. Chad quickly turned and tackled the intruder.

Desperate to help, CiCi struggled to her feet and eased her way toward the dark foyer where Chad exchanged hard jabs and punches with a formidable opponent. Her head reeled as she picked up the flashlight from the floor. She held her breath and took aim. As she swung with all her might, a shot rang out. A windowpane shattered. Chad gasped and fell to his knees. Footsteps raced out the door. Chad struggled to his feet and staggered in pursuit.

Outside, she scanned the lot. Her attacker and Chad were nowhere in sight. The brunt of the storm had passed, leaving a steady shower and darkness in its wake. A car door slammed in the distance. An engine revved as a car raced from the far end of the lot.

Chad reappeared at her side, bent at the waist and panted from the chase. When he straightened, she wrapped an arm around his waist. "Chad, are you hurt? Were you shot?"

"No, I'm good, Sugar. The shot fired was from *my* gun." He checked his pockets. "My phone must've slipped out. Go to the complex office and call 9-1-1. Stay there while I search the house." He pushed her forward, checked his weapon, and headed toward her townhome.

CiCi stumbled across the grassy area that stretched across the front of the building. Brian, the complex manager, stood under the shelter of his porch sweeping a high-powered flashlight across the area. The earth seemed to shift with each step she took. The shocked look on Brian's face barely registered as her legs folded beneath her. Every bone in her body seemed to evaporate. The wet grass cushioned her fall as she slumped face first to the ground like a rag doll. A familiar voice shouted her name, and heavy footsteps pounded across the waterlogged turf. Gentle hands rolled her over and frantically inspected her body for wounds. Rain pelted her face and lightning flashed across the sky as a flurry of activity and voices erupted around her. Her body felt weightless and her mind at peace as she slipped into total darkness.

She struggled to open her eyes, and when she did, it took a few moments to comprehend where she was. To her right, a nurse checked her vitals and adjusted the pillow under her arm. To her left, a bag of clear fluid hung from an upright pole. Tubing from the bag snaked through a portable monitor and into an IV in her arm.

Chad paced at the foot of her hospital bed, talking on the phone. A bandage covered one side of his forehead. He quickly ended the call when he noticed her taking inventory of her surroundings. He closed the void and gently kissed her temple. Perplexed, she looked from him to the massive bandage that encased her right arm from elbow to fingertips.

"Don't worry, Sugar. Your surgery went fine," he said.

She had questions, but her throat ached, her tongue stuck to the roof of her mouth, and her eyelids were heavy. Chad stroked her cheek and held her hand as she drifted away.

Even with his eyes shut, Chad detected someone monitoring his every breath. He leapt from the chair, ready for battle, but the spinning room hampered his efforts. He closed his eyes and took a deep breath as strong hands helped guide him back into the chair.

"Take it easy, champ. Looks like you got clocked by someone almost as tough as me," Mark whispered in a joking manner. He picked up the blanket that had fallen to the floor and tossed it on an empty chair.

Chad opened his eyes and blinked against the early morning sunlight streaming through the window. With a weak smile, he rubbed the stiffness from his neck. His head throbbed something fierce. With scraped fingers, he gingerly touched his swollen lip and the lump under his eye. He glanced down at his shirt, still stained with blood from the night before. He slowly stood when Megan rushed into the room. She handed Mark a carryout tray holding three cups of hot coffee, then wrapped her big brother in a gentle hug.

"You had me worried. Are you okay? How's CiCi?" she asked.

"Yeah, I'm good. Her injuries were the worst, but she'll heal in time."

"Her doctor stopped by, Chad," Mark said, "but you were out cold."

"Yeah, I took a fairly solid hit to the head. Apparently, my head isn't as hard as we all thought. The ER doc told me to lay off work for a couple of days."

"That's probably a good idea."

"Yeah. The nurses woke me every two hours, so I didn't get much sleep. Neither did CiCi. She was in a lot of pain." Chad sneezed and immediately looked over to see if he had awakened her.

"Her doctor said he wants to check on her again before he thinks about releasing her. She's one lucky gal. He said she might have bled out if you and Brian hadn't been there."

Chad's heart dropped into his stomach. He shook his head and imagined what could've happened if he hadn't insisted on going inside for the motel receipt.

"Why don't you let Megan take you home?" Mark suggested. "Eat something. Take a nap. Shower and get yourself cleaned up before you come back. You're scary enough as it is, even without the bloody clothes. If you feel up to driving later, I'll have someone drop you by CiCi's to pick up your truck. I'll stay here. When she wakes up, I have a few questions for her."

Chad felt better by the time he arrived back at the hospital. At the nurse's station, he ran into Tasha, who offered him a friendly hug.

"How are you feeling?" she asked.

"Fine, except for a pounding headache. Where's Mark and Megan?"

"Megan brought CiCi some clean clothes to wear home, but she had back-to-back clients this afternoon. I called Pastor Young. He and his wife came by for a short visit. Mark had to leave, so I offered to stay until you came back."

"Thanks. How's she doing?"

"Sleeping. The nurse gave her a pain pill after Mark left. I've got to go, too, but keep me updated if anything changes." She rattled off her phone number and waited while Chad added her to his contact list.

After Tasha left, he tiptoed over to CiCi's bedside and watched her sleep. A short time later, her eyes fluttered open. He smiled and gave her a kiss. As he pulled back, her eyes took in his swollen lip and black eye. When her gaze landed on his bandaged forehead, a troubled look crossed her face. "It's not as bad as it looks," he said.

She burst into tears. "I'm so sorry."

He frowned, confused by her reaction. "Calm down, Sugar. You've nothing to be sorry for."

"Yes, I do," she wailed. "*I'm* the one who hit you with the flashlight. I missed him and hit you by mistake."

He slowly shook his head and chuckled. "Don't worry about it. Just remind me not to pick a fight when you've got something in your hand."

TWENTY-ONE

A distinguished-looking gentleman entered CiCi's hospital room without any hesitation or pause. His clothes were casual, but expensive. The creases in his slacks were as sharp as his blue-eyed gaze. The stethoscope around his neck gave the only hint as to his occupation.

"Afternoon, CiCi." He gave her a warm smile as he flipped through her medical chart.

"Doc? What are you doing here? I heard you were thinking about retiring."

"You can't believe everything you hear in this town," he chuckled. "I cut the hours at my practice in order to work a couple of nights a week in the emergency room. They were short-staffed, and I needed a change of pace. It's a win-win for both of us."

"Chad, this is Doctor Cunningham, a family friend and my physician. Doc Cunningham, my boyfriend, Chad Cooper." She watched the men assess one another over a handshake.

"Call me Doc; everyone does. Are you by any chance Greg's son?"

"Yes, sir, I am."

"I hear he and your mom moved out of town recently. Give him my regards and remind him he still owes me a pair of Royals tickets." He smiled, then turned his attention to his patient. After he checked her vitals, he peeked under the bandages and made a few notes on the chart.

"CiCi, would you prefer we talk in private?" He glanced over the rim of his glasses at her, then directed his gaze to Chad.

"No, he can stay." Chad moved forward and gently squeezed her hand.

"All right then. Your arm was slashed in several places from hand to elbow. You lost a lot of blood by the time you arrived in the ER. The surgery went well, but tendon damage might be our next concern; only time will tell. After I sign the discharge papers, you'll be free to leave once the nurse gets the proper paperwork logged. A rigid brace will keep your wrist and hand immobile, and a semi-soft, removable splint will cover the bandages up to your elbow and provide added protection. Keep the stitches dry and the hand elevated as much as possible. Use ice packs if you notice swelling. You aren't to do any lifting, and you're not to return to work for at least two weeks. Is your vehicle automatic or manual?"

"It's a stick. Why?"

"No driving, either." He shot her a stern look when she started to protest.

Doc paused before looking squarely at Chad. "Would you mind if she and I had a few minutes alone?" Chad nodded and left the room. Doc's faint smile faded and his eyes filled with sadness. "I'm sorry to hear of your mother's passing. Regretfully, I was out of town and didn't make it back for the funeral. I'll miss her."

"Thanks, Doc. I know how much she valued your friendship over the years, and she so looked forward to your visits at Hospice House."

"I wish I could've done more to help, but her treatment was out of my realm of expertise." He shook his head before steering the conversation in a new direction. "You haven't been to my office for quite some time."

She shrugged. "I haven't been sick, not that I wouldn't mind seeing you."

"You came to the clinic fairly often back when you were in high school. The moment you left home, your need for my medical intervention suddenly stopped. Why is that, CiCi?"

Does he know? But how, and why now? Her heart skipped a beat and her throat turned dry. She looked away, debating whether or not to answer. "I don't know."

"I do. I treated your dad a month ago in the ER after he'd been injured in a bar fight. He'd been drinking, of course. In passing conversation, I asked about you. His comments shook me up enough that I went back and reviewed your medical history. To say I was shocked and angry would be an understatement. I vaguely remember having doubts about your explanations near the end of your senior year. Instead of pushing for answers, I chose to believe the excuses you gave. If I could go back in time, I'd do things much differently. I apologize for failing you, Cecilia."

"Doc, please, don't blame yourself."

"But I do. I have to shoulder some of the responsibility. Considering the circumstances, I think I deserve to finally hear the truth."

Chad leaned against the doorjamb and glanced again at his watch. *Thirty minutes. How much longer?* His casual stance belied his inner turmoil. He straightened as the doctor approached. "Sir, if you don't mind, I have a couple of questions."

Doctor Cunningham raised his eyebrows and stared intently into Chad's face. He turned and led the way to his office at the end of the hall. There, he offered Chad a chair and a fresh cup of hazelnut-flavored coffee. He nodded when Chad pulled out his badge and offered it for inspection. "Somehow I guessed you to be in law enforcement."

"A keen sense of observation is helpful in my line of work, so pardon me if I don't apologize for eavesdropping. I overheard bits of your conversation with CiCi, but not enough for my liking. Something happened to her in the past that involves her father, and

I'd like to know what." Chad leaned forward. "I'm not asking as a detective. I'm asking as a man who's deeply in love with her."

"I want to help, but I can't ignore the privacy issues. Have you asked her?"

"Not in so many words. She avoids any discussion that involves her dad."

"That's not surprising." Doctor Cunningham leaned back in his chair and steepled his hands over his midsection; thumb to thumb, finger to finger, pinkie to pinkie. His blue eyes narrowed as he remained deep in thought. "How long have you two been together?"

"We've been dating for a year, exclusively for about eight months. We've known each other since seventh grade and dated on and off all through high school."

"From your recollection, what was she like back then?"

Chad smiled as he thought back to high school. "She was smart, beautiful, and a lot of fun. She hasn't changed. Although back then she was a bit clumsy...well *a lot* clumsy, actually. She was considered the class klutz." His laugh faded and he stared off into the distance. "She was always getting hurt, but now...I don't know." He turned to look squarely at the physician. "Or maybe I do, and don't want to believe it's possible."

"As a detective, you sense there's more to her past than you perceived at the time, and you're right. Her mother's death has opened old wounds she would rather ignore and brought her into contact with people she would rather avoid."

"Jack?"

Doc nodded. "In my opinion, it would be best if you hear about it directly from her."

"I would do anything to be able to help, and nothing will ever change how I feel about her. I want to propose, but not in the shadow of her mother's death."

"Considering the current circumstances, you're wise to hold off on a marriage proposal. You couldn't have picked a sweeter girl. I've watched her grow up, so naturally she holds a soft spot in my heart.

Don't push her too hard. She'll open up when she's ready, and I have a feeling it will be sooner than you think."

Doc checked his watch and rose to indicate he had other patients to see. He shook Chad's hand as they left the room together.

Chad stood in the hall and mulled over the scant information he'd received. He compared it to Mark's theory concerning CiCi's estrangement from her dad. The very thought made his chest burn with anger. Theories and guesses weren't enough in his line of work. He needed to hear CiCi confirm or deny his suspicions. Waiting would be the most difficult part.

TWENTY-TWO

While the nurse helped CiCi dress, Chad stepped into the hallway outside her room and tapped a two-digit number on his cell phone. "Hey, Mark. Any news?"

"We've asked around," he said. "No one heard a thing. Her residence is adjacent to the wooded area and the occupant next door is out of town. The complex manager had been watching a ballgame on TV. When the electricity went out, he stepped outside to check on the storm."

"Any fingerprints?"

"Nope. The way this guy trashed the place, I'd say he was looking for something. Her dad left a message on the answering machine while I was there. She has something he wants, and he wants it bad. I stopped by his automotive shop. His lead mechanic said he didn't show up for work today."

"Maybe I should—"

"*No*, you shouldn't. The Chief wants you to stay away from her dad and concentrate on the Reynolds murder. And aren't you supposed to lay off work for a few days?"

"Yeah, yeah."

"I wonder if her break-in is connected to the murder. What if

Julie Reynolds tried to tell CiCi something about an actual *key* and this guy is looking for it?"

"Anything's possible."

CiCi held the post-op instructions in her lap as the volunteer wheeled her to the entrance of the hospital. Chad pulled his truck as close to the door as possible and helped her into the passenger seat before driving from the lot.

"While you were sleeping earlier, the nurse showed me how to clean around the sutures and change the dressings. I see she found a soft cast and a sling in your favorite shade of blue. Nice." He smiled and patted her thigh.

"It's hardly what I'd consider a bonus. The splint is awkward, and the brace won't let me move my hand at all." She leaned her head back against the headrest. "I'm so glad I took my appraisal test yesterday. There's no way I could type wearing this thing."

"Doc wants you to take it easy." His tone was firm, but gentle. "You're not to do any physical work for a while. Keep that in mind when you see your place."

"It can't be that bad."

"Have you remembered anything that might help identify the attacker?"

"No. I've tried not to think about it. Can we stop by the pharmacy to pick up my pain meds? I have a feeling I'm going to need them soon."

"Sure," he said, turning the truck toward the nearest drugstore.

Chad helped her from the truck once they arrived at her home. As if on cue, Mark pulled alongside them and stepped from his vehicle. He gave Chad a questioning look, but stopped when he caught her watching their silent exchange.

Chad removed the crime scene tape and led the way into the building. CiCi followed, and Mark brought up the rear. Not wishing to draw attention to her horrible aim, she silently sidestepped the infamous flashlight on the floor. She averted her eyes from the trail of dried blood that streaked the hallway, and instead surveyed the damage in the kitchen and living room. Chad wrapped an arm around her as she choked back a sob.

In the kitchen, most every drawer and cupboard had been emptied. Beyond the breakfast bar, one door of the china cabinet hung precariously from a single hinge. Her heart ached when she saw the fractured pieces of china that once belonged to her grandmother. Dried blood dotted the jagged pieces of the crystal goblets that lay shattered where she fell during the attack. In the living room, cracks snaked across her TV screen. The sofa cushions were slashed open, and the bookcases toppled. She blinked rapidly to keep the tears at bay.

The cleanliness of the stairway gave her a false sense of hope. The level destruction on the second floor appeared to be the same as downstairs. Her computer tower and monitor sat helter-skelter on the floor, the cords ripped from each unit. The contents of her file cabinet were scattered across the room, dresser drawers had been emptied and chucked aside, and her bedside lamps were nothing more than pieces of fragmented pottery.

She slumped on the edge of the off-kilter mattress, while the men left to inspect the guest bedroom. Tears formed as she scanned the room. *Who would do something like this? And why? Haven't I had enough to deal with over the last few months?* She straightened and brushed away the tears, determined not to wallow in self-pity. Her grandmother always said, "Honey, nothing good ever comes from feeling sorry for yourself. Tough times don't last, but tough people do." Grandma Agnes was a resilient woman, and CiCi aimed to follow in her footsteps.

She glanced down and picked up a small framed picture that once sat on the dresser. She ran a thumb over her mother's smiling face. She looked around for the box containing her mother's necklace and caught a glimpse of blue a few feet away. As she reached for it, a clothes hanger snagged her foot. Pillows cushioned her fall, but the sound brought Chad and Mark rushing into the room. Mark took the picture from her hand and Chad gently lifted her to her feet.

"What the hell are you doing?" Chad asked. "You're supposed to take it easy. Are you okay? Did you hurt yourself?"

"I'm fine." She leaned against the empty dresser and rubbed her injured arm. "Speaking of taking it easy, would you and Mark straighten the mattress so I'll have a place to sleep?"

"Mark and I've talked. We think you should make other sleeping arrangements. Find a bag and pack whatever clothes you might need for a few days."

Her head snapped up. "What're you talking about? I can't leave. There's work to be done. It looks like an F5 tornado ripped through here. "

Chad turned and looked at Mark. She watched the silent communication between the two. Chad shook his head and sighed. "Sugar, I know how badly you want to get this mess cleaned up, but you just had surgery and you're supposed to take it easy." His gaze swept the room before his eyes locked with hers. "Besides, do you really think you'd be able to get a good night's sleep after what's happened?"

CiCi massaged her forehead with her only good hand as she looked around the room. Her shoulders sagged with despair and her resolve began to weaken. "I'd stay at Megan's while she's in Florida, but her roommate doesn't like me all that much. Maybe I could stay with Tasha."

Chad shook his head. "Not a good idea."

"Why not?"

Mark shot a glance at Chad before speaking. "In my professional opinion, this is more than a simple vandalism. You have something this guy wants. When he didn't find it, he went ballistic and tore the place up. What if he comes looking for you, thinking you have it?"

"That's crazy. There's nothing here worth stealing. But I also don't want to put Tasha in danger. I'll stay here and sleep with one eye open. I'll be fine."

"CiCi—"

"Chad, I'll be fine."

Chad crossed his arms over his chest. The look on his face dared her to argue. "Remember when I said I wouldn't cross the line

146

unless it became necessary? Well, *now it's necessary*. Pack a bag. You can stay at my place, where I know you'll be safe. Besides, I'll need to change your bandages every day."

Her eyes widened, her cheeks flushed with heat. "You think that's a good idea?"

"I do. Mark and I knew you'd put up a fight. You either stay at my place, or we'll temporarily set you up with one of our female officers. Those are your choices. You decide."

She wrinkled her nose. "That's hardly what I'd call a choice."

"We're trying to keep you safe, CiCi," Mark interjected. "By the way, Chad said you own a couple of guns. Where do you keep them?"

She pointed to the general vicinity. Chad, being the closest, proceeded to move aside pillows and articles of clothing. She quickly stepped forward and snatched her lingerie from his hand. He chuckled softly and his eyes danced with amusement. When he raised his other hand, a pair of red panties hung from his wrist, the delicate lace caught on the stem of his watch. As she worked to unhook the undergarment without damaging the material, her face flushed from the heat of his gaze. The search for the guns continued, but they failed to find either weapon.

"Well," she said, "I suppose I had something worth stealing after all."

"If you have the serial numbers, I'd suggest you go down to the station and report them stolen," Mark said. "By law, you're not required to do so, but it's a good idea."

"I will," she said. "I think the serial numbers are in my safe deposit box."

Chad raked a hand through his hair. "I wonder where that motel receipt is. That's what I came in for the other night, remember?"

"It was in my desk drawer, but I don't see the drawer anywhere in this mess. Is it that important?"

"It is, especially since there's no record of Ivan having used a credit card at the motel."

CiCi nodded wearily and gathered tops and bottoms that would be easy to slip on using one arm. She packed the clothes, along with shoes and a few toiletries, into a suitcase. Mark took the suitcase and headed downstairs. She followed, with Chad not far behind. At the door, she turned for one last look at the damage.

Chad gently wrapped his arm around her shoulder. "It's going to be okay, hon. You know that, right?"

She gave a weak sigh and nodded.

He bent and picked up something from the floor. With a grin, he placed the flashlight in her hand. "You can keep this, but you really need to work on your aim before you use it again."

She followed Chad inside after he unlocked the door to his apartment. He scooped up dirty socks and an undershirt from the floor and two shirts draped over a recliner and carried them, along with her suitcase, to the one and only bedroom.

His rental occupied the main floor of an older two-story house. She and Chad were both fans of the open floor plan. Gleaming hardwood floors in the living room flowed seamlessly into the dining room. A breakfast bar separated the living room and dining room from the dated, but functional, kitchen.

"Make yourself at home. If there's anything you need or can't find, just ask," he said as he took a large stack of newspapers off the coffee table and dropped them into an empty cardboard box in the corner of the room.

"Looks like you've started packing."

"A little." He stared at several boxes stacked against one wall. The contents of each box had been marked on the outside with a black marker: books, blankets, winter gear, coats. His landlord had hinted that he wanted to make the rental property his primary residence in the near future. Finding another apartment and moving was unavoidable.

He glanced at his watch. "It'll be time for your pain meds soon. Why don't you relax while I make a quick run by the grocery store? You need anything while I'm out?"

"No, I'm good."

After he left, she placed a call to her insurance agent, who agreed to meet the following morning. From her earlier observations, very few of her furnishings would be salvageable. As Chad had suggested, she arranged to have a dumpster dropped off in the parking lot of her complex. By the time she had notified several friends about her release from the hospital, Chad had returned from the store, his arms loaded with groceries. She put the canned goods away while he started dinner. They washed down grilled ham and cheese sandwiches and chips with ice-cold milk. Chad wiped his mouth after the last bite and leaned back in his chair.

"You look horrible," she said. "You either have gas, or a headache. Which is it?"

He chuckled. "Both."

"Take a couple of pills and go lay down."

Without any argument, he went to the bedroom and flopped across the bed. CiCi settled back on the buttery-soft leather sofa, pulled the bookmark from a library book and began to read. Her eyes fluttered open a short time later when she felt a light throw cover her body.

"Sorry, I didn't mean to wake you," he said.

"I didn't intend to take a nap. The snoring from the bedroom lulled me to sleep."

"*My* snoring? *Your* snoring was the last thing I heard before I drifted off."

She puttered around the apartment, finished reading her book, then flipped through a magazine. While checking for phone messages, she cast furtive glances in Chad's direction. Though emotionally and physically drained by the end of the day, she felt reluctant to settle in for the night.

"You're not nervous about us sleeping under the same roof, are you?" He chuckled when she shrugged and looked away.

"You're not the only one with needs and desires. I love you, Chad, but I don't want to do something I'll regret later. I'm sorry if—"

He held up a hand. "There's no need to apologize. I'm not

saying it'll be easy for either one of us, but trust me, I'm a man of my word."

She nodded, grateful for his patience and understanding. "If you'll get me a couple of blankets and a pillow, I think I'll turn in. This sofa looks plenty comfy. I promise not to drool on it."

"Not gonna happen. You're taking the bed. I've already changed the sheets." He held up a hand when she started to protest. "I'll be fine. I crash on the sofa all the time."

Chad checked on her before turning in for the night. Under the soft glow of a nightlight, she looked like an angel. Her wavy hair lay feathered across the pillow and her chest rose and fell with each gentle breath.

She's so beautiful, inside and out. I know we agreed to refrain from getting intimate, but I never thought it would be so difficult. Sometimes I can hardly contain my love—or my lust—for her. But, if holding back is what it takes to prove my love and commitment to her, so be it. It's a small sacrifice for the amount of joy she brings into my life every day. If I could spend the rest of my life with her, I'd count myself as the luckiest man alive.

After grabbing a few blankets and an extra pillow from the hall closet, he settled in on the sofa and drifted off to sleep thinking of what married life would be like with her as his wife. When a piercing scream shattered his dreams a couple of hours later, he knew her demons had returned.

TWENTY-THREE

CiCi angled herself out of the unfamiliar bed, slipped on a robe, and padded down the hall to the kitchen. Chad sat at the table hunched over his laptop, a cup of coffee in his hand. He wore a simple white T-shirt, jeans, and a pair of rugged work boots, a combination she found wildly attractive on his well-toned body. Her heart fluttered at the possibility of spending the rest of her life with him. "Morning," she said.

Chad set down his coffee cup. His warm brown eyes slowly roamed her body from head to toe. She self-consciously ran a hand through her sleep-tousled hair, but his dimpled grin melted away any concerns she had about her appearance.

"You should've gotten me up earlier so I could help fix breakfast or make coffee."

"After the last couple of days, I thought you could use the extra sleep. And you don't need to worry about cooking. I've already made breakfast."

He slid an arm around her waist and pulled her in for a kiss.

"What a great way to start the day." She smiled and nodded toward the rental listings on the laptop. "Having any luck?"

"Not yet. I want an older home with yesteryear charm, but most of the properties advertised are too small for my needs or too modern to suit my taste." He reached out and gently stroked her cheek with his thumb. "How's your arm feel this morning?"

"It throbs—*a lot*. I need to eat something so I can take a pain pill. Sorry about last night. Being attacked a second time must've pushed my mind over the edge."

"Don't worry about it, although we may want to send a peace offering to my upstairs neighbor. We'll pick up a bottle of sleeping pills for tonight," he said with a wink.

"That might be a good idea."

"We need to get a move on if we plan to meet the insurance man at ten." He reheated her omelet in the microwave and served it with a devilish gleam in his eyes. "If you need help getting dressed later, just let me know."

"In your dreams."

"Every night."

When they arrived at her complex, she immediately took notice of the green dumpster in the corner of the parking lot. As they exited the vehicle, a car pulled in and parked next to Chad's truck. The driver's door opened and out stepped her insurance agent. CiCi and Chad escorted him inside, where he took notes and numerous photos of the damage. He processed the space in quick order and left a folder of instructions and blank inventory forms on his way out.

As she and Chad stood in the doorway and watched the agent leave, Mark parked at the edge of the lot, a few spaces away from the dumpster. Fellow officer Frank Guzman pulled in a few seconds later and parked alongside Mark. The two men got out of their vehicles and approached CiCi's townhouse. Each man wore scruffy, torn jeans, work boots, and ratty T-shirts.

"What are you two doing here?" she asked. "You're clearly not on duty."

"When I heard about the break-in," Frank answered, "I thought Chad might need help clearing out the damaged furniture. Mark had the same idea, so here we are."

"Thank you. At the moment, it's more than one person can handle."

Frank inquired about her injury, and then turned his attention to Chad. "If you ask me, the stitches and black eye are a big improvement." His comment made everyone chuckle.

Once inside, the men turned quiet. Cryptic looks were exchanged as they pointed here and there, silently communicating with one another in a language known only to them. After agreeing on a plan of action, each man pulled on a pair of leather work gloves and attacked the piles of debris. They rebuffed her feeble attempts to help. After slipping and stumbling against the breakfast bar, Chad's patience evaporated. He wiped the sweat from his brow, took ahold of her good arm, and led her over to the stairs.

"You're not supposed to be working. Doctor's orders," he said.

"But—"

"But what? You're supposed to take it easy." He turned and grabbed a pen and a few sheets of paper from the kitchen counter. "Here, if you need something to do, work on this."

"Good idea." She took the inventory forms left by the insurance agent and listed the items that were damaged beyond repair.

A short time later, Chad leaned in and whispered, "We're going to head to the second floor when we're finished with lunch. If there's anything you don't want the guys to see, now might be the time to take care of it. But—no heavy lifting, and be careful where you walk." His warm breath tickled her ear and a sexy smile played at the corners of his mouth.

Understanding dawned slowly, but when she caught his meaning, she rushed upstairs to pick up the undergarments scattered across the bedroom. Although glad for the recent upgrade in her lingerie, she would be embarrassed beyond words if his friends were to see some of her skimpier pieces. Not that they would mind.

At noon, a local sandwich shop delivered foot-long hoagies, chips, a couple of liters of pop, and bottled water. Once the men finished eating, they pulled on their gloves again and headed to the second floor. While they worked, she lowered herself onto a wayward sofa cushion in the living room. She rubbed her throbbing arm and closed her eyes. Then, a familiar voice filtered through the fog.

"Wake up, Sugar. All the large pieces that were damaged have been removed, and we've done all we can for today."

She opened her eyes and found Chad looming overhead. *I must've fallen asleep.* He helped her from the floor and gave her a gentle squeeze. A quick glance at his watch indicated she had slept for nearly an hour. "Chad, it's still early. Why don't you go home without me? You can shower, take a nap, and pick me up later."

He shook his head. "Not gonna happen."

She met his stern look with a frown, which did nothing to change his mind. She turned and expressed her gratitude to Mark and Frank. They each nodded and grabbed a bottle of water on their way out. She shut off the lights, locked up, and followed the weary crew outside.

"Chad, she's got company," Mark warned.

CiCi looked at Chad, then followed his gaze. Thirty feet away, her dad exited his truck and stomped across the parking lot toward her. She froze. Her heart raced and her pulse quickened. He wore a scowl on his face and had a noticeable wad of chew tucked into his cheek. She briefly thought of asking about her grandmother's ring, but quickly dismissed the idea. Chad and Mark positioned themselves to her left and right. Frank casually drifted away from the group and slipped around behind Jack.

"You could at least answer the damn phone," he snarled. "You got an answering machine, and probably caller ID, so don't lie and tell me you didn't know I was trying to get ahold of you." He briefly glanced at her dirty work crew and the over-flowing dumpster. "You didn't waste any time, did you? Looks like you're getting ready to buy new furniture."

Her stomach knotted. "What do you want?"

"Don't play stupid with me! You know what I want. You stole it out from under my nose, and I aim to get it back, one way or another." Contempt rolled off his tongue with ease. He glared and spat a brown stream of tobacco juice on the pavement.

Chad took a step forward. "You need to calm down, or leave."

Without glancing at Chad, Jack said, "I'll leave after her and I have a talk."

She held tight to Chad's arm to keep from shaking. "There's nothing I can do to change things, Dad. Call Mr. Browning; he'll explain it to you again. And for whatever its worth, it might help if you were sober when you talk to him."

"I don't have to put up with your smart mouth." Jack's face contorted with anger. His meaty hands closed into fists as he took a step forward. "Tell your hired help to leave so we can have ourselves a little talk."

Chad freed himself from her grip and immediately moved to shield her from an attack. "You heard her, Jack. She doesn't want to talk to you. The last time you *talked*, she ended up with bruises around her neck. That won't happen again."

"Do I know you? If I do, butt out. If not, get lost." Jack glanced dismissively at Chad, then settled an evil eye on CiCi.

"You surely remember *me*, don't you, Jack?" Mark asked, drawing Jack's attention away from his daughter. "I questioned you recently about a murder."

Recognition washed over Jack's face. He looked back at Chad, then snuck a glance at the man behind him. CiCi saw the wheels turning in his mind, wondering if they were also cops. Anyone could tell they were by their haircuts, the stony set of their faces, and their manner of stance.

"In fact," Mark continued, "I've been looking for you. I have a question about another case I'm working on. Where were you Thursday night, say between nine and midnight?"

Jack narrowed his eyes and spat on the pavement. He swiped a hand across the brown spittle that dripped from the corner of his mouth. "I don't have to say nothing without my lawyer present. But, to show you how obliging I am, give a shout to Tipsy's Bar. Ask for

Eldon or Goldie. I gave you something, now I want something in return. Ten minutes with her, alone. We got some family business to discuss."

"You don't make the rules here, Jack."

"Dad, please. I don't want any trouble." Her fingernails dug into the palm of her hand as the knot in her stomach tightened.

Chad's gaze focused on Jack like a hawk on its prey. "You don't have a hearing problem, do you, Jack? She doesn't want anything to do with you. I normally don't get in the middle of family business, but make no mistake about it, I will if I have to. It'd be in your best interest if you get in your truck and leave." When Jack didn't budge, Chad took two steps forward. "That was *not* a suggestion."

Jack rubbed a hand across his whiskered chin, then slowly turned and walked toward his red pickup. He jumped into the cab, slammed the door shut, and whipped out a cell phone. After he disconnected from two short calls, the engine of the rusty old truck roared to life. As he slowly cruised by, he cocked a forefinger and pointed at CiCi. "We're not finished, you and me. We're gonna talk real soon, just like old times."

His words were thick with malice and full of promise. He gave a wicked grin, gunned the engine and peeled out of the parking lot, nearly sideswiping a parked car. Frank waved goodbye and jumped in his truck to follow.

The tension melted from CiCi's body and her legs felt like rubber. She leaned against Chad for support.

"I think you've had enough excitement for today, Sugar. Let's get you home."

She thanked Mark again for his help, then climbed into Chad's truck. During the drive to his apartment, an awkward silence filled the cab. "I'm sorry if my family drama caused you any embarrassment in front of your friends. I'm sure by now they're questioning your taste in girlfriends."

"Why would you even say that? You had three of Ripley Grove's finest ready to do serious battle if he so much as laid a finger on you. If I know Frank, he'll tag your address for extra patrols starting tomorrow. CiCi, *never* apologize for your dad. Don't you get it? You're not responsible for his behavior." His words hung heavy in the air.

"I never expected him to show up. In fact, I'm surprised he even knows where I live. To my knowledge, it's the first time he's ever been to my place, unless—" She stopped short. From the look on Chad's face, he could have easily finished her sentence.

"Yeah, I thought of that. I find it odd he didn't say anything about your arm being in a cast. It's almost as if he already knew about your injury. I also noticed he had some visible cuts and scrapes."

"True, but that's not to say he hasn't been in a bar fight or two lately."

"You can be sure Mark will check his alibi. On a positive note, Jack doesn't know you're staying elsewhere. That should put your mind at ease."

"It does. I suppose it *was* a good idea to stay at your place."

His hand took a firmer grip on the wheel as he drove the next several blocks in silence. "When he said he wanted to talk 'just like old times', what did he mean?"

She stared out the window and shook her head.

"Every time he comes up in conversation, you shut down. It's obvious there's something you're not telling me." He expelled a heavy sigh at her continued silence. "I'll leave it be, but I'm here when you're ready to talk."

After dinner, CiCi assembled the necessary materials to change her bandages. She removed the soft splint while Chad slipped on a pair of latex gloves as directed by the nurse to keep the risk of infection to a minimum. She swallowed hard as he gently removed the dressing. A single glance at the discarded gauze caused her stomach to lurch. She quickly clamped a free hand over her mouth and looked away.

"Got a queasy stomach, huh? Take a couple of deep breaths. It's oozing a bit. Maybe you shouldn't look until the stitches come out. I'll try to be easy, but I can't promise it won't hurt. Did you take a pain pill?"

She nodded and focused on keeping her meal down.

After the last strip of tape was affixed, he inspected his handiwork and gave a nod of approval. He put away the medical supplies, gave her a kiss, then flopped on the sofa to make his weekly call to his parents, who lived out of town. She, in turn, retreated to the front porch with a white chocolate-macadamia nut cookie and a glass of iced tea. She nibbled on the cookie while she chatted on the phone with Tasha, and then took a call from Floyd. He and his wife, Margaret, were concerned about her situation and relieved to hear that Chad had stepped in to help.

The neighborhood may have grown quiet as the day drew to a close, but a war waged in her heart as she mulled over her father's unexpected and unwanted visit.

If I'm able to confront Keenan in a dark parking lot and stand my ground against a fierce detective who practically accused me of murder, why do I refuse to stand up to my dad? I can't blame Chad for not understanding. I don't understand it myself. But somehow, filing charges and taking my father to court feels like the ultimate act of betrayal, regardless of the fact he has betrayed my love and trust for years. I suppose it proves that deep down, I still yearn for his love and affection.

Am I subconsciously trying to earn that love by not pressing charges? Maybe, but it makes no sense, unless you take into account my deep-seated fear of him. Though I've tried to ignore it, I can't deny it. And he is just smart enough to use that fear against me to get what he wants.

She popped the last bite of cookie into her mouth and brushed the crumbs from her fingertips.

The inheritance simply puts another wedge in our damaged relationship. Mom had to have realized that leaving me the estate would cause more animosity —and yet, she still followed through with her plans. It seems Mom's ultimate goals had been to protect the family fortune and sever my ties with my dad forever. It's the only conclusion that makes any sense.

The important things in life seldom come easily, or quickly. By the time the streetlamp flickered on, she had made a momentous decision. She shook her head in disbelief.

Mom always had been full of surprises, but never more so than after her death. Her actions have finally forced me to examine my feelings and take charge of my life. That is a major accomplishment for someone who is dead.

TWENTY-FOUR

After church, she and Chad shared a quick bite to eat before he left to wash his truck, run a few errands, and then hit the gym. That gave her a bit of free time to watch a chick flick on TV. Later, using one of Chad's favorite recipes, she assembled a basic meatloaf for dinner that evening. Even without the chopped onions or green peppers, measuring and mixing the ingredients took longer than usual. In the end, the loaf didn't look half bad for a one-armed chef. She covered the meat and popped the baking dish into the fridge. When the throbbing in her arm became impossible to ignore, she ate a granola bar, washed down a pain pill, and retreated to the bedroom to let the meds do their magic.

She awoke to the delicious beefy aroma of meatloaf. Inhaling deeply, her stomach growled. She went to the kitchen, where Chad sat at the table, drinking coffee and pecking away on the laptop. She walked over and gave him a kiss on his forehead.

"I'm glad you started dinner. I'm starved," she said. The cell phone in her back pocket rang. She looked at the screen and hit the ignore button. She fixed herself a glass of iced tea, then took a seat at the table. The phone rang again. She checked the caller ID and pursed her lips.

Chad stopped typing and leaned back in his chair. "Your dad?"

"Not exactly." She slid the device across the table.

He picked up the phone as it rang a second time. His brows pinched together when he saw the caller's name. "You want me to handle this?"

"I do."

He answered and put the call on speaker. Instantly, the line went dead.

"I can't imagine why Richie would call," she said.

"I suspect he's calling on your dad's behalf, since you won't answer his calls anymore."

She sighed. "You're probably right. They're drinking buddies, you know. I bet he enlisted Richie's help since he knows Richie still holds a grudge over our divorce settlement. You had every right to suspect Richie after the tires were slashed on my Jeep. After all, he drove Dad to the lawyer's office."

"Speaking of Jack. Mark called earlier and asked if he could stop by for a chat. I invited him for dinner and—"

The doorbell rang and Chad went to answer it. Mark joined them at the table and CiCi poured him a cup of coffee. He thanked her and smiled, though it never reached his eyes. Clearly, there was something on his mind.

"Chad said you wanted to talk?" she asked as she refreshed Chad's cup.

"I do. I want to talk about your dad."

She stiffened. "Not exactly my favorite topic of conversation."

Mark nodded as he took a drink. "I checked your dad's alibi for the night of your break-in. According to Eldon, the bartender, Jack took up drinking with Goldie from eight until the bar closed. Of course, he could've made up the story to cover for his war buddy. Goldie is a whole another story. I think 'alibi' might be her middle name."

"So, he's in the clear."

"Seems that way for now, although a few regulars I spoke with were iffy on what time he arrived." He exchanged glances with Chad over the rim of his coffee mug. "After listening to your dad's phone message and witnessing his behavior firsthand yesterday, I don't think you're taking his threats seriously enough."

"I thought if I ignored him, things would eventually die down."

"Apparently that's not going to happen," Chad interjected.

"From what you've told me," Mark said, "your relationship with him has been practically non-existent since you moved out after graduation. Other than his wife's death, what's happened recently to push him over the edge?" He drained his cup and waited for a response.

Drops of condensation trickled down the side of her glass as she considered the question and collected her thoughts. *I knew this moment would come and questions would arise—questions that deserve an honest answer.*

Mark persisted. "CiCi, your dad is like a dog after a bone. He's focused on getting his hands on something you have. What does he think you stole from him? We need to know in order to put a stop to this harassment."

She took a deep breath and lifted her eyes to meet his. "Here's the abbreviated version. Mom left nearly all of her assets to me. For all practical purposes, she disinherited her own husband. If that isn't enough, I'm legally forbidden to give him any part of it, which he refuses to believe. He has every right to feel angry and cheated, but he's wrong to think I influenced her decision. I hoped he would come to terms with the situation, but how do you reason with an alcoholic who feels he's been double-crossed?"

Chad shook his head. "Alcohol makes people stupid, and money affects their judgment—or is it vice versa?"

Mark rested his forearms on the table. "We'll keep this strictly confidential, but can you give us a ballpark figure of what your inheritance is worth? Sometimes the larger the amount, the more effort the perpetrator puts into getting it."

She hesitated, reluctant to speak. Both men leaned forward ever so slightly.

"The entire estate is estimated to be worth...around three million dollars."

Chad reeled back in utter disbelief and raked a hand through

162

his hair. It took a few seconds before he found his voice. "Are you kidding me?"

"I know. I can hardly believe it myself," she said. "It's embarrassing, and yet ironic at the same time. I never chased after the almighty dollar. As long as I have what I need, I'm happy."

A trace of shock lingered on Mark's face. He leaned back in the chair and rubbed a hand across the base of his thick neck. "Now I understand why he's so angry. With that much at stake, he might do about anything. Maybe he broke into your house looking for a hidden stash of money. You don't keep a boatload of cash at home, do you?"

She shook her head. "I'd have to be an idiot to keep that much money around, and most of the inheritance is tied up in property and investments."

"I'm not trying to frighten you, but what happens to your inheritance if something were to, you know, happen to you? Who would it fall to?"

Her eyes darted to Chad, then to Mark. "As the trust stands, it would fall to my heirs, if and when there are any."

"Here's what I suggest. Change your phone numbers, and then file for a PFA. The threat of going to jail might make a difference."

"What's a PFA?"

"PFA," Chad said, "stands for Protection from Abuse, although most people refer to it as a restraining order. I agree with Mark. I think it's something you need to do."

She let out a deep sigh. "I'm such a hypocrite. I encouraged Julie to stand up for herself, yet I've been unwilling to follow my own advice. You're both right. It's time I faced the situation head-on and file for a restraining order."

Mark nodded his approval. "Good. Be at my office around eleven. I'll have a couple of documents to attach to your petition." He drained his cup. "One more thing. I wouldn't tell anyone about your inheritance. News like that can spread like wildfire and the outcome might not be so good."

"I'm fine with that, but there's no telling who Dad and Richie have told."

The timer dinged. Chad rose and took the food from the oven. Mark tossed a salad while she set the table. Judging from the men's appetites and their request for seconds, her meatloaf was a hit.

She ate half-heartedly, barely touching the food on her plate as the men talked sports. Her thoughts remained elsewhere, on a deeply personal subject that weighed heavy on her heart. She forced a smile when she caught Chad staring at her with a concerned look on his face.

After dessert and another cup of coffee, Mark rubbed his midsection and expressed his gratitude for the home-cooked meal. Glancing at his watch, he stood and announced he had better get home. She and Chad escorted him out and waved goodnight as he pulled from the driveway. They stood holding hands on the covered porch until Mark's taillights disappeared down the street.

Chad pulled her into a gentle hug, then tilted her chin up and looked into her eyes. "Are you going to tell me what else is troubling you, Sugar?"

She nodded. "Yes, but only if you promise to leave Detective Cooper outside."

Chad nodded and followed her back inside the house.

TWENTY-FIVE

She didn't speak, nor did he, as they sat side by side on the sofa. She took a deep breath, and then exhaled, hoping to gather the unwavering strength needed to tell him something she'd never shared with anyone.

"You've been more than patient with me and deserve to know why my dad and I have such a rocky relationship. It goes beyond the inheritance, and has haunted me for years. I've tried to ignore it, but I can't any longer, which is why I decided to file for a restraining order."

Chad drew her close, then kissed the top of her head. "I love you with all my heart. Nothing you can say will change that."

Her eyes misted at his words. She paused and took another deep breath.

"As a child, I was a daddy's girl through and through. He held my hand when we went for walks around the block, attended every grade school play I was in, and cried with me when my hamster died. We never missed a daddy-daughter dance. He taught me how to ride a bike and how to change a tire. He laughed at my corny jokes, and took me out for ice cream every Friday night. It's no wonder I have a sweet tooth." She smiled at the distant memories.

"I love the dad from my childhood, the dad of my teen years—not so much. It started during my sophomore year of high school, after Mom had been diagnosed with cancer. I think working long hours and caring for Mom in the evenings took its toll on him. He began to drink heavily, and his resentment over my so-called freedom grew into a bitter hatred of me as I matured. It didn't help matters when Mom gave me the Jeep as an early graduation present and offered to pay for my college education. At one point, he said I reminded him of his first wife—spoiled and always expecting a hand-out. His words were grossly unfair and hurtful. And now? My inheritance seems to validate his opinion of me—at least in his mind."

Her voice crackled with emotion and pressure built within her chest. Putting the past into words proved to be more difficult than she thought.

"The attack at the attorney's office wasn't the first time I've been the target of his anger. Early on, I would get smacked for getting a 'C' on a report card, or a chore not done fast enough. His discipline, as he called it, became more violent as time passed. On many occasions, he woke me from a sound sleep and beat me just because he could. He sometimes locked me in my closet or in the garden shed for entire weekends without food or water. I never knew what to expect."

Chad's arm tightened around her, but he remained silent. For that, she was grateful. Tiny sobs bubbled from deep within as painful details poured from her lips. With a trembling hand, she accepted his handkerchief and dabbed at her eyes. When she continued, her voice sounded as distant as her thoughts.

"After I was pushed down the basement stairs, I went to see Doc Cunningham. I lied and told him I forgot to turn on the light and missed a step in the dark. A broken arm, and later a sprained wrist, were passed off as sports mishaps after school. When Dad slashed my thigh with a knife, I told Doc I got cut while building props for the school play."

"Why didn't your mother kick him out and report him to the authorities?"

"She never witnessed any of his abuse. For the most part, his violent episodes happened when she was in the hospital, or during one of her many stays at the cancer center in Texas."

"Didn't she ever wonder about your injuries?" he asked.

"She did. Dad told her I was a clumsy, accident-prone teenager. She loved him, and there wasn't any reason at that time for her to believe otherwise."

"I'm not asking this to place blame, but why didn't you tell her the truth, or at least report him to the police or a school counselor?"

"He threatened to beat her if I told anyone. It terrified me and I stayed silent to protect her. Besides, if he went to jail, he would've lost his job and the insurance that paid for her treatments. As a teenager, the repercussions seemed overwhelming."

"By law, Doctor Cunningham should have involved the authorities."

"He only learned of it recently. He deeply regrets he didn't recognize what was happening at the time, but it wasn't his fault. He was a victim—a victim of my lies."

He tenderly brushed a tear from her cheek with his thumb, then exhaled heavily. "You fooled everyone at school, teachers and friends alike."

"It was the only way I knew how to deal with it—to act like it never happened. I desperately needed at least one part of my life to be normal. If my friends had known the truth, they would have treated me differently. I didn't want anyone to look at me with pity, or gossip about me behind my back. The fallout would have felt like another fist in the face."

Chad's jaw clenched and his dark eyes glistened with moisture. He cleared his throat and swiped a hand down his face. "I am so sorry. If I had known, I would've done anything to help."

"It's not your fault. I'm as much to blame as my dad is. My silence let it continue."

His hands cupped her face. With a fierce intensity, he stared into her eyes. "Listen to me. You were not responsible for his despicable behavior then, and you're not responsible for it now. Don't *ever* feel guilty about what happened or try to take the blame. Do you hear me?"

She nodded and rested her head on his shoulder.

"It took a lot of courage to share something so painful," he said, kissing her temple.

"A crushing load has been lifted from my shoulders. I guess what they say is true: confession is good for the soul. I wish now I'd done it years ago."

"The important thing is you did it, and on your own terms."

"It helps to have someone in my life who loves me unconditionally." She stood and wiped a hand across her face. "I'd better wash up. I must look disgusting."

When she returned, she found him leaning against the kitchen counter, deep in contemplation. With his hands splayed on either side of the sink, he stared at nothing in particular. He glanced up when she entered. His eyes were stormy and dark, and the muscles in his jaw tight and rigid.

"How could he do that to you? I swear, if he ever lays a hand on you again, I'll…"

The fury in his voice filled her with worry. "Chad, don't make me regret telling you. Promise you won't do anything stupid." Her demand was met with silence. "Chad, promise me!"

Seconds ticked by before he released a tension-filled breath. "I promise."

TWENTY-SIX

Though CiCi arrived at the Ripley Grove police station on time, Mark's conference call ran longer than expected and delayed their meeting. She waited near the front desk, where Officer Frank Guzman bantered with Stacy, the officer who manned the front desk. When their topic of discussion turned to Chad, they commented that the detective looked as though he hadn't been getting enough sleep. CiCi smiled but held her tongue. *If they find out Chad's sleeping on the sofa, he'll never hear the end of it.*

Ten minutes later, Frank escorted her down the hall to Mark's office. Her chest tightened with each step and her hands began to perspire. Mark stood when she entered and gestured to an empty chair. She tucked a strand of hair behind her ear, wiped a hand on her slacks, and chose the seat closest to the door.

"How're you feeling this morning?"

"Anxious."

"That's perfectly normal. Did you print the online PFA form and fill it out?"

"I did."

"Good." He pulled out a folder and hunkered down to business. "All right, I'll give you a quick explanation of how this is going to play out. I've pulled a couple of supporting documents to attach to your application. The form needs to be filed at the courthouse. The court clerk will present the petition to the judge, who will review your request. Due to Jack's attack at your lawyer's office, his threatening phone calls, and his visit to your home the other day, I'm certain the judge will grant a temporary order of restraint that will go into effect immediately. A deputy will notify you once Jack is served. A date will be set for a court hearing. At that time, Jack will be given the opportunity to contest the petition. The judge will then determine whether or not to extend the PFA order for a full year. Any questions?"

"No, but I worry filing this petition will just make him angrier."

"Don't worry about how he feels about it. Concentrate on the positive outcome it'll provide for *you*. Once you've taken legal action, he'll think twice about making further contact. Any violation is a criminal offense. I'll be honest, there's no guarantee he'll pay attention to the order. You'll need to stay alert." A hard rap sounded on the wooden door. "Enter."

Officer Guzman stepped inside and handed a folder to Mark. "Hey, CiCi. Mark, I finished filling in a few details on the Jackson burglary. Thought I'd drop it off before I head back out on patrol."

"Thanks." Mark scanned the first two pages before closing the folder and tossing it on the desk. He glanced at CiCi as she sat massaging her arm, then turned back to Guzman. "Would you mind giving CiCi a lift to the courthouse?"

"Sure, be happy to."

"Thanks, but that's not necessary," she said. "It's only a few blocks away."

Guzman clutched his chest and exclaimed, "Ouch! The pain of rejection."

CiCi chuckled and shook her head. "Okay, you win. Let's go."

Chad looked up in surprise when CiCi entered his office and took a seat. He glanced at his watch and frowned. "Took longer at the courthouse than I expected. Was there a problem?"

"Sort of. I had a lot on my mind this morning and forgot to take a pain pill, so I took one while I waited to speak with Mark."

"Let me guess. You took it on an empty stomach." Chad shook his head.

"By the time I arrived at the courthouse, I was nauseous and lightheaded. A court clerk gave me a banana and a few crackers to eat. I sat in his office until it passed, and I lost my place in line. One of Ripley's finest gave me a lift back to the station."

"Are you feeling better?" Her simple nod erased his concern.

"The process was simple. I have a copy of the order in my purse. I filled out a Request for Service form, allowing a deputy to serve the papers to Dad at work."

Mark entered the office and took a seat. He glanced at his watch and frowned without saying a word. He looked at Chad and raised an eyebrow. "Did you mention…"

Chad shook his head and apprehensively studied a folder on the desk. *She's not going to like what I have to say, any more than she liked me telling her she couldn't stay at her townhouse after the break-in. I won that battle, but will my luck hold a second time?*

"What's going on?" she asked.

Chad cleared his throat, then turned a steady gaze on her. "We've never determined if Julie was the intended target…*or you—*"

"It wasn't me." She spoke assertively, with a hint of defensiveness in her tone.

"And then someone vandalized your home. The two incidents may or may not be connected, but Mark and I think you should have someone stay with you during the day—"

"Oh, no you don't! Stop right there. I don't need a babysitter. Julie's murder has nothing to do with me. Either my dad trashed house, or some thug too stupid to realize I have nothing worth stealing. If it's the latter, I'm sure the creep has moved on by now. If it was Dad, my life will go back to normal…well, almost normal, after the restraining order is served."

"CiCi, don't be so stubborn. Try to look at this from our point of view."

"Stubborn? I'm not stubborn! You're overly protective."

"Maybe I am, because when I love someone, I'll do everything in my power to protect them. I'm worried for you, and with good reason." Chad shot an exasperated look at his co-worker. "I told you she wouldn't go for it."

She turned to Mark. "I expect this from Chad, but you surprise me."

Mark remained unruffled. "Huh. Then you don't know me very well."

Chad turned and threw up his hands in surrender. Deep in thought, he ran a hand across his jaw as he looked at the paperwork spread across the desk. "CiCi, do you mind giving me another minute or two? I need to tie up a loose end before I take you home."

"Sure. I'll be at the front desk, chatting with Stacy." She frowned at them before she turned and left the room.

"She's under a lot of stress." Mark looked pointedly at Chad. "I'm no shrink, but I think she's in denial. I'd keep an eye on her if I were you."

"You're right, and I plan to do just that, regardless of what she says. With a killer on the loose and her dad's aggressive behavior, I'd say she has a double threat lurking on her doorstep. I love her too much to let anything happen to her."

After Mark left the room, Chad picked up the phone and placed a quick call.

There were several things she had difficulty doing with her arm in a sling. Climbing into Chad's truck was one of them. He gave her a boost into the passenger seat and snagged a kiss as he leaned across to fasten her seatbelt. Being at his mercy had its advantages. She offered an apologetic smile as he climbed into the driver's seat. "Sorry I snapped at you earlier."

"Me, too. Let's forget about it and move on."

"Okay, good. You know, your co-workers have noticed the dark circles under your eyes. The sooner I get my place cleaned up, the sooner you get your bed back."

"I'm perfectly fine sleeping on the sofa. You don't hear me complaining."

"No, you don't, but your sofa can't be that comfortable. Why don't you drop me off at my place so I can start cleaning?"

He slid his sunglasses on and casually brushed back a wayward lock of hair. "I'd rather you wait until you have help. You're someone who doesn't know when to quit once you start on something. That's an admirable trait, but not when you're recovering from a serious injury. Let's talk about you moving back into your place after the restraining order is served and the place gets cleaned up."

She huffed with impatience.

"You struggle getting dressed in the morning, you can't tie your own shoes, and you need help cutting your food. How are you going to clean up a two-story townhouse with your arm in a sling? Sugar, you're going to have to accept the fact that you can't do it alone."

"I know." She slid her sunglasses on with a resigned sigh.

"Look, I promise it'll get cleaned up. Maybe not as fast as you want, but it'll get done." He reached over and patted her thigh. "How would you like to stop for lunch?" he asked, flashing a dimpled smile. "A banana and crackers are hardly what I'd call a meal."

She glanced down to where his hand rested. The heat from his touch traveled upward and spread into dangerous territory, making it hard to stay focused. At the moment, food was the last thing on her mind. Without waiting for an answer, he turned the truck toward a local diner.

A half an hour later, the waitress brought their dessert to the table. As he picked up a spoon, his phone rang. He looked at the screen and walked outside to take the call. By the time he returned, she had eaten his half of the chocolate sundae. She grinned sheepishly. He chuckled and reached across to wipe a smear of chocolate from the corner of her mouth.

"Sorry, we need to go."

"Something to do with Julie's murder?"

"Something like that," he said as he paid the tab and left a nice tip.

When they drove from the lot, they headed in the direction of her home. As they parked in front of her townhouse, she noticed a man sitting at the small patio table on her front porch. Her grip on Chad's hand tightened as they neared her unit. The stranger, who looked to be in his upper fifties, unfolded himself from the chair and stood as they approached.

His well-lined face had pale blue eyes that practically twinkled, and a nice smile framed by a graying mustache that trailed down to his jawline. Wavy salt and pepper hair curled over the neck of his navy T-shirt. His long legs were clad in faded denim jeans and a pair of worn work boots completed the look.

"How're you doing, Pete?" Chad parked his sunglasses atop his head and gave the older gentleman a firm handshake that transitioned into a brief semi-embrace. Pete returned the gesture with an added slap on Chad's back. Chad smiled. "Pete, this is my girl, Cecilia. CiCi, this is an old friend of mine, Pete Mason."

"Hey, kid, watch your mouth. I'm barely cresting the top of the hill." He turned and shook her hand firmly, but gently. A startled look crossed his face, then quickly disappeared.

"Is something wrong?"

"No, ma'am. You reminded me of someone, that's all. I'm pleased to meet you."

"Likewise," she said. "Any friend of Chad's is a friend of mine."

"Hey, what happened to your head?" Pete asked, after giving Chad a second look. "And a shiner, too. You didn't tell me you both got banged up."

"Yeah, I ran into a little trouble." Amused, Chad looked pointedly at CiCi, causing her face to heat with embarrassment, before changing the direction of the conversation. "CiCi, I've come up with a plan that will make us both happy. I asked Pete to meet with us because he does odd jobs for folks now that he's retired. He's available this week and willing to help clean up your place. Don't worry about the cost. I'll take care of that."

"Oh, Chad, that's sweet of you, but I don't think I need—"

"You're going to need help and I can't take any more time off work at the moment." he said. "Pete's the perfect solution, and he'll do pretty much whatever you ask. The choice is yours. You can work with Pete or go back to my place."

She'd been backed into a corner and from the look on Chad's face, he knew it. She pressed a finger to her lips as she reassessed the situation. *I could fight him on this, but it's obvious I need help. Besides, the only other handyman I know is Keenan, and hiring him is definitely out of the question.* "Well, I suppose we could give it a go for a day or two. If you're like most retired folks, you could use the extra money."

"Yes, ma'am. A little extra cash always comes in handy," Pete said.

"But, there's one condition. Call me CiCi, not ma'am. So, how long have you and Chad known each other?"

Pete stroked his mustache thoughtfully. "About seven years or so. We also work out at the same gym," he answered. "I try to stay in shape so I don't turn into a couch potato."

"If you don't mind me asking, what kind of work did you do before you retired?"

"I spent thirty-four years working for the city of Ripley Grove. I kept the streets clear of rubbish and trash, which was a never-ending job."

Several questions later, Pete held up a hand and shook his head. "I wasn't prepared to do a job interview. How about I answer all your questions when we start work in the morning?"

Chad chuckled. "I should have warned you. She likes to ask lots of questions."

"Ha, ha. You'd better watch out. I knocked you for a loop once, and I can do it again," she said jokingly.

TWENTY-SEVEN

She awoke Tuesday morning to find Chad gone. According to one of two sticky notes on the fridge, he'd been called into work early, and Pete would arrive at eight-thirty to give her a lift to the townhouse. The scribbled message on the second note made her face flame with heat. She crumpled the tiny paper into a ball and threw it in the trash. Over toast and orange juice, she fumed over the insulting words. She pulled it from the trash bin, smoothed out the wrinkles, and tossed it into her purse. True to Chad's first note, Pete arrived at precisely eight-thirty.

At the townhouse, she led her new helper on a brief tour. Afterward, he shook his head and let out a long, low whistle. Fingers crossed, she hoped he wouldn't tuck tail and run. "I know it's a big job. If it's more than you want to take on…"

"I can handle it," Pete said with confidence. "Where do you want to start?"

She breathed a sigh of relief. "I thought we might start in the foyer and work our way through the lower level. That would give us a clear path out to the dumpster."

"Sounds like a plan."

They worked steadily, talking and bantering back and forth.

After they finished the foyer, half bath, and closet, they moved on to the kitchen. She attacked each area with gusto, anxious to have her place back in order. Though Pete tried to keep her activity to a minimum, she wasn't about to be called lazy or be shown up by someone twice her age.

They took a well-deserved break on the front porch. Pete lit up a cigarette and they talked over coffee, tea, and the scones she had taken from the freezer earlier that morning. As she laughed at one of Pete's jokes, an old red truck slowed to a crawl as it passed her complex. The driver looked in her direction, lifted an arm out the window, and gave a single digit wave.

Pete stood, matched glare for glare with the driver, and watched the truck speed off. He snuffed out his cigarette butt and turned to her. "Friend of yours?"

"Hardly," she said. It was only a matter of time before the harassment stopped, and it didn't feel right to burden someone she'd just met with her tale of woe. To avoid the questioning look in his eyes, she pointed at the last scone on the plate. "Why don't you finish that off. I've had enough."

"If you insist."

He snatched it up and followed her back into the house to pick up where they'd left off. While he took a full trash bag out to the receptacle, she spotted a flash drive on the floor. She dropped to her knees and searched for others. As she placed each one in a pile, a shadow fell across the floor. Startled, she looked up and threw a hand over her heart.

"You scared me half to death!" she exclaimed.

The two men who loomed overhead looked like giants. Side by side, Floyd and Rex were polar opposites. Floyd stood roughly six-foot-tall and wore dress slacks, a crisp white shirt, and a tie. His graying hair indicated he was a man comfortable with his age. Rex, on the other hand, topped his business partner by several inches, dyed his hair, and favored casual designer clothes that emphasized his muscular build.

"Sorry," said Floyd. "The door was open and I thought you heard me call your name."

Pete rushed in, took one look at CiCi on the floor, and asked, "You okay, missy?"

"I'm fine. Pete, meet Floyd and Rex, the two senior partners of Five Star. Floyd, Rex, this is Pete; he's helping clean up the place."

Pete shook Floyd's hand first, then extended his hand to Rex. After eyeing Pete's dirty hand, Rex nodded and turned away. CiCi shook her head. *Typical Rex.* It was then she noticed the faint purple and yellow ring around one eye.

"What happened to you?" she asked.

"I got elbowed playing basketball at the gym. I'm not as aggressive as the younger players seem to be these days." He looked away, embarrassed by his admission.

"I spoke on the phone with Margaret earlier," Floyd said. "When she found out I would be in your neighborhood, she insisted I stop by and check on you."

"Your wife is such a sweetheart. Assure her I'm fine and on the mend."

His eyes widened as he took in the condition of her residence. "I can't believe someone would do this much damage. Certainly you're not staying here. It doesn't look safe."

"No, I am staying elsewhere until things are back in order," CiCi answered as she continued looking for the rest of her flash drives.

"Good idea. Are you staying with Tasha or Izzy?" Rex glanced about the room. His mechanical inquiry indicated he had little interest in her answer, as usual.

"Neither," she said, still brushing aside magazines and books. She stopped suddenly and looked up. "Where are my manners? Would either of you like to sit? I'm sure I can find a chair. How about something to drink?"

"No, but thanks. Actually, we came by to make you an offer you can't refuse," Floyd said, giving his best *Godfather* impression.

"Cut it out, Floyd, and get to the point," Rex groused.

"Sorry. Sometimes I can't help myself. Anyway, considering how you found Julie, and then were suspected of her murder, we thought you might need a couple of weeks off, with pay of course, for a mental vacation. Now that you have the vandalism and injury to deal with, four weeks sounds more reasonable."

CiCi struggled to wrap her mind around the offer. "Thank you for being so generous, but I doubt I'll need that much time off."

"Other than Norma, you have the most seniority and have proven yourself to be an asset to the company. We want to help any way we can."

"I promise I'll be back to work as soon as I'm able," she said as her hand brushed aside a few loose papers.

"Are you looking for something specific?" Floyd asked. "Maybe I can help."

"Thanks, but I can manage. I thought there might be another flash drive in this area. Some have photos on them, like this one shaped like a guitar from my trip to Graceland. I've found most of them, but I don't want to lose one."

The two men stared at the small mound of flash drives, then at each other. Finally, Floyd spoke up. "You have *more* of those crazy things? But, there must be at least two dozen here."

She laughed and shook her head. "Yes, I do. I have a few upstairs at my computer and several on my key rings. It's nothing compared to your Godfather memorabilia." She halted her search and leaned back against the wall to rest. Nearby, Pete worked at a steady pace, silently gathering books and stacking them in a pile.

Floyd smiled as he picked up a flash drive shaped like a flip-flop from under a pillow. "You and I do share a fondness for unusual collectibles. Your infatuation for these must have rubbed off on Julie. That Thursday night, her last night at work, she had a flash drive shaped like a pink pig on her desk. Said she bought it for a nephew."

CiCi frowned. *I've met the nephew, and a two-year-old child is hardly old enough for a flash drive.* She started to ask a question, but Rex spoke first.

"Bruce said he ran into you and Julie at Stella's."

"He did."

"Speaking of Bruce," Floyd interjected, "he mentioned Julie had come to him with a concern over an account entry. Do you know what she was having trouble with?"

"No, I don't. She gave me a hard copy, but I barely glanced at it. At the moment, I don't even know where it is. We intended to discuss it…well, *that* night, but…" Her employers nodded with understanding. "By the time we met up, she said she'd found a solution and it wasn't an issue any longer."

"I told you there was nothing to worry about," Rex said to Floyd. "Are you satisfied now?"

"No, I'm not. In any case, CiCi, I want that copy back when you find it."

"Quit obsessing about it," Rex said. "She clearly has enough to worry about."

"I understand, but company documents shouldn't be floating around. Not only is it against company policy, it isn't ethical," Floyd snapped. "CiCi, call me when you find that copy. The sooner, the better. I don't want it falling into the wrong hands."

CiCi, taken aback by his tone, struggled to her feet. As a friend and mentor, he had never questioned her judgement in the past. Before she could explain, he turned on his heels and left.

"Don't mind him," Rex said. "This whole ordeal has him on edge. Give me a call when you find the document and I'll smooth things over between you and Floyd." A car horn honked several times outside. Rex shook his head, turned, and walked out the door.

After lunch, she and Pete picked up where they left off. Their steady pace throughout the afternoon produced amazing results. They managed to finish the living room before the throbbing in her arm brought her to a stop. She tried to ignore it, but couldn't. She leaned against a wall and winced in pain.

"You take your meds? I heard Chad mention them earlier. From the look on your face, I'd say your arm is giving you a fit. You might be pushing yourself too hard, missy."

"It's hurting, but I hate to take another pill. They make my head fuzzy."

"We've done a lot of work today. Take a pill and rest while I finish up."

"I feel guilty sitting down while you're working."

"That's what I'm getting paid for, remember?"

———

After she got situated in Chad's truck, she kept her eyes forward and responded to his questions about her day with short, curt answers.

"What's the matter with you tonight? Did I do something wrong?"

"Like you don't know! You could have at least told me to my face. And for your information, I shower every day."

"Okay," he said, still puzzled. "But I still don't know what you're talking about."

She pulled the crumpled sticky note from her purse. "Your note telling me I *stink*."

He took the note from her hand and read it. He laughed so hard, tears sprang to his eyes. "Sugar, you're hilarious. Read what this says—out loud."

"I know what it says. It says, pee-yew, you stink!"

"Look closer. It reads 'P/U your suit', as in, pick up your suit from the dry cleaners. Remember? The one you wore to your mother's funeral?"

She squinted at the scribbled message, then laughed until her cheeks hurt. "I know your handwriting isn't the greatest, but this takes the cake."

"What can I say? I was in a hurry." He grinned and gave her a wink. "Are we good?"

"We're good," she said, placing her hand in his.

TWENTY-EIGHT

S till woozy from the pain killers, CiCi headed for Chad's favorite leather recliner and promptly fell asleep. She awoke to the aroma of warm garlic bread and the sound of Chad talking on the phone. She stilled when the name Hughes came up in the conversation. Stretched out in the chair with her eyes closed, she continued to listen.

"You say you got a positive match for the prints in the accounting office? Ivan Hughes, huh? Did you get a warrant for his phone records? Yeah. Something's not right. Check again and have it on my desk in the morning."

Pushing aside the guilt from eavesdropping on his conversation, her mind whirled with questions. *Why would Ivan's fingerprints be in the accounting office? He told me he hadn't seen Julie since their argument at the HideAway Inn.*

Only after Chad disconnected did she stand and stretch, awkward as it was with one arm in a sling. She went to the kitchen and set the table while Chad filled their plates. Judging by the portion of spaghetti and meatballs on his plate, he was ravenous.

"How'd your first day with Pete go?" he asked as they ate. He listened and nodded occasionally while she told him about their progress.

"Enough about my day," she said. "Are there any new developments in Julie's case?

"That's not for you to worry about," he said, reaching for the mozzarella cheese.

"Have you been to the HideAway Inn?"

As he reached for the last breadstick to squeegee his plate clean, he chuckled. "We interviewed flirty Gertie. That gal's something else. She took a shine to Mark. Offered him a free night's stay with a complimentary bottle of bubbly."

"She's old enough to be his mother. Besides, isn't she married?"

"I don't think she cares."

"Any other news?"

He stared at her over the rim of his tea glass. "Let's finish eating so I can change your bandages. Your hand looks swollen."

Her hand and arm were swollen, much more than she thought. When he unwound the gauze, she moaned with relief.

"I'd say you overdid it today. Jeez, CiCi, why didn't you say something, or have Pete bring you back here?"

She gritted her teeth and closed her eyes as he swabbed and cleaned. "How would it look if I bailed on my helper the very first day? I'm not a wimp. I can handle a little pain."

"That mindset may have served you well at one time, but those days are over. You should tell someone if you're having a problem. There's no shame in that."

"I know, but it's my home and I need to shoulder some of the work."

He fastened the last strip of tape over the gauze, then repacked the medical supplies.

"You need to keep it elevated and iced this evening. If the swelling hasn't gone down by morning, think about taking tomorrow off and seeing the doc. I can let Pete in before I go to work. He'll know what needs to be done."

"I'll think about it."

"Do you want me to set you up on the sofa? There's a baseball game on TV, and our boys in blue are playing."

"As much as I love the Kansas City Royals, I have a few calls to make."

She took an ice pack and padded down the hall to the bedroom, where she could lie on the bed in comfort. As soon as she hung up from talking with Megan, Ashley, the college student working part-time at Five Star, called. CiCi barely heard her weepy voice over Chad's yelling at the TV. She got up and closed the bedroom door. "Hey, Ashley. Yeah, I'm fine. What's going on with you? You sound like you've been crying. Are you all right?"

"No, I'm not. I got fired today. I can't believe it. Everyone said I did a great job." Ashley choked back a sob.

The hurt in her voice tugged at CiCi's heart. "Fired? But, why? Did they give you a reason?"

"No. Rex promised I would get more hours now that the school year is over. When Norma said my services were no longer needed, I was like, totally shocked. I wanted to talk to Rex, but she said he'd left early and wouldn't return until tomorrow. I called his cell several times, but he never answered."

Called his cell? Why would Ashley have Rex's cell phone number? Maybe she copied it down from the office records before Norma ushered her from the building.

CiCi's words of encouragement and offer to help polish Ashley's resume were quickly dismissed. Her determination to be rehired at Five Star made CiCi wonder about the college student's involvement in the workings of the accounting office.

"Ashley, Julie had concerns about an expense account. Did she mention why?" The long, drawn-out silence indicated Ashley knew something, and CiCi refused to drop the matter. "Ashley? It's obvious you know what I'm talking about, so talk."

"When Julie started working on those accounts, I figured one of the bosses had her on a special project. When I asked if I could help, she flew off the handle and threatened to…"

"She *threatened* you? What did she threaten to do?" Her heart rate hiked with every second the line remained silent. Finally, Ashley spoke.

"She...she somehow found out I bought the answers to one of my finals. I know I shouldn't have, but I was desperate. She threatened to report me to the dean. I...I couldn't let that happen."

"What did you do, Ashley?" CiCi held her breath, wondering if she were going to hear a confession to murder.

Small sobs filtered through the earpiece and distress saturated Ashley's voice. "I'm sorry for what happened to Julie, but at least I don't have to worry about her destroying three years of hard work over one stupid decision."

It didn't escape CiCi's attention that Ashley skirted around the question. "Ashley, did you tell this to the police?"

A loud gasp echoed through the phone. "Are you crazy? If Julie's not around to spill my secret, why should I?"

Certain she would learn more if they talked face to face, CiCi quickly put together an enticing proposition. "Can we meet up and talk? Julie was supposed to make me a copy of the problem accounts. If you help me find it, I'll talk with Floyd about getting your job back."

"Didn't she give it to you? I heard her mutter something about giving it to you at Stella's. She copied a bunch of stuff to a little flash drive shaped like a pig. You know, like the ones you carry on your key ring."

"No, she didn't give it to me." CiCi sighed. "Well, can we meet?"

Ashley hesitated, but finally agreed. "I guess. How about nine o'clock tomorrow morning? Flat Rock Apartments, unit 2B."

CiCi hung up, pleased she had persuaded Ashley to meet, especially since the young woman had been adamant about not talking to the police. She leaned back against the pillow as questions ran rampant through her mind. *Why did Five Star fire Ashley after knowing they would be short-staffed? Earlier, my paid leave seemed generous. Now it reeked of suspicion.*

She yawned as other questions floated to the surface. *Since when did Julie start using the same type of novelty flash drive that had become my quirky trademark? Would Julie's threat provide Ashley with a motive for murder?*

CiCi quickly called Tasha for the latest news at Five Star, and Tasha didn't disappoint.

"I'd say Izzy's embarrassment over her and Ivan being escorted by police from the funeral is a distant memory. Ivan bought her a new diamond ring, and she's been flashing it under my nose every chance she gets."

"I'd say she's reaping the benefit of having the upper hand on Ivan." Another call beeped in, but CiCi ignored it to hear the rest of Tasha's news.

"The real excitement came at the end of the day. A loud argument erupted in the accounting office between Norma and Ashley. With the door closed, I couldn't hear what they said. A short time later, Ashley marched from the room carrying a small box of her personal stuff and left. I don't know whether she quit or was fired, and I wasn't about to ask Norma."

By the time CiCi disconnected, she could barely keep her eyes open. A short time later, her eyes fluttered open when Chad walked into the room. She gave him a slow, sleepy smile when he placed a gentle kiss on her forehead. Her eyelids were nearly closed when he set the phone on the nightstand and threw a light blanket across her body. He turned the lights off and tiptoed from the room.

TWENTY-NINE

The next morning dawned bright and beautiful. As she approached her townhome, the morning breeze carried the sweet scent of peonies. The bushes at the corner of the building were in full bloom and the stems sagged under the weight of the large blossoms. Pete, who had been sitting on the porch reading the paper, followed her inside. While he waited for a fresh cup of coffee to brew, CiCi took a glass of juice and a croissant to the porch, eager to feel the light wind brush against her cheeks. As she ate, the manager of the complex made his way across the lawn.

"How are you doing, CiCi?" Brian asked.

"Much better." As she finished giving a brief update, Pete joined them on the porch, carrying his cup of coffee.

"Hey, Pete. Long time, no see." Brian extended a hand.

"You two know each other?" she asked, the surprise evident in her voice.

Pete smiled and took Brian's hand in a firm grip. "Yep. We met several years ago. I've removed trash from here on more than one occasion."

To Brian, she said, "Now that Pete's retired from the Public

Works Department, he's taking on odd jobs. Chad hired him to help clean up my place."

Brian ran a hand across the stubble on his chin. "Hmm. Sounds like Chad had an excellent idea. If there's anything you need, let me know."

"I'd say you've gone above and beyond when you helped save my life. I owe you my deepest thanks. Since I don't have the authority to give you a key to our fair city, the best I can do is offer you baked goods."

"I'll gladly accept your offer." He rubbed his hands together in anticipation. "Speaking of offers, I have one for you. Your neighbor, Diane, took a sudden job transfer and moved out of state. She called last night and told me to sell the furniture, take a commission for my trouble, and send her a check. I know you don't mind buying second-hand if it's quality stuff. I thought you might want to see if she has anything you want. If so, it could be a win-win for both of us."

Brian, Pete, and CiCi walked next door to look at the contents.

"Brian, this is too good to be true. Her style is similar to mine, and most of the pieces are better quality than what I own. I'd like purchase the entire lot, depending on the price." She nearly jumped for joy when Brian told her the asking price. "That is more than fair, and I have enough cash in my savings. The insurance company can reimburse me later."

She smiled at how easily she had kept the inheritance out of her thoughts, while maintaining the thrifty attitude she was known for. A plan formed in her mind as she tapped a finger against her cheek. She glanced at Pete and Brian.

"I'll pay top dollar if you guys will take any furniture I don't need from both units to the donation center, and then move Diane's furniture into my place. I'll pay to rent a moving van and additional help if you need it. Professional movers are fine, but I'd rather give you fellas first shot at the extra cash. Don't feel obligated. Think about it and let me know."

Without hesitation, both men agreed. She promised to call Brian after she returned from an errand. Brian nodded and waved as he went to check the availability of the furniture dollies owned by the complex. Pete crossed his arms over his chest and used a thumb and forefinger to smooth down the sides of his mustache. He gave her a quizzical look.

"You going somewhere? I thought you weren't supposed to drive."

"I need to pick up doughnuts and pay a quick visit to a friend who lives on the other side of the square. I thought about asking if you'd give me a lift, but figured you'd rather keep working. I don't mind walking. It's not that far and the exercise will do me good."

"I'll drive. Just tell me where."

When they arrived at Ashley's apartment complex, Pete stayed in the car with two powdered doughnuts and a fresh cup of coffee. CiCi climbed the stairs to the second floor. With a bag of glazed doughnuts in hand, she knocked on Ashley's door and waited. When she failed to get a response, she perched her sunglasses atop her head and peeked through a broken slat in the mini-blind covering the window. The apartment appeared to be empty, except for the drab, worn-out furniture. She frowned. *Did I misunderstand? Did Ashley say 2B, or 2D?* The gentleman in 2D assured her 2B was the right apartment. Puzzled, she walked down to the first floor and back outside. She passed Pete's car and pointed to the leasing office. He nodded and waved back.

Inside, the receptionist rolled her eyes at CiCi's request and made it clear she would rather finish painting her fingernails. She stopped just long enough to make a quick call before returning to the task at hand, literally.

Minutes later, a heavyset man with a bad comb-over waddled toward the front desk. Red suspenders held up a pair of ill-fitting pants and a wide tie tried, but failed, to hide a large stain on the front of his shirt. He smiled and shook CiCi's hand.

"What can I do for you? If it's a furnished apartment you want, you're in luck. We have three vacancies. Vera can give you a tour and a list of the amenities." His offer prompted Vera to roll her eyes again, letting CiCi know it would be a huge imposition.

"No thanks. I'm looking for a tenant by the name of Ashley

Morgan. Her apartment looks empty. It's important I contact Miss Morgan. Can you help, please?"

At the mention of Ashley's name, his face paled. "Well, maybe. My girlfriend, who lives across the hall from Ashley, called me last night around eleven o'clock and said Ashley and some dude were having a big argument. A little later, when she returned from taking Muffy for a walk, she calls back and says Ashley is carrying clothes down to her car, like she's moving."

"Did she see who Ashley had been arguing with, or notice a car in the parking lot that wasn't familiar?"

"Sorry. I asked. Anyway, I didn't wanna get stiffed on rent, so I hurried upstairs. Ashley handed me the apartment keys, five one hundred dollar bills, and told me to keep her security deposit. What could I say, but good luck?" He shrugged while eyeing CiCi's bag of goodies.

"Did she leave a forwarding address, or say why she decided to move?"

His eyes never strayed from the grease-spotted bag. "She didn't say nothing, but I could tell she'd been crying. She looked scared, if you ask me."

"Does her application have the name of a relative, or maybe a contact number?"

His eyes became as glazed as the doughnuts in the bag. "Nah, but she did give me an envelope to mail. Hang on, I'll get it."

As he waddled back to his office, CiCi glanced out the window and noticed Pete had moved the car to a parking spot just outside the door. She gave a little wave and held up a finger to show she'd be another minute. He nodded. When she turned, the manager had returned and held a long, stamped envelope in his hand.

"Here we go; it's addressed to a gal named Winslow. She doesn't live too far from here. Maybe she can help you out."

"I don't think she can." CiCi sighed and pulled out her identification. After a quick peek, the manager traded the letter for the doughnuts. Happy to have his sugar lust satisfied, he headed back to his office.

CiCi opened the envelope and read the hastily scrawled words on the folded sheet of paper: "Sorry, I can't help you after all. Your friend, A." The note provided none of the information she needed. *Where did Ashley go, and is she okay?*

CiCi slid into the passenger seat as Pete finished the last of his coffee. He brushed the powdered sugar from his shirt and started the car.

"What happened to your friend?" he asked. "Did she forget you were coming this morning?"

CiCi nodded and slid her sunglasses in place, hoping they would conceal her worry.

Having the meeting with Ashley suddenly cancelled, CiCi and Pete arrived back at the townhouse sooner than expected. Brian, who had changed into a pair of torn jeans and a stained T-shirt, pulled a dolly loaded with moving blankets across the lawn. Brian's brother had dropped off a small moving truck he had sitting idle at his warehouse. Pete and Brian loaded the unwanted furniture onto the truck and delivered the items to the donation center. When they returned, the job of moving the furniture from one unit to the other began. Luckily, the floor plans were identical, eliminating the need to take measurements.

"While you two hook up the TV and electronics, I'll pick up in the bedroom."

"Don't you dare be lifting anything heavy," Pete ordered.

She promised, then climbed the stairs to tackle the master bedroom. She gathered up her lingerie and various articles of clothing, files, and office supplies that still littered the floor. Around lunchtime, Brian left to check on a tenant and grab a sandwich. CiCi wanted to continue working, but Pete insisted they stop to eat. They went to the kitchen, where they made turkey and cheese sandwiches. Chips, a pickle, an oatmeal cookie and a glass of cold milk finished off the meal.

As they sat on the porch, she came to realize how much she appreciated Pete's steady presence. He was easy to talk to, quick-witted, and a hard worker. Despite his knack for telling a good story, CiCi's thoughts veered off in another direction.

"What're you thinking about? You haven't heard a word I said for the last five minutes, not that any of it was important," he chuckled. He took a drag on his cigarette, then blew out the smoke and watched it drift up and away from CiCi.

"Sorry." She sat forward and brought her focus back to her lunch companion. "A friend of mine was murdered at work a little over a week ago." She absently took a bite of her sandwich and stared off into the distance. "Her killer also attacked me, but I fought back. After he ran off, I tried to help her, but..."

"That must've been terrifying. I'm sorry for your loss."

"If I hadn't loaned her my key to the building, she'd still be alive. I need to figure out who murdered her. Chad and Mark think there's a possibility I had been the intended victim, but they're wrong, and I intend to prove it. I have a few pieces of the puzzle tumbling around in my head, but I can't quite fit them together."

"You need to shake those images and puzzle pieces out of your head and let the police do their job. *Your* only job right now is to give orders, and my job is to follow those orders."

"It's scary how much you sound like Chad."

He smiled. "I'll take that as a compliment."

The phone rang. True to Chad's suspicions, Richie offered to negotiate a time when she and her father could talk and settle matters concerning the estate. She choked back a laugh, knowing most of his negotiating skills were honed in the back seat of a car. When she refused, he became belligerent. He and her dad had a lot in common.

After she disconnected, she stored the leftovers from her sandwich in the fridge while Pete carried a box of trash to the dumpster. Brian returned after lunch, and he and Pete finished transferring the furniture, leaving only the smaller, more manageable pieces for the next day. She and Pete managed to log a few more hours of work in the master bedroom.

"Well, this looks special," Pete said, holding out his hand.

DOUBLE THREAT IN RIPLEY GROVE

Draped over his fingers was a necklace—a silver chain paired with a beautiful diamond pendant.

CiCi gasped. "Oh, you found it! Thank you." She gently took the treasure from his hand. "It belonged to my mother. Last I saw, it was in a small blue box. I worried it had been taken during the break-in."

"I'm surprised it wasn't." Pete brushed a few things aside and found the container.

She tucked the box into the far back corner of a drawer in the bathroom for safe keeping until she found a permanent place to keep it. When Chad arrived, her eyes were immediately drawn to his forehead. "Hey, you got your stitches out. I'm jealous," she said.

"Took care of it during lunch." After a quick tour of the interior, he remarked how impressed he was by the speed of their progress and the quality of the new furniture.

CiCi locked up and everyone headed home for the evening.

THIRTY

CiCi took a sip of tea and watched Chad turn the brats on the grill. Flames shot up between the grates and smoke wafted through the air. He looked perfectly at ease wielding a pair of tongs and wearing an apron that read, "Light My Fire." *With pleasure,* she thought.

"So, have you cleared everyone at Five Star from your list of suspects?"

"Hardly. There's still a lot of leg work to do and some of the alibis seem a little shaky," He squinted and coughed when a sudden flare-up sent a cloud of smoke into his face.

"I still have a hard time believing someone I work with could be a murderer."

"The door was unlocked when you arrived, and there were no signs of forced entry. Like it or not, it's a possibility. On the other hand, your dad could've driven by and seen the Jeep out front. If he were drunk enough, one black Jeep would look like any other black Jeep. He might have thought you were alone and decided to have one of his *talks* with you, as he calls them."

"It's hard enough knowing I put her in that deadly situation by giving her the key to the building, but the thought she might've died instead of me makes me sick to my stomach. *If* your flimsy theory turns out to be true, but I don't think it is, how could I live with that?" Tears formed in her eyes as she stared solemnly at the table. Chad reached down and gently lifted her chin.

"Don't blame yourself for her death. The guilt lies with the murderer, not you. I promise we'll catch whoever who did it. If it happens to be your dad, so be it. Knowing what I know now, I can't say that I'd be broken up to see him put away for a long, long time."

She squared her shoulders and swiped at the corners of her eyes. "I'm not the only one affected by her murder. It's had a negative impact on every employee and could hurt the business as a whole. Five Star is the closest thing to a family I have. If there's a wolf in sheep's clothing among us, I want that person behind bars before any more damage is done."

"I understand how you feel, and we're doing all we can."

"I know you are." She set a plate on top of the napkins to keep them from blowing off the table. "Why don't I fix us some lemonade?"

"Sounds good."

She hopped up and went to the kitchen, where she stirred a packet of dry lemonade mix into a pitcher of cold water. Heading back out to the deck, she paused when she overheard Chad talking on his phone. *I've got to quit eavesdropping—later.*

"Has the Reynolds' home computer and finances been checked yet? How big was the life insurance policy?" He paused and let out a long, low whistle. "Wow. Okay, so we know Keenan went inside and argued with his wife, but that's not enough to make an arrest. From what I gather, Keenan left before Ivan showed up. You need to find out if either of them came back later. Yeah, keep me posted."

As she shifted the pitcher to her hip, the floorboards beneath her feet squeaked. Her heart stopped. She held her breath and took a step back into the shadows.

Chad paused and turned his head in her direction. "I'll call you back."

CiCi took a deep breath and walked outside. After placing the pitcher on the table, she made a return trip for the potato salad.

Chad studied her with a suspicious eye. "How much of that did you hear?" he asked as he turned the brats. Flames kissed the juices dripping from the casings, scenting the air with the aroma of charcoal and spicy meat.

"What?"

"Sugar, I know every creak in that house. The floorboards near the back door, where you were standing, sound different from those in the kitchen or hallway."

"I shouldn't have listened, but I couldn't help myself. I caught everything after the part about checking the Reynolds' computer and finances. So, I take it Keenan is still on your radar."

"We have *several* suspects."

"I'm surprised about Ivan, though. At Julie's funeral, he claimed she still loved him and set him up to destroy his marriage to Izzy. He swore he never saw Julie again after that night at the motel. He *lied* to me. Why would he do that?"

Chad shrugged. "People lie to law enforcement all the time. It's a lot more work than you realize to separate a lie from the truth, not to mention time-consuming."

"The more I learn about Julie, the more I regret suggesting that Five Star hire her, even temporarily. Julie was a different person back when we were in college. Of course, she was married to someone else at the time. I wonder if their divorce was amicable. Have you talked to her ex?"

"We have. Let's just say she decided somewhere along the way that fidelity was not for her. The ex seems like a nice guy. He's remarried and has a child."

"I heard Julie had at least one other affair before she started at Five Star, not counting the affair with Lesley." Chad's delayed eye contact indicated her statement had been correct. "I called a friend who works for one of Julie's past employers, and she said Julie left under suspicious circumstances."

Chad lifted one eyebrow and stared at her. "That's what we call hearsay."

"I know, but let me tell you what I think. Julie supported a number of top-level executives in the past, but never worked longer than six months at any one place. Knowing her view of fidelity, I'm guessing she had an affair with a member of upper management at each company. The executive in question probably paid Julie to keep the matter quiet so as not to put his job or reputation in jeopardy. That would explain how she afforded the expensive cars and designer clothes."

"You have an amazing knack for connecting the dots."

"Did Keenan know about the affairs?"

He pressed his lips together and refused to answer. He squinted when the smoke drifted into his eyes again. After pulling the meat from the grill, he grabbed a few sides, chips, and condiments from the fridge. "Let's eat."

"Okay, so let me ask you this," she said. "Have the crime scene techs found a pig-shaped flash drive at Julie's house, or at Five Star?"

"Not that I recall." He forked a brat into a bun on his plate and added a spoonful of potato salad and baked beans. "Why? Is it important?"

She reached for a brat and added ketchup. "It contains financial information Julie wanted me to look at. All three owners saw the flash drive on Julie's desk before she left work, and Ashley confirmed Julie intended to give it to me that night at Stella's. I've been trying to locate it, but so far, I haven't."

"Our department isn't big enough to have a dedicated Financial Crimes Unit, so we had to send Julie's computer to another agency. They're running behind. Why are you so concerned about it? Is there something I need to know?"

"No. Yes. I don't know. I can't shake the feeling that I *need* to get my hands on that flash drive. Maybe Julie's murder is connected to the financial dealings at work."

"I said if you came to me with something, I'd look into it. I'll put word out that we're looking for that flash drive. That'll give me a reason to have another chat with Ashley. I think she's hiding something." He took a large bite of a brat covered with a mountain of condiments.

"Ashley's gone, Chad." He stopped mid-chew, and his posture

alone demanded the rest of the story. "They fired Ashley yesterday afternoon. Her apartment manager said she moved out last night without giving any notice."

"And how do you know that?" He gave her a withering look.

She took a deep breath, and then recounted Ashley's distraught phone call the previous night, and the trip to her apartment complex earlier that morning.

"If she's holding back information, she could be putting herself in danger. We need to locate her, and the sooner, the better." Chad got up from the patio table and stepped inside to make a phone call. He returned, wearing a stern look.

"Cecilia, please, take a step back and get this investigation out of your head before someone decides they don't like you snooping around."

THIRTY-ONE

The following day, Pete and Brian dismantled the antique iron bed frame that once belonged to CiCi's grandmother and hauled it to the basement. After a few more trips between the two units, they had CiCi's new bedroom furniture in place.

As Pete carried over a slipper chair from the vacated unit, he caught a fleeting glimpse of a figure in dark clothing enter CiCi's townhouse. Recalling the nasty phone calls he'd overheard and the mysterious truck that drove by, he set the chair aside and bolted across the lawn. At the door, he bent and removed a pistol from his ankle holster. With movements quieter than a whisper, he crept down the hallway toward the kitchen. From his vantage point, the unexpected visitor and CiCi were nowhere in sight.

He whipped around the corner, careful to keep his gun hidden until he assessed the situation. With swift actions that were a near match to his own, his opponent spun around and instinctively placed a hand on the weapon attached to his belt. Both men let out a sigh of relief when they realized they knew one another.

"You scared the crap out of me, Neil," Pete whispered as he holstered his weapon.

"Same here, Pete." Neil relaxed and withdrew his hand from his firearm.

Pete's gaze darted around the room. "Where's CiCi?"

"Cecilia Winslow? She stepped out back to finish a private phone call. What the heck are you doing here?" Neil stared at Pete with a confused look. "And why are we whispering?"

Before Pete could respond, CiCi entered the living room through the patio door.

"Thanks for waiting, Officer," CiCi said. "Now, what can I help you with?"

"Miss Winslow, I'm Deputy Neil Arnold from the Sheriff's Department." He withdrew his identification and offered it for her inspection. "I'm here to inform you I served Jack Parker with a restraining order this morning. I need your signature, acknowledging you've been notified the party listed has been served. The bottom copy is yours. As a reminder, they set your court date a week from tomorrow."

Neil turned to Pete while she read and signed the document. "So, Pete, I ran into Bleu the other day. He said business has been brisk lately with your—"

"My handyman business. Yep, things are picking up. I've been working this week with Miss Winslow. Her boyfriend hired me to help clean up her place after a nasty break-in."

She stared at the two men. "You know each other? Pete, you must have been the most popular guy at the Public Works Department."

Pete smiled. "People appreciate someone who's willing to keep our fair city free of trash."

The deputy glanced from Pete to CiCi, and back again. He returned CiCi's smile and nodded as he tipped his hat. "Have a good day, ma'am. Good to see you, Pete, and good luck with your, uh, handyman business." Deputy Arnold shook his head and left.

CiCi held the papers in her hand and turned her attention to

Pete. "Pete, I'm sorry. I should have told you what's been going on." Without going into every detail, she filled him in on her dad's recent threats. "If the situation makes you uncomfortable, I'll understand if you want to call it quits. No questions asked, no offense taken, and you'll be paid just the same."

Pete guffawed at the suggestion. "I'd rather go up against your father than quit this job and have to face Chad." His grin turned serious as he stared into her eyes. "You've had quite a time lately, haven't you? Yesterday I learned you were attacked, and your friend murdered. Today I find out you've been receiving threats from your dad. Is that why Chad thinks her murder might've been a case of mistaken identity?"

"I suppose, but I think he's wrong," she said as she slipped the document into her purse. "Well, what would you like for lunch?"

After they ate, she and Pete picked up where they left off in the master bedroom, but her mind never strayed far from Julie's murder. They moved their focus to the designated office area on the opposite side of the bedroom. CiCi sorted through the mound of paperwork, while Pete tucked folders into the new file cabinet. When she came across the handwritten motel receipt and Julie's tampon holder containing the copy, she stashed them in a desk drawer. The only items she needed now to make her work space complete were a computer, a printer, and a swivel chair.

As quitting time neared, Pete place his empty coffee mug in the sink and followed CiCi to the porch. They sat on the porch in companionable silence and watched squirrels chase each other around a tree trunk in a game of tag. A train whistle sounded in the distance. A neighbor walked by with her dog and waved. CiCi leaned forward suddenly and focused her attention on her dust-covered Jeep in the corner of the parking lot.

"What are you thinking about now? I can see something's got your attention."

"I keep a spare key to my Jeep taped under the bench in the foyer. I wonder if it's still there." She started to rise, but Pete jumped up ahead of her.

"Sit back and relax. I'll take a look for you." He returned a few minutes later, empty-handed. "Sorry. Didn't see it. Besides, what do you need it for? I thought you weren't supposed to be driving."

"True, but I should be able to drive after I get my stitches out tomorrow. By the way, you don't need to show up until noon. That'll give you the morning to do as you please. If you're anxious to be cut loose, I'm sure I can manage the rest of it on my own."

"Are you trying to get rid of me? I'll be here 'til we're finished, and I'm not leaving a minute sooner. If I start a job, I stay with it to the end." She smiled at his dedication.

As soon as Chad pulled into the lot, CiCi rose and went inside to shut off the coffee maker. She grabbed her purse and sunglasses and returned in time to catch an amused look pass between the two men. Not wanting to intrude on a private joke, she resisted the urge to ask what they found so funny. Pete turned and tossed a hand up in farewell as he walked to his truck.

THIRTY-TWO

CiCi sighed. Chad's cryptic answers to the work-related call he received after dinner left a stern look on his face. He wrote down an address on his way to the bedroom and returned with a shoulder holster strapped in place and a shiny badge clipped to his belt. He gave her a quick kiss, grabbed his RGPD jacket, and locked the door on his way out.

She roamed the apartment, searching for something to occupy her time. The new library book failed to hold her interest. If she'd read the blurb on the back instead of being dazzled by the cover, she might've left the book on the shelf at the library. She picked up the TV remote and surfed through the channels. Boring, unless you loved reality shows, which she didn't. Life itself was more reality than she could stand at the moment.

Her cell phone rang and her spirits lifted when Tasha's name appeared on the screen. "Hey, how's it going?"

"Crazy is how it's going. It's hard to cover your job in addition to mine, especially when I don't understand half of what you do. I'll have you to thank for the overtime on my next check. Can you believe I just got home? I'm exhausted."

"I hope to be back at my desk next week."

When CiCi inquired about the current happenings at work, she learned Norma might resume her accounting duties soon, despite wearing a cast on her arm, and Bruce had found a potential candidate to purchase his share of the business.

"And I couldn't believe my eyes," Tasha continued. "This afternoon, Detective Sullivan took Izzy into the conference room and shut the door. Before long, she stormed out of the room, shut down her computer, grabbed her purse and left. I peeked out the window and watched as he put her in his car and drove off. What do you suppose that means?"

"I'm not sure," CiCi answered, not wanting to reveal what she'd overheard.

Immediately after hanging up, she received a brief call from Chad telling her not to wait up. Then, the phone rang again.

"CiCi, this is Floyd. I've been looking for the Remington work file and can't find it anywhere. Tasha's been swamped, or I'd ask for her help."

CiCi smiled but sighed inwardly. Life would be so much easier if Floyd would go digital, but being older and set in his ways, he resisted change. "Is that the job the lender put on hold a few weeks ago because the city rejected the original construction plans?"

"That's the one. New adjustments were made and approved, and the lender has requested the appraisal move forward. Could you possibly stop by the office tomorrow and find it for me? I'd really appreciate it."

"I'd be happy to."

"Fantastic. I'd rather not have a lost file hanging over my head all weekend."

She said goodbye and disconnected. In the kitchen, she rummaged through the fridge, freezer, and cabinets, looking for something to appease her sweet tooth. Her nose wrinkled at Chad's meager selections. *If I were up to baking, I'd stock his freezer with goodies.* She glanced at the clock on the wall and strummed her fingers against her splint. She grabbed her purse, locked up, and left the house on a mission to satisfy her craving. Her feet carried her a half a mile away, toward a shop that sold gelato, sorbet, and ice cream.

The breeze ruffled her hair as she walked the short distance. The trip there and back wouldn't begin to wipe away the empty calories, but it felt good to stretch her legs and be outdoors.

After purchasing a chocolate ice cream cone, a seat became available on the crowded patio. Around her, families, couples, and teens enjoyed every flavor imaginable. As she took in her surroundings, she realized Five Star was only a mile away. Images of a pink pig flashed through her mind and drew her attention back to the murder.

I need to find that darn flash drive. With Chad working tonight, this may be the perfect opportunity to search for it at Five Star. Floyd's request to find the missing Remington file gives me a legitimate reason to be there. Besides, having the file on his desk when he arrives in the morning might put me back in his good graces. It's not that far of a walk. and I can surely be back at Chad's before dark. She grabbed an extra napkin and headed out.

As expected, there were no vehicles in Five Star's parking lot. She went inside and locked the door behind her. She turned on the lights and stood for a moment, taking in the silence. A trickle of fear took hold, but she shook it off and walked straight to her desk. It took longer than expected, but she finally found the file. She scanned the documents and put the originals on Floyd's desk. Done.

Back at her desk, she checked her emails, left a couple of suggestions for Tasha concerning a new account, and made sure things were in good order. Glancing around the room, her thoughts turned to Izzy. She stared at the cubicle across the aisle from hers. Curiosity got the best of her. A brief inspection of Izzy's work space turned up nothing out of the ordinary.

She surveyed the room once more before making her way to the accounting office. A final search for the pig-shaped flash drive netted zero results. She drummed her fingers on the desk, noting that the computer and all of Julie's personal effects were gone. With the absence of the computer, her mind went to the only other option to access the accounts: the laptop she had seen earlier on Floyd's desk.

Moments later, the five fingers on her left hand stumbled over the laptop's keyboard, trying to do the work of ten. *Dang it! I forgot Julie changed the password. Wouldn't Rex have had the password reset by now?*

Probably, but I can't call and ask for it without raising questions as to why I need it.

As she pondered what to do, she glanced at the framed photo on Floyd's desk. It was a lovely picture of Floyd and Margaret on their thirtieth anniversary. Suddenly, a vision popped into her mind. A few years back she happened upon Floyd as he replaced the backing that held the frame in an upright position. She assumed then it might be a hiding place for his passwords. She crossed her fingers and hoped that assumption had been correct. Gently laying the frame face down, she removed the cardboard holding the picture in place. There, on the back of the photo, was a sticky note with several passwords. The first four had a line drawn through them, but the last one had not. She copied down the code and replaced the picture in its original position.

She typed in the password and held her breath. *Bingo!* As far as she could tell, everything looked in order. She had only gotten three pages in when she heard a series of sharp raps on the front door. Her heart jumped into her throat and she froze in place. Again, the raps sounded on the door, this time louder and more insistent. She quickly logged off and powered down the laptop. She glanced at the clock. *Where had the time gone?* She hurried from the room toward the front of the building. The knocking continued with increased intensity. Then, she heard a voice.

"Ripley Grove Police. Open up."

She rushed to the door and peered through the blinds at the badge on the other side of the glass pane. She sighed with relief as she twisted the lock and opened the door.

"*You?*" he said. "What are *you* doing here?"

THIRTY-THREE

"I'm working," CiCi replied as she stepped aside to let Mark in. "And *you?*"

"I had dinner with my parents tonight. On the drive home, I saw the lights on and thought one of the owners might be here. I have a couple of questions." His eyes darted around the room, as though expecting Floyd, Rex, or Bruce to appear.

"Sorry, it's just me. Is it something I can help you with?"

He shook his head. "No. Why aren't you at Chad's curled up with a book?"

"Um…I decided to go out for ice cream."

"Ice cream? They serve ice cream at Five Star now? That excuse sounds about as good as picking up a pair of sunglasses."

"Very funny. Floyd asked me to stop by tomorrow to find a missing report. When I realized the ice cream shop wasn't that far away, I decided to take care of it tonight."

"I thought we asked you to stay away from here."

"You did. It was a spur of the moment decision."

"So, you were just getting a report for Floyd, huh?"

"Yes." She walked back to her cubicle, and he followed. "See, here's the folder I took from my file cabinet. The originals are on his desk."

He nodded toward the hallway. "So why are the lights on in the accounting office?"

"Oh, I…I must've forgotten to shut them off."

He turned to her and narrowed his eyes. "Uh-huh. And just what were you looking for?"

"Nothing." She walked down the hall. He followed and watched her every movement as she shut the lights off in the back offices. She and her shadow then walked back to her desk. As she shut down her computer, she glanced up at Mark.

His stare turned hard-core cop. "Are you interfering with my investigation again?"

"No, and I haven't done anything wrong. Call Floyd if you don't believe why I'm here."

"I have no doubt he'll back up your story. I just don't believe that's all you did."

She picked up her purse and headed to the entrance. "I'm sure you have other things to do, and I need to get back." She turned out the lights, leaving Mark standing in the dark. He shook his head and sighed. She locked up after he exited.

Outside, darkness had fallen. Had she really been in Five Star that long? She said goodnight and took several steps before Mark called out to her.

"Get in. I'll give you a lift."

"Thanks, I'm fine."

"Don't test my patience tonight," he said harshly. "It's dark out and it's over a mile to Chad's house. Get in the car."

She slid into the passenger seat next to her fuming chauffeur. "Are you going to tell Chad where I went tonight?" Whoever said there's no such thing as a dumb question should have seen the look on Mark's face. If *he* were this upset, she could imagine what Chad's reaction would be.

She thanked him for the lift as he pulled to the curb in front of Chad's apartment. She glanced at the house. The faint glow from the streetlight two houses away shed minimal light on the porch.

When Mark exited the car, she said, "You don't have to walk me to the door."

"Why didn't you leave any lights on?"

"I expected to be home before dark."

"You would have if you hadn't been snooping."

As they reached the porch, a truck pulled into the driveway. The beam from the headlights panned across their bodies and their shadows seemed to dance against the clapboard siding. She stifled a groan when Chad slid from the driver's seat.

"What's going on?" Chad's confused gaze darted from Mark's face to CiCi's.

"Let's take a walk," Mark said. CiCi followed, but he whipped around to face her. "*Not you!*"

She went inside, peeked through the curtains and watched as the two men leaned against Mark's car. As Mark talked, Chad's earlier look of confusion turned to one of anger. By the time they parted ways, Mark had calmed down considerably. Chad, not so much.

He entered and slammed the door hard enough to rattle the windowpanes. With a stony silence, he removed his jacket and threw it over a chair. Next came the badge and the revolver, which he took to his bedroom and locked away. He returned to the living room wearing a glare worthy of cutting a diamond in half.

"Chad, let me explain."

The muscles in his jaw were clenched so tight, she feared he might crack a tooth. "Cecilia, what the hell were you doing at Five Star after we told you to stay away? Do you know how dangerous that was, especially at night and by yourself?"

"I had no intention of causing trouble. Like I told Mark, I went out for ice cream and ended up at Five Star to find a file Floyd needed. I thought I could take care of Floyd's problem and still be back before dark."

"I heard that same story from Mark, but we both know you were there longer than a few minutes." Chad said, his eyes never leaving hers.

"Okay, so I looked around after I found Floyd's report."

"And?"

"And what?"

"What were you looking for?"

"I was looking for that flash drive. With Julie's computer missing, I used the company laptop in Floyd's office. I had hoped to check for anything that might've caused Julie a problem, but I didn't finish because Mark showed up. Don't ask me why, but I believe the information on that flash drive might somehow be connected to Julie's murder."

"If it is, then you're playing with fire. Maybe that's what the person who tore apart your house had been looking for. What if they think you still have it and come after you again? Huh?"

"I don't think—"

He swung around and his voice echoed in the room. "That's the problem, Cecilia. You *don't* think! You're putting yourself in danger and don't even know it."

"Are you calling me *stupid?*" A fire erupted deep inside her. She snatched her purse from the couch and marched toward the front door. She barely had the door ajar when an arm shot overhead, forcing the door shut. She turned and found herself pinned between his arms.

"Where do you think you're going?" he demanded.

"For a walk," she snapped.

"Damn it, you're going to drive me crazy," he said, his voice barely containing his anger. "You've already put yourself in a dangerous situation once tonight. Don't push your luck."

"I can take care of myself." She raised her chin in defiance.

"Yeah? Prove it."

She lifted a knee, but he pressed her body against the door, foiling her attempt to make a solid impression where it would hurt the most. Her fist shot upward, but in less time than it took to blink, his fingers snapped around her wrist. She struggled and pushed against him, but with one hand still in his grip and her injured arm wedged between their bodies, she was powerless to do anything more than glare.

"This is exactly what I'm talking about. You're a very capable woman, CiCi, but at this moment in time," he said, "it wouldn't

take much for a bad guy to overpower you. I love you, and I can't—
no, I *won't*—ever let that happen."

She sagged against the door, surrendering to the reality of her
limitations. When she looked up to meet his gaze, she found something she hadn't expected to see: fear and regret lurked behind the
anger in his eyes.

"It's late, and we both need time to cool down. We'll talk in the
morning." Without saying another word, he released her and
stepped back.

Still angry, she brushed past him and stormed to the bedroom.

THIRTY-FOUR

"I'm sorry, Chad," CiCi said over a half-eaten plate of scrambled eggs the next morning. "If I could undo my decision to go to Five Star last night, I would."

"I'm the one who should apologize. I let my emotions get the best of me. Just thinking of you getting hurt again drove me crazy, and I overreacted. You simply responded to my insanity. It was me who asked you to prove you could take care of yourself, remember? Although after I cooled down, I found it amusing that you thought you could overpower me."

She shook her head. "What was I thinking?"

"You're a strong and independent woman. I expect nothing less."

"I don't like it when we argue. I was so upset, I barely slept a wink."

"I didn't sleep much either. I worried my aggressive stand would stir up painful memories and have you comparing me to your father."

"Chad, you're *nothing* like him. It never crossed my mind, because I know you would never hurt me."

Chad reached across the table and lifted her chin, forcing her to look at him. He tenderly traced his thumb along her jawline. "CiCi, listen to me. We're bound to have fights and disagreements, but I'll never hurt you and I'll never stop loving you. What we need to do is learn to handle our differences in a way that will strengthen our relationship."

"Agreed. Now that we've both apologized, what's next?"

"This," he said, walking around the table and pulling her into his arms. He kissed her, softly but passionately.

"Perfect." She wrapped her arm around his neck and returned the gesture. Then, her dreamy expression turned to one of concern. "Will Mark hold my visit to Five Star against you?"

"Things will be fine between me and Mark, but we're still not happy you insisted on going to Five Star."

"I couldn't help myself. Sometimes the guilt is overwhelming. I should never have given Julie the key to the building. No matter what, she didn't deserve to die. I want to help make things right."

"I know, but this is a murder investigation. Trust me enough to let me do my job."

"I do trust you, Chad, but I haven't had a lot of success in that area. I loved and trusted my dad, but he betrayed me. Then, my husband strayed and betrayed. At times, I wonder if my mother betrayed me. Did she harbor suspicions about my injuries? Was my inheritance given out of guilt over what she'd failed to protect me from?"

"I wish I could give you answers, honey, but I can't."

Chad glanced at his watch and quickly sobered. "We'd better get going. You don't want to be late to your doctor's appointment."

Her incisions hadn't healed as quickly as Doc Cunningham had hoped, and the disappointment of not getting rid of the splint or being cleared to go back to work hung over her head like a black, angry cloud. She sulked in the truck while Chad went inside a deli and selected a couple of sandwiches and sides for her and Pete's lunch. When they pulled in front of her townhouse a short time later, they found Pete on the porch, reading the morning paper and smoking a cigarette.

Chad held up the bag sporting the deli's logo. "We brought lunch."

"I love that place."

"Why are you here?" she demanded. "It's barely eleven o'clock."

"I had a hunch you'd get here early. I could just imagine what you'd be doing if you were left on your own."

"I'll do whatever needs to get done. No one's going to call me a slacker."

"Didn't say you were." His cool blue eyes narrowed, and the corners of his mouth twitched upward. He took a drag on his cigarette and exhaled. "Didn't expect to see you wearing the splint. I assume you still have restrictions."

"Maybe. Why?"

"I like to know what I'm dealing with. Chad told me not to let you lift too much, and I take my job seriously."

"And was it your job to tell Chad I wanted to find my spare car keys?"

"It worried me since he said you weren't supposed to drive yet. And just for the record, I report to Chad, not you." The twinkle in his eyes disappeared.

"Humph!" she grunted. With a hand planted firmly on one hip, she countered back. "So, you were just looking out for me, huh? Well, let me return the favor," she said, as she snatched the cigarette from between his lips and threw it on the ground, "because this nasty thing is going to kill you one of these days."

She grabbed the deli sack from Chad's hand and went inside to make a pot of coffee. She hadn't taken but three or four steps when she heard Chad's words of caution.

"Well, Pete, do I need to warn you she's not in a good mood?"

She pursed her lips together, closed her eyes in shame. *What's gotten into me? Why am I taking my frustrations out on Chad and Pete?* She turned to go apologize, but stopped when she heard Pete's hearty chuckle.

"Don't worry, I won't charge you extra. I've put up with worse before," he said. "It might be a good thing you bought our lunch today. She's mad enough to spit nails and they might've ended up in my sandwich."

She smiled and shook her head, grateful for his forgiveness and sense of humor.

She took a call from Bruce that afternoon, inquiring if she'd found Julie's copy of the account. After she said she had, he promised to swing by to pick it up. She disconnected and wondered if Rex would take offense that she hadn't notified him first. A short time later, Bruce called to report he had been detained by a client and would be running late.

When a car screeched to a halt outside, CiCi opened the front door just as Bruce slid from behind the wheel of his convertible. She ushered him inside, where he gave an approving nod. She couldn't imagine what he expected to see, nor did she care. Pete came down the stairs carrying a box. She introduced the two and watched as they sized each other up over a simple nod of the head.

She offered Bruce a seat in the living room, then went to the second floor and retrieved the copy from the desk drawer. Before heading back downstairs, she pulled out her cell phone and took a photo of the document. Bruce and Pete discontinued their discussion of the Royal's latest game when she reentered the room. Pete nodded and went about the business of shifting things around in the hall closet to make room for the box.

Bruce scanned the account and voiced his displeasure that she and Julie had taken it from the workplace.

"I know I shouldn't have. I promise you, it won't happen again." As Bruce studied the copy, she asked, "Why was Julie so concerned about that?"

He shrugged. "Don't know. She wanted to talk about it, but I got sidetracked."

"Did she happen to give you a flash drive at Stella's, one shaped like a little pig? It may contain additional information."

He frowned. "No, she didn't. I wouldn't worry about it if I were you. Besides, didn't you tell Floyd she had the problem solved?" He stopped suddenly and studied her intently. "Why the sudden interest in the account?"

"Just curious. By the way, who's covering the accounting position? I heard Ashley was let go."

"Rex assured me Norma can handle the job, just at a slower pace." Bruce let out a heavy sigh. "She'd be alive if it weren't for me."

"Who? Julie?"

"Yeah."

"What do you mean?" she whispered. *Am I about to hear a confession of murder?*

"Maybe if I'd have taken care of this when she first brought it to my attention, she'd still be alive." His demeanor now wavered between grief and guilt. He cleared his throat to regain his composure. "If I had done my job, she wouldn't have gone to Five Star that night."

"I could say the same thing. I should never have given her the key to the building."

"I guess we both have regrets to deal with." Bruce suddenly looked up and blinked, as though a light switched on. "Hey, there's an auditor coming next week. I'm going to have a quick look at the books on Sunday. Why don't you join me? Together, maybe we can discover what had Julie puzzled."

She hesitated, recalling Chad's admonition. "I'll have to get back to you on that."

He straightened, glanced at his watch. "I need to go. Let me know what you decide," he said as he strutted out the door.

THIRTY-FIVE

I n need of a diversion, she turned to Pete. "I need to get out of the house." She smiled, knowing Pete would take her anywhere she wanted to go.

"You have someplace special in mind?" he asked.

"I do. I'd like to stop by the bank, and then go shopping. Megan and I stopped at a store last week, and there's a couple of little numbers I've had my eye on."

Pete raised his eyebrows and stroked his mustache. A nervous expression inched across his face. "I'm not too keen on girlie shopping."

"You'll be fine. Besides, I need a man's opinion for this particular purchase." She chuckled, half expecting him to break out in a sweat.

Pete drove and followed her directions with a certain amount of tolerance. As they neared her destination, he tightened his grip on the wheel and slowed the car. He propped his sunglasses atop his head and shot her a stern look. "I think I know where you're headed, and I don't know that I should be doing this."

"What's the matter?" she teased. "Afraid Chad will chew you out?"

"No, it's not that, but...well, yeah."

"If you don't want to go in, that's fine. You can wait in the car." She turned and looked him squarely in the eye. "I'm not going home empty-handed. I'll buy something with or without your help."

Pete parked and let loose a heavy sigh of defeat as he slid from the driver's seat. CiCi smiled and murmured her thanks as they walked into the shop. Pete shoved his hands deep into his pockets and grumbled to himself as he followed her lead. He drew a few stares, but for the most part, kept his head down and his eyes averted. When her turn came, he focused his attention on the two pieces the clerk brought out. They both agreed the second option seemed to be a perfect fit. Excited, she paid while he took her merchandise to the car.

"Mind if we stop at Art's Hardware?" she said, sliding into the passenger seat. "I have several lightbulbs that need replacing."

"Sure," he replied. "I've been needing to pick up a new O-ring to fix a leaky faucet."

Art, standing at his usual post behind the front register, greeted them warmly as they entered and directed them to the appropriate aisles for their particular needs. Pete veered to the left in search of plumbing supplies, while CiCi headed to the right. After she studied the various lighting options, she grabbed a multi-pack of LED bulbs from the shelf. During the few moments it took to make her selection, a large pallet of incoming merchandise had been parked in the center aisle of the store. She scooted around the blockade and scanned each aisle she passed, looking for Pete. At the end of the small sporting goods section, a head of tousled red hair caught her attention. Keenan had his back to her, listening to one of the sales clerks point out the merits of the newest fishing reel model.

Hmm. He refused my casserole and ignored me at Julie's funeral. Perhaps he'll be in a more sociable mood today. Taking a right, she walked down the aisle. "Hello, Keenan."

Keenan turned and waved the clerk away. "Well, if it isn't Miss Goody Two Shoes."

"My name's CiCi, in case you've forgotten. How are you?"

"Get to the point. What do you want?"

Sociable, he's not. "Okay. I went to Five Star and noticed Julie's personal effects were gone. I wondered if—"

"Yeah, Floyd dropped them by the house, along with Julie's final paycheck. That guy had a lot of nerve keeping the bonus she had coming."

"Bonus? What bonus?"

"Don't know. I'm just going by what Jules told me that last night I saw her alive. I think she meant it to be a surprise, but she let it slip that she was expecting a big bonus on Friday."

Bonus, my eye. She probably found someone new to blackmail. Perhaps one of Five Star's owners? "Anyway, I wondered if you'd found that flash drive—the one shaped like a pig? I thought it might've gotten mixed in with Julie's personal effects."

"Nope, haven't seen it. Still willing to pay if I find it?"

"Yes, I am."

"Being stiffed out of the bonus makes me wonder if I can trust anyone who works for Five Star. If I find it and hand it over, are you going turn me in for stealing company property?"

"What? Don't be absurd. If I said I'd pay you, I'll pay you." A sound behind her made her turn. The same clerk from earlier wiggled a hand truck out from underneath a stack of boxes, which he left sitting in the middle of their aisle.

"I could sure use the money. The life insurance won't cut a check because I'm still a person of interest in her murder."

"Is that so?" *Why am I not surprised?*

"Yeah. I found the receipt proving I bought beer on the way to the cabin, and I also found the knife I'd lost, the one identical to the murder weapon. My alibi should be tighter than last month's budget, but your cop buddies just won't let it go," he said angrily. "They seem determined to pin the murder on me. You got anything to do with that?"

"No. Why would you think that?"

"It's odd that you're in the clear, but I'm not. Did your cop boyfriend cover up your involvement in my wife's murder? After all, it was *your* fingerprints they found on the knife."

"Don't be crazy! I had nothing to do with her murder."

"And yet I hear you been snooping around Five Star when no one's there. Scared you left behind a piece of incriminating evidence they haven't found yet? I'd watch my back if I were you. You might find yourself on the receiving end of trouble."

"Don't threaten me, Keenan."

"Is there a problem?" The deep voice over Keenan's shoulder ended the conversation. Pete's icy stare and fisted hands challenged any intentions Keenan may have had.

"Just having a friendly chat," Keenan said casually.

"Ready to go, CiCi?"

"Yes," she said.

"I'm sure we'll be talking soon, and I'd prefer my finder's fee in twenties." Keenan winked at CiCi, then turned and brushed past Pete.

Pete shook his head and watched him go. "You shouldn't be talking to that guy, missy. He's nothing but trouble and has already proven he doesn't like you—or women, period."

"I couldn't help it. Anyway, I doubt I'll hear from him again unless he comes across a flash drive I'm looking for. He's not the type to pass up easy money."

A short time later, he parked in front of her townhome. She put the lightbulbs away while Pete carried her other purchases to the master bedroom. "All righty," he said upon returning to the kitchen, "I've put everything away where it where I think it should go. You can check later and see if you're okay with it."

"Thanks, Pete."

"I sure hope Chad doesn't think I overstepped my bounds."

She gave him a reassuring smile. "Don't worry! It'll be our little secret."

The rest of the afternoon went smoothly. While Pete carried a box of winter blankets to the basement, she sat at the kitchen table and sorted her cash withdrawal into two envelopes. She called Brian over and handed him a check for the furniture purchase and an envelope of cash for his labor. He thanked her and left with a plastic container of chocolate chip cookies. She gave the remaining envelope to Pete. He slid it back across the table.

"Chad has paid me more than enough. I'm not about to double dip."

"But—"

"No buts about it."

"Thank you. Would you be offended if I send a loaf of banana bread home with you?"

Pete grinned. "Offend me all you want."

She laughed at his eagerness to be offended. "Let's get something to drink and sit on the porch. It's too nice to sit inside." She led, and he followed. An easy silence fell between them, and she used the opportunity to clear her conscience and make amends. "Pete, I apologize for being so rude this morning. You shouldn't have to put up with my foul mood."

"That's all right. I know this past month has been rough for you. Besides," he grinned, "I've been trying to quit smoking for some time now. I needed someone to give me a kick in the pants as a reminder."

"I'll admit I wasn't keen on having your help, but I never could've managed without you. To be honest, I'll miss having you around."

"Missy, I appreciate that, and the feeling's mutual."

"You're welcome to stop by any time you're in the neighborhood."

"I guarantee you'll see me again," he said with a playful wink, "especially since you keep a freezer filled with baked goods." He smiled, then lifted his coffee cup in a mock toast.

When Chad's truck pulled into the lot, she reminded Pete not to mention the shopping trip. She gathered up her stuff while he and Chad talked. She returned, purse in hand and her sunglasses on. "Ready to go?"

Chad eyed her curiously on the drive to his apartment "You're awfully quiet. What are you thinking about?"

"I have something to run by you. I'd like to avoid another fight, if possible." She smiled and Chad's mouth twisted into a grin. "Bruce stopped by today and said he's going to look over Five Star's books on Sunday. He asked if I'd help."

221

He angled his head toward her. She couldn't see his eyes, only her reflection in his mirrored sunglasses, but the tightness in his jaw indicated what he thought of Bruce's offer.

"We've already discussed this. Mark and I want you to stay away from Five Star, at least for now. There's something shady going on there and we don't want you in the middle of it."

She expected the answer, but wasn't one to give up easily. "But who knows? Come Sunday, you and Mark might have the murderer in custody."

"Why don't you ask Mark tomorrow night?"

"Tomorrow night?"

"We're double dating with Mark and Stacy. Remember? And just for the record, I appreciate you asking. We wouldn't insist you stay away, but we still believe the vandalism to your home is somehow connected to the murder."

"I don't see how, but you've proven me wrong before."

"Do you need to pick up lightbulbs on the way?"

"No, Pete and I picked them up earlier. In fact, I ran into Keenan at the hardware store. He had the nerve to suggest I killed Julie, and you covered for me."

"Stay away from him, CiCi. He's bad news."

"Speaking of bad news, Tasha said Mark escorted Izzy from work yesterday. What was that about?"

"We needed clarification on some new information we came across. That's not for you to worry about," Chad said. "So, what are you hungry for? I have ground beef in the fridge. Will it be tacos or burgers?"

"Surprise me."

THIRTY-SIX

The next morning, after Chad left to run errands, CiCi dialed Izzy's number.

"Sorry, Miss Winslow. My mom just took my brother and sister to the library for some class she signed them up for. She should be back in a couple of hours."

"Thanks, TJ." Disappointed, she disconnected the call. *I guess any questions about why Ivan's fingerprints were found in Julie's office will have to wait.*

The doorbell rang repeatedly, and she rushed to answer the door. She squealed when she saw Megan leaning against the door-frame. "You're back from Florida! Oh my gosh, you look wonderful," CiCi said. She pulled Megan into a hug.

"Thanks. I would have returned your texts, but a tan like this takes work."

"I'm sure it did," she said, pulling Megan inside and shutting the door.

Megan threw her purse on the sofa and cast a questioning gaze around the apartment. "Where's that brother of mine? I thought he'd be here to greet me."

"He left earlier to run errands, wash his truck, and spend a few hours at the gym."

"Have you decided to stay here permanently?" Megan wiggled her eyebrows.

"No, and don't give me that look. Chad's been a perfect gentleman and a tremendous help. He even hired a handyman to put my house back in order. The place looks wonderful, and I can't wait for you to see my new furniture."

"You've always had great taste. Why don't we stop by your place later?"

"Sure. Hey, would you mind if we swing by the library first? I shouldn't be more than ten or fifteen minutes."

"Not a problem. In fact, I have three books I need to return."

"Perfect. Afterward, let's stop by that little consignment shop on Thistle Avenue. They have an office chair in the window I want to check out. If I decide to buy it, we'll need my Jeep. Your trunk isn't big enough." CiCi frowned as her eyes darted around the room. "Let's see, where did Chad put my car keys?"

She searched, but came up empty-handed. She took the next best course of action and pulled out her cell phone. "Hey, Chad, where are the keys to my Jeep? I've looked and can't find them anywhere." A heavy and somewhat exasperated sigh filtered through the earpiece.

"CiCi, you know you're not supposed to drive."

"I know that. Megan's back and she'll drive. We'll need my Jeep if I decide to buy that office chair I told you about."

"Well, you'll need to make other arrangements because your car keys are in the glovebox of my truck. I, uh, must've forgotten and left them there after Shiner's detailed your Jeep."

"That excuse seems a bit weak. Were you afraid I'd find the keys and go for a drive?" His silence spoke volumes and CiCi imagined him grinning from ear to ear. "I thought so."

"Look, why don't you and Megan go shopping instead? Take two hundred dollars from my emergency stash tucked inside my steel-toed work boots and buy yourself a new dress for tonight."

"Are you trying to divert my attention away from my car keys?" she chuckled.

"Maybe."

"You know what? That sounds like a great idea. I remember seeing a dress advertised in the paper I think you'll appreciate."

"You and Megs have a good time. You and I can check on the chair tomorrow."

The phone rang seconds after she disconnected. She answered without hesitation, thinking the caller to be Chad. "Did you change your mind already?"

"CiCi, don't hang up!" The words spoken held a sense of urgency.

"Give me one good reason why I shouldn't, Richie," she said.

"Hear me out, okay?" He paused and cleared his throat. "I saw your dad at the bar the other night, drunk and angry as usual. He belly-ached most of the evening about you and the inheritance. I think he's willing to do almost anything to get it. He offered me a hundred bucks if I could get you to talk to him without the cops hanging around."

"What did you say?" Though her voice remained calm, she felt anything but.

"I turned him down. Even so, you need to watch yourself."

"Did he tell you I have a restraining order against him?"

"He did, which is another reason I refused. That's not the kind of publicity I need. I've had to work my butt off to get the business back where it was before you walked off with half of it."

"In case you've forgotten, the business was a marital asset, jointly owned, and split fifty-fifty. I'm sorry you're not happy the way things turned out, but you need to let it go."

"That's easy for you to say now that you're loaded." He chuckled, but the sarcasm in his voice couldn't be ignored.

"I appreciate the heads up," she replied, purposely skirting around his last comment. *There must be an ulterior motive lurking behind his good deed.*

"A monetary gift would be a good way to show your appreciation."

And there it was. His ulterior motive in all its glory.

"Just for once, would it hurt you to do the right thing without expecting something in return?" It wasn't surprising he hung up without saying goodbye. She turned to Megan and shrugged. "Typical Richie. Forget him. We have the whole afternoon to spend together."

At the library, Megan turned in her books and headed straight to the romance section. CiCi inhaled, taking in the unique aroma of imagination put to paper, and let her eyes wander over the rows and rows of books. In a Non-Fiction aisle, Izzy trailed her fingers along a section of cookbooks and tilted her head to read the titles. CiCi quietly headed in that direction.

"Hmm. Looks like you're planning to try a few new recipes," she whispered.

"Hey, CiCi. I am. I thought I'd look for some inspiration while Beth and Billy take a class on hacking musical cards."

"Hacking?"

"They take used musical greeting cards and reuse the circuitry in stuffed animals, or something like that." Izzy stepped to the side as another library patron tried to squeeze by.

"Let's move out of the aisle and have a seat."

CiCi led the way to a nearby table. Izzy reluctantly followed and settled into a chair. She opened a cookbook and flipped through the recipes, her eyes never spending more than ten seconds on any one page. The silence didn't deter CiCi. "Wow, is that a new ring?"

Izzy smiled. "An anniversary gift from Ivan."

"It's beautiful. So, how are things at work?"

"Fine." Izzy's mouth opened, then shut. She paused, then said, "I suppose you heard the police took me in for more questioning."

CiCi's eyebrows lifted. "Yes, I heard."

"They found Ivan's fingerprints in the accounting office. Yes, I know. He told you he'd never seen Julie again after that night at the trashy motel." A tear trickled down Izzy's cheek. "That's also what he told the police, but when they confronted him about finding his prints in the office, he confessed to being there that night, shortly after Keenan left. Ivan had finished a late night call to fix a client's electrical problem, and spotted her Jeep at Five Star on his way home. He decided to talk with her one last time, but only to tell her to leave him alone, that he would take his chances and tell me himself about the motel. All they did was talk. He didn't kill her."

"If he's innocent, he has nothing to worry about. Although, he'll certainly look guilty after having lied about it. The police frown on that sort of thing." CiCi pulled a wad of tissues from her purse and pressed them into Izzy's hand.

"Ivan loves me and was only trying to protect me."

"Protect you?"

"Yes, because Julie and I got into a fight after Ivan left."

"What are you saying? You didn't—you couldn't have…"

CiCi's raised voice caught the attention of the head librarian, who shushed her and threw in a scowl for good measure.

"I left TJ in charge and went to the convenience store for toilet paper. On the way home, Ivan drove past. I followed, assuming he would head home. But no, he made a stop at Five Star instead. Julie's car was in the lot. I had suspected for weeks she'd been trying to lure Ivan away from me. I felt so angry and hurt. I parked across the street, not knowing what to do." A tear trickled down her cheek. "After he left, I went over and confronted her. She laughed in my face and waved the receipt under my nose. I lost control, and we got into a fight."

"Those scratches on your neck—"

"Julie put them there. I'm guessing the DNA under Julie's fingernails will be mine. It'll only be a matter of time before the police charge me with murder." Izzy's dropped her head into her hands. "I swear to God, CiCi, I didn't kill her."

"What time did you get back home?"

"I don't know. Maybe around ten? I pulled in the driveway as Ivan got out of his car. And no, I don't have any witnesses unless you count Ivan, or the beady little eyes peering out from behind our hedge. I doubt a possum or raccoon would count as a witness. What does it matter? Do you really think the police will believe anything we say now?"

Children poured from the craft room, each clutching a stuffed animal. Izzy stood, wrapped CiCi in a hug, and thanked her for listening. She turned and hurried to claim her kids.

Megan slipped behind CiCi. "I've never seen anyone cry at the library."

"Me, either," CiCi replied as she watched Izzy walk away.

THIRTY-SEVEN

CiCi and Chad sat with Mark, Stacy, and two other couples around the hibachi grill at the Bonsai Japanese Steakhouse and watched their chef performed a culinary magic show. The chef's skill at juggling cooking utensils and flipping cooked shrimp into a patron's mouth delighted and amazed the small group. At the conclusion of the meal, everyone gave a round of applause.

While Chad, Mark and Stacy waited in the lobby, CiCi excused herself to use the ladies' room. Upon her exit from the restroom, she walked past a row of private rooms that lined the perimeter of the main dining area. As she rounded a corner, she bumped shoulders with another patron.

She looked up in surprise. "Rex? It's a small world, isn't it?"

"Hmm, I suppose it is," he said coolly.

"I didn't see you seated at one of the grills. Are you here with friends?" CiCi followed his nervous gaze to one of the private alcoves at the back of the room. A half wall and the upper Shoji divider obscured his dinner companion, but the shadow cast on the translucent panel had a feminine profile.

"Yes, I'm here with…a friend."

Stacy appeared and touched CiCi's arm. "Are you ready? The guys want to go to the Silver Saddle next. Sounds like fun."

"I'll be along in a minute," she said as Stacy hurried off. "Rex, you and your friend are welcome to join us."

"Thanks, but country music really isn't my thing," he said.

"Are you planning to help Bruce tomorrow—"

"CiCi." Unbeknownst to her, Chad had slipped up behind her. He glanced at her employer and gave him a forced smile. "Rex."

"Detective." Rex's reply remained crisp and contained.

"Ready, CiCi? Everyone's waiting." He nodded once to Rex, and then gently steered her toward the exit.

"Why the hurry? I wanted to ask if he was going to help Bruce look at the books tomorrow." She looked over her shoulder and waved goodbye. Rex stared at her quizzically, then turned and walked back toward his private table.

At the Silver Saddle, customers occupied nearly every table that circled the large wooden dance floor. A local band played a mix of country songs, ranging from the newer hits to the older classics. They were lucky to snag a table along the edge of the room. A waitress wove her way through the crowd and quickly took their orders. A slow, sultry tune began to play. Chad pulled CiCi to the dance floor and into his arms.

"Did I mention how beautiful you look tonight?" he asked.

His smoldering gaze skimmed over her nearly bare shoulders and traveled down to linger on a hint of cleavage. She smiled, pleased that he liked the dress she had chosen on her shopping excursion with Megan. The flirty skirt hit just above the knee and the bodice fit like a glove. The plunging neckline and thin straps exposed a little more skin than she was used to showing, but his reaction made it worthwhile. Next to the cobalt blue dress, her blue splint seemed to disappear. "Thank you, and thank you for the dress. I hoped you would like it."

"Are you having a good time?" He pulled her close. She rested her head against his shoulder and fluidly followed his every step.

"I am. Good times, good friends, and the man I love holding me close. What more could I ask for?"

"Well, I imagine there's plenty, but…" He stiffened slightly, then relaxed.

She looked up, perplexed by his response. "But what?"

"Forget it. Let's just enjoy tonight. I know this has been a hard week for you, but I have to admit I've loved having you so close. Of course, it's not as close as I would like."

His hungry gaze spoke volumes as they swayed in sync to the music, his hard, muscular body pressed against her soft curves. He slowly placed a kiss on her neck, sending shivers down her spine. Her breathing quickened as he nibbled on her ear, then brushed his lips against hers. He parted them slightly before giving a soft, yet passionate kiss. She responded with lustful enthusiasm. The heat rose between them; the enormity of his desire became unmistakable. She gazed longingly into his eyes, keenly aware of what they both wanted.

It became almost too much to bear…until Mark and Stacy danced over and cut in. Mark laughed as he whirled CiCi away.

"I think Chad needs time to cool off. I'm happy you two have fallen in love, but I have to admit, I'm jealous. Whatever you're doing works. You may have to give me some pointers."

"You won't find our method on any checklist of how to bond with your soul mate. Let's see," she said, counting from memory, "there's been an assault, a murder, a restraining order, a break-in, and my surgery."

Mark stifled a laugh. "You're right. There's no way I'd want to duplicate that."

"So, are you thinking about getting married again?"

A momentary shadow of pain crossed over Mark's face. "It's been three years this month that a drunk driver killed my wife and son."

"I'm sorry. I didn't mean to bring up painful memories."

"That's okay. Something like that is hard to forget. I'm finally ready to get married again, but I haven't found a woman willing to put up with me."

"What about Stacy?"

"Nah, we're just two co-workers who have a good time together. We both know it's not meant to be. That deep connection is missing."

"You're handsome, smart, and compassionate. And a good dancer, I might add. When you find that special someone, you'll know it in here." She clumsily patted his chest over his heart with her splinted hand. "In fact, I know a gal who'd jump at the chance to go out with you." She smiled with amusement at the surprised and hopeful expression on his face.

"Yeah? Who?"

"Have you forgotten flirty Gertie? I'm sure she'd *love* to hear from you."

Mark tilted his head back and roared with laughter, drawing attention from nearby dancers. CiCi struggled to keep her own amusement in check.

"Sorry, I couldn't help myself," she said with a tiny snort. "And speaking of apologies, I owe you one for the other night. My poor judgement put you and Chad in a bad position."

"Trust me. We've seen over and over how quickly things can change from innocent to deadly. We don't want you caught in the middle."

"Um, by the way, has there been any progress in the investigation that would change your mind about me going back to Five Star? Bruce asked for my help when he looks over the books."

Mark dropped his smile and left her momentarily dancing with Detective Sullivan. He cocked a menacing eyebrow and stared down at her. "Nothing has changed my mind. Stay away from there, CiCi."

The music stopped. She thanked him for the dance and they walked back to their table.

The next few hours flew by. As they prepared to leave, CiCi discovered her clutch missing. They sought out the manager after a fruitless search. He, in turn, walked off to canvass his employees. A short time later, he returned with good news. A customer had found her purse and its contents scattered at the outer edge of the parking lot and had turned it over to the bartender. Relieved to find her wallet, cell phone, lip gloss, and house keys were all accounted for, she gave the bartender a healthy tip.

Chad locked eyes with Mark. "You ever hear of a purse snatcher walking away empty-handed?"

"Never."

CiCi from the doorway as waved as Mark and Stacy drove away from Chad's apartment. She glanced at her watch. One o'clock in the morning. She hadn't stayed out dancing this late for some time. She kicked her shoes off and went to the kitchen, where she poured herself a glass of water. Chad removed his jacket and leaned against the counter. She took a sip and admired his handsome profile as her thoughts replayed the events of the evening.

"Earlier when I said 'what more could I ask for', what were you going to say?"

He stiffened, the question clearly catching him off guard. He fixed a half-hearted smile on his face and avoided eye contact. "Nothing...just forget it."

"We've talked about being honest with each other. I think I deserve to hear what's on your mind. Don't you trust me?" He flinched, and she almost felt guilty. Almost. She stared, waiting for an answer.

He sighed and ran his fingers through his hair. He glanced at her and then paused, as if wondering whether to express his thoughts out loud. "Okay, if you must know. When you asked what more you could ask for, I wondered when you'll realize I don't measure up financially. I can't give you everything you want or deserve. It scares me that tomorrow, or next week, or next year, I might lose you."

His answer was unexpected, and left her nearly speechless. "Do you really think I'm that shallow?"

"What? No! CiCi, you're anything but shallow, but…think about it. With a three-million-dollar inheritance at your disposal, I pale in comparison."

"How would you feel if I said you love me *because* of my money?" she countered. He reeled back as though she had punched him. "I don't believe that for one minute. Look at the last few weeks. You've cared for me after my surgery. You've given up your bed instead of dropping me off at a hotel. You paid Pete out of your own pocket. Never once have you asked for a single dime or made me feel like I owe you in return. In spite of my stubborn and sometimes foolish ways, you always try to protect me. Everything you do shows how much you love me. *That's* the kind of man I want to spend the rest of my life with."

He sighed. "I guess I had that coming. I, of all people, should know there are two ways to look at everything. When I heard how much you inherited, the doubts set up camp in my head and convinced me you'd eventually want someone who's equally well-off. I do all right on a detective's salary, but money-wise, I'm highly inadequate to give you everything you deserve."

She stepped closer and placed her hand on his cheek. "Don't *ever* think of yourself as inadequate. Rich or poor, you are the only man I love. The money shouldn't change anything."

"Maybe, but—"

"You worry too much." She lovingly stroked the side of his face.

He smiled and kissed the palm of her hand. "I love you so much, sometimes I think I'll explode."

"I love you, too, and dancing with you tonight almost made me want to renege on my promise. It's probably a good thing Mark and Stacy came over when they did." She smiled and glanced up at him.

"They're not here now, are they?" He moved closer with a hungry grin plastered on his face. He set her glass aside as his gaze swept across her bare shoulders and down to her chest. He nibbled on her ear lobe and smiled when a soft groan bubbled up from her throat. His lips grazed against her neck before kissing the soft mounds peeking above the low neckline of her dress. His eyes locked on her lips. He freed her hair from its clip and plunged his fingers into the silken tresses. When his hand moved to caress her neck and shoulders, her body shuddered at his touch. His mouth captured hers, and the kiss turned savage as his tongue found its way deep into her mouth. His body pressed against hers and his breathing became ragged.

Suddenly, he pulled back.

"As much I want you right now," he gasped, "I'm also a man of my word. If I disregard your feelings on something so important to you, how will you ever trust me in the future?"

CiCi closed her eyes and leaned against the counter, panting. "You're right. Neither of us wants to do something we'll regret later." She gave him a weak smile. "Unfortunately, I now have a bit of a dilemma. Megan helped me get dressed for our date tonight."

A look of confusion washed over his face as she held up her splinted arm. She turned her back to him and held the bodice of her dress in place with her splinted arm. With her free hand, she twisted her hair up and away from the zipper of her dress. A few tendrils came loose from her grasp and swept across her bare shoulders.

He planted a soft kiss on the crook of her neck and unzipped her dress. She heard his breathing hitch. With movements that were slow and steady, he began to unhook her strapless bra. As his hands came in contact with her bare skin, she closed her eyes and savored the warmth of his touch. After he finished, he kissed her shoulder and whispered in her ear.

"I'm going to need a cold shower."

When she turned, she found herself standing alone in the room. From down the hall, the sound of running water broke the silence.

THIRTY-EIGHT

"Cooper," Chad grumbled into the cell phone. His groggy, sleep-deprived brain wondered why Mark would be calling at six in the morning.

"It's Mark. Let me in."

Chad scrambled from the sofa, padded to the front door, and slid back the deadbolt. Mark stood on the threshold, bleary-eyed, but fully dressed. Mark stepped into the living room, gave a second look at the pillow and blankets on the sofa, and threw a questioning look at Chad.

"She kick you out of bed? That must've been some fight."

"Jerk. She didn't kick me out," Chad said grumpily.

"You telling me you two don't sleep together? You've got to be kidding! I thought you were going to jump her bones right there on the dance floor last night." Mark planted his hands on his hips and stared at the rumpled mess on the sofa.

"If you and Stacy hadn't cut in, I might have," he said with a half-grin.

"Yeah, well, Stacy didn't mind." Mark chuckled.

"What's up? I'm sure you didn't come here to discuss my sex life."

"I wanted to give you a heads-up. The shift sergeant notified Lieutenant Cabrillo of a call that Detective Logan responded to tonight...ah...I mean this morning," he said, glancing down at his watch. "Cabrillo called and wants me at the scene before they move the body. He's certain the death is connected to our Five Star case. Thought you'd want to be there."

"Sure."

"Logan has tentatively identified the guy as——"

A muffled moan came from the back of the apartment. Chad hurried toward the bedroom, and returned after a couple of minutes. "She has occasional nightmares, ever since the murder. Last week, my neighbor upstairs heard her scream and called the cops." Chad stifled a yawn and scratched his head. "Lucky for me, Baker responded to the call and knew about the case. He came in to make it look like he took the call seriously, then went upstairs to explain the situation."

"You're sleeping on the sofa, not getting any sleep, and not getting laid. No wonder you look like hell. You're nothing but a time bomb waiting to explode."

With a roll of his eyes, Chad sighed. "As you were saying earlier?"

"Possible suicide at Five Star," Mark whispered. He paused and rubbed a hand over his weary face. "The cleaning lady found the body. The victim is Bruce Owens."

Chad stood and fixed his eyes on Mark. "Let me get dressed."

Mark grabbed Chad's arm as he turned to leave. "I've changed my mind. You stay here with CiCi. I'll call when I know something definite."

———

Detective Mark Sullivan pulled his car into the commercial parking lot, looked around at the familiar setting, and felt a small measure of relief. If the incident had occurred on any day other than a Sunday, extra officers would've been needed to keep a curious crowd at bay. It was a mystery why people pushed and shoved to view a horrific crime scene, only to wish they could later erase those same images from their minds.

The victim's car sat in the exact spot Julie Reynolds had parked her car the morning of her murder. Sullivan approached the main entrance, where Detective Logan stood speaking with a patrol officer. Logan stopped, surprised by Sullivan's arrival. He nodded and grudgingly handed Sullivan a pair of booties and gloves. He slipped them on and followed Logan inside and down the hall toward the victim's office.

With years of experience under his belt, Sullivan knew things were not always as straightforward as they first appeared. The fact that a murder had recently been committed here and both victims were employees of Five Star had him on edge. He wasn't inclined to believe in coincidence. The easiest outcome, of course, would be for the death to be ruled a suicide, but he suspected nothing about this case would be that simple.

Careful not to disturb evidence, Mark entered the room and surveyed the scene. The body sat slumped in the leather executive chair behind the desk, the handgun loosely held in his right hand. The crime scene tech finished taking photos of the body, and turned his attention to the objects on the desk. The right side of the desk held a jar of peppermints and a framed photo of an elderly couple, presumably the victim's parents. Several folders were open and the contents spread across the blotter centered in front of the computer monitor. On the left-hand side of the desk sat a half-full cup of coffee, a stapler, a pen and note pad, and the printer. The printer tray held a computer-generated suicide note.

Sullivan's eyebrows rose as he scanned the desk. "The victim was left-handed."

"Yeah?" Logan scoffed at the assessment.

"Mark my words." He and Logan stepped outside the room. Two EMT's stepped inside and loaded the body onto a gurney. Sullivan looked at the people standing nearby. "Where's the woman who found the body?"

"She's been taken to the station."

"Isn't it unusual to clean an office on a Sunday?"

"She normally cleans Five Star on Saturday mornings, but she didn't feel well and put it off until this morning. Couldn't sleep, so she came in early."

Mark watched as the two men pushed the gurney into the hallway and toward the exit. He stepped back into the room and spoke to the tech. "Be sure to get a photo of the keyboard and dust it for prints."

Logan growled, "I took the call. This is *my* case, so don't start ordering people around or questioning how I do things."

"Sorry. Habit, I guess."

As the group stepped outside, Lieutenant Cabrillo arrived on the scene. After a short and heated discussion, Cabrillo ordered Logan to turn the investigation over to Sullivan and assist as needed, which hinted to the Lieutenant's lack of confidence in Logan's abilities. Logan nodded in compliance, but grumbled under his breath after the senior officer left. Sullivan ignored the tension in the air and set about taking command of the crime scene.

CiCi showered and dressed and entered the kitchen at ten the next morning. Chad sat at the table, nursing a cup of coffee and reading the paper. She smiled and brushed a light kiss across his cheek. "Apparently I was dead to the world this morning. Did you eat already?"

"Not hungry."

Someone's not in a good mood. CiCi shrugged and grabbed a container of yogurt from the fridge and added a spoonful of granola. Though Chad appeared to focus on the Sunday comics, she noticed that he checked his watch several times. Mark called twice, and each call left Chad more distracted than before.

Something is brewing, and it isn't a pot of coffee. "Is everything okay?" she asked.

"We need to talk."

The serious expression on his face and the tone of his voice sent a chill down her spine. She listened in stunned silence as he told her of Mark's early morning visit and Bruce's death. She stood and paced the length of the room, trying to process the news.

"This can't be happening." She shook her head in disbelief. "It doesn't make sense. Bruce wanted to meet me at Five Star today to look over the books. That doesn't sound like a man wanting to commit suicide. And why would he have gone there so early?"

"I don't know. Mark will find out. This is a perfect example why Mark and I wanted you to stay away. You never know what can happen."

"But don't you see? If I had met him there, maybe I could've stopped him from…" She closed her eyes and her mind reeled at the thought.

Chad pulled her into his arms. "You don't know that. It could've just as easily turned into a murder-suicide, and there's always the possibility it wasn't a suicide."

Her phone rang. She pulled away from his embrace, and he reluctantly let her go. "Hey, Tasha. Yeah, I just heard." She choked back a gasp as she settled on the sofa and listened. After she disconnected, she remained seated, too numb to move.

Chad took a seat beside her and tucked a strand of hair behind her ear. "You okay?"

"The police just left Tasha's house and they're headed to Izzy's. Tasha said they plan on talking with every Five Star employee. If Bruce committed suicide, why would they do that?"

"Suicides are treated the same as homicides until the evidence, witness statements, and the medical examiner's report confirms suicide as the cause of death. Everything will be given extra scrutiny since Five Star was the site of a recent murder, which is still under investigation."

"Since I haven't been at work for some time, will the police still want to talk with me?"

He replied with a sigh, "Yeah, I'm afraid so."

"Well, I'm not about to sit here on pins and needles, waiting to be questioned. Why don't I pack up and take my belongings back home? Later, maybe we can look at that office chair. That'll keep my mind occupied until I hear otherwise."

"Considering what's happened. I think you should stay another night or two."

"I shouldn't move back home because someone committed suicide? That doesn't make any sense." She listened to his reasoning, and reluctantly agreed he might be right. An hour later, as she admired her new second-hand office chair, Chad received a call to report to the station. He dropped her back at his apartment on the way to work.

Too jittery to spend the afternoon alone, CiCi called Megan. With the furniture aspect of her home office complete, CiCi decided a second set of eyes would be helpful when shopping for new electronics. She also hoped to take advantage of the Memorial Day sales. They looked at several computers, and CiCi opted for a sleek laptop, something that would take less space than her old bulky desktop. She also purchased a wireless router, all-in-one printer for her home office, and a flat screen TV for her bedroom. Using every square inch of free space, they managed to fit the merchandise into Megan's car.

While Megan carried the boxes to the second floor of CiCi's townhouse and stacked them in an empty corner of the bedroom, CiCi pulled up the Tech Trio website on her phone and booked an appointment. She would rather have an expert handle the technical details than attempt the job herself. They had a Tuesday opening and she grabbed it.

After dinner, Megan dropped her off at Chad's. During the course of the evening, her calls to Floyd went directly to voicemail. She took several calls from co-workers and friends. Tasha and Izzy never meant to be insensitive, but each expressed concern about the effect Bruce's death might have on Five Star, and ultimately their livelihood. The situation at Five Star looked bleaker by the moment.

THIRTY-NINE

Memorial Day morning. CiCi reached over and squeezed Chad's hand as he drove through the cemetery. Colorful bouquets dotted the recently mowed grounds, and miniature flags waved in the breeze above every veteran's plot. They left an array of mixed flowers on Chad's grandfather's grave, then walked to where CiCi's grandparents were buried. She filled the bronze vase on the headstone with yellow tulips, her grandmother's favorite. Her eyes pooled with tears as she moved to her right, where young, tender blades of grass sprouted from the slightly mounded soil where her mother had been buried. She bent and brushed away the grass clippings from the granite marker. A flood of emotions overwhelmed her as she placed the rest of the flowers in the vase.

She stood, and Chad wrapped a comforting arm around her shoulder as they walked back to the truck. He helped her into the passenger seat and shut the door, but stopped as he passed in front of the vehicle. Something had drawn his attention elsewhere. CiCi followed his gaze. An old red truck sat parked at the entrance to the cemetery. Her dad stood outside the cab, leaning against the open door, watching their every move. She hadn't realized Chad had slid into the driver's seat until he slammed the door shut. Without a word, he started the engine, made a U-turn, and left the cemetery using the exit on the far side of the grounds.

"I wish I could join you at the church picnic today, but duty calls," he said.

"I understand. Will you be investigating Bruce's suicide?"

"I doubt it. Something came up yesterday that has Mark on edge. He said he would know more today. Until I hear otherwise, he wants me to verify an alibi in the Reynolds case."

"Speaking of alibis, I ran into Izzy at the library the other day. She told me about her fight with Julie. Do you think she had anything to do with the murder?"

"No comment. You want me to drop you off at Tasha's?"

"Please. We're going to whip up a fruit salad for our contribution to the picnic."

"Sounds like you'll be busy most of the day. I'm glad you'll have something to keep your mind off murder and suicide."

Chad arrived at the station before eleven. The team gathered around a large table in the briefing room. Two new faces had joined the group—detectives borrowed from neighboring cities. Detective Mark Sullivan cleared his throat and the room quieted. He read the preliminary autopsy report aloud.

"I'll summarize what we know so far. The bullet entered just behind the right ear and exited through the left front side of the forehead. The trajectory of the bullet makes it impossible to duplicate as a self-inflicted wound, especially considering the victim was left-handed." He paused and looked straight at Logan. "In the suicide note, Owens apologized for stabbing Julie Reynolds in a fit of rage after she fought off his sexual advances. He also admitted to destroying Miss Winslow's residence, but gave no motive for doing so. However, the suicide note didn't have any blood splatters on it, though it was in the printer tray on the desk. That means it was printed after the fatal shot had been fired. Bruce Owens' death is now officially classified as a homicide. Are there any questions or observations so far?"

Chad scrutinized Mark's face, his voice, his mannerisms as he fielded questions and responded with clear and concise answers. Chad knew his co-worker like the back of his hand. Something was off. He felt it the moment he arrived at the station yesterday. But what?

"All right," Sullivan said. "We're looking for a killer, and there's no doubt in my mind we'll find a connection to the Reynolds murder. I've got a warrant from the judge to search the victim's residence. Wicks, I want you to take another officer and get started on that." Wicks nodded, and Mark continued passing out assignments to various individuals.

"Detective Logan, see if anyone has located Ashley Morgan yet, and then help finish up on the interviews we didn't get to yesterday. Detective Cooper, see me after the meeting. Everyone be safe and keep me posted." Sullivan dismissed the meeting with a nod. The room emptied and each person left to complete his assigned task.

Chad walked to the front of the room. "What's up?"

"Are you still canvassing the Hughes' neighborhood? The sooner we tie up that loose end, the better." Mark stared absently at the papers scattered on the desk.

"I'm on it." Chad paused and crossed his arms over his chest. "Come on, Mark. Out with it. What's on your mind?"

The phone at Mark's waist vibrated. He glanced at the screen and then answered, staring at the floor as he listened. "Okay, send it to me." He disconnected, then pulled up a text. He ran a hand down over his face and handed the phone to Chad. "I suspected as much yesterday, but I wanted confirmation before I said anything. For now, this information is on a strictly need to know basis. Understand?"

Chad read the message and his jaw dropped. The name of the registered owner of the murder weapon turned out to be someone they both knew. He looked at Mark and nodded.

After putting the fruit salad on the table designated for side dishes, CiCi and Tasha set up their folding chairs under the shade of a large pin oak. From there, they had a perfect view of the gazebo, where a group of veterans were giving a short concert. Picnic tables, along with blankets spread open on the grass, were full of families waiting for the food lines to open. Parents pointed upward and children watched the colorful kites twist and dip in the sky. A line of kids waited to get an up-close look at a fire truck and have their picture taken wearing a firefighter's hat. A dozen toddlers shrieked with excitement inside an inflatable bounce house.

After they had eaten and listened to the band, Tasha decided to wander the park grounds and visit with friends. CiCi waved her away, content to relax and let her meal settle. Her gaze briefly landed on a woman sitting about thirty feet away. Two beady eyes beneath the woman's folding chair caught CiCi's attention. The woman's black dog had taken full advantage of the deep shade underneath her owner's seat. CiCi smiled, tipped her head back against her chair and closed her eyes behind her sunglasses. A minute later, she bolted upright.

Resting her sunglasses atop her head, she took a closer look at the little black ball of fur. In the shadows, the dog's eyes seemed to glow in the dark. *I have a hunch those beady little eyes Izzy saw in the bushes wasn't a possum or raccoon. It's a long shot, but what have I got to lose?* She lowered the sunglasses to shield her eyes from the harsh sunlight, and wove her way around the small clusters of attendees until she reached the woman and her furry little companion. "Hello, Mrs. Harmon. Are you enjoying the picnic?"

"CiCi, how delightful to see you. Yes, I am." She reached over and removed a tote bag from the chair beside hers. "Please, have a seat."

"Thank you." The moment CiCi sat, the small dog scurried out from under the chair and jumped into her lap. She laughed and gave the dog a good scratch behind the ears. Her thanks? Several wet kisses.

"Inky, stop that! If she bothers you, say the word b-a-t-h. She'll dart under the chair quicker than you can blink."

"She's no trouble at all. I'm surprised at how friendly she is toward me today. When I stopped by your house to return your dish, she barked at me."

"She only barks when we're at home and someone she doesn't know well encroaches on her territory." The woman reached into her pocket and gave Inky a treat. "I'm sorry to hear about your boss, and so soon after that woman's murder. What a tragedy."

"Yes, it is."

"It must be terribly upsetting. I spoke with Tasha earlier, but I haven't seen Izzy today. Perhaps she and the family decided not to come."

"You live around the corner from Ivan and Izzy, don't you?"

"I do. Inky and I pass by their house on our daily walks around the block."

"What time do you and Inky normally walk?"

"Unless something comes up, we usually walk around ten in the morning, and again at six in the evening. Of course, we sometimes walk later than usual because I played Bunco with friends on Tuesdays, and a couple of weeks ago Alice Sallee and I went to dinner and a movie."

CiCi straightened in the chair, her mind quickly doing the calculations. "Oh? Do you recall what night you went to the movie?"

"A Thursday, if I remember correctly. It was pretty late when I came home that particular night. I was tired, but I didn't want to miss our evening ritual, so we went for a walk anyway."

I knew it! "Do you remember what time that was?"

"I suppose it was around ten o'clock, maybe a little after."

"Did you happen to see or hear anything unusual that evening?"

Mrs. Harmon leaned over and whispered, "I probably shouldn't say, but I overheard Ivan and Izzy having a big fight in their front yard."

"Really?"

"Yes, and it was a doozy." Mrs. Harmon settled back into the chair, but kept her voice low. "On our second trip around the block, Inky stopped to do her business just on the other side of their hedge. When they pulled into their drive, I had knelt to pick up Inky's deposit, and neither of them saw us tucked away in the shadows. She got out of the car screaming at him about seeing someone else. He said it wasn't what she thought and he could explain. They yelled at each other for several minutes, then took the fight inside."

"What happened next?"

"It's anyone's guess. Inky and I continued on our way. By the time we finished our last lap, all the lights in their house were off. Both cars were still there, but I'd bet money he ended up sleeping on the couch." Inky began to whimper and strain at the leash. "Well, it looks like she needs to go take care of business. Stop by the house sometime when you have a chance."

So much for Chad thinking the picnic would get my mind off of murder and suicide. As soon as the pair left, CiCi pulled out her phone and relayed the conversation to Chad. "Is there any way you can talk to Mrs. Harmon without mentioning my name?"

"Yeah, I'm sure I can find an excuse to talk with her."

"Good. And Tasha will drop me off at my place after the picnic."

"Be sure to keep the doors locked, okay? And CiCi? Thanks for the tip."

She smiled. "I'm always happy to assist the RGPD."

FORTY

Late that afternoon, the man who stood on CiCi's porch introduced himself as Detective Logan and offered his badge for inspection. Thickset and in his late forties, his black eyebrows and mustache were a stark contrast to his shaved head. She led him into the living room where he took a seat in a chair at the end of the sofa. The buttons of his shirt strained around his ample midsection. His eyes made a quick sweep of the room as he accepted an offer of a soft drink. When she returned from the kitchen, he accepted the glass with a nod of thanks and took a sip. He pulled a small notebook from his shirt pocket and patted several pockets before asking to borrow a pen.

"I assume by now you've been in contact with your co-workers and heard about your boss, Bruce Owens. I've been assigned to the case and have a few questions."

"I don't think I'll be much help. I haven't been to work in over two weeks." She smiled nervously and took a seat on the sofa.

A persistent buzzing of the doorbell interrupted their conversation. CiCi excused herself and hurried to the door. Mark gave her a tight smile when she let him in. His unexpected arrival drew a grimace and a few grumblings from Detective Logan. Mark nodded to Logan and ignored the chilly reception.

"I was in the area and thought I'd sit in."

"I'm good. Don't need any help." He glared as Mark took a seat on the sofa, completely disregarding his preference to conduct the interview alone. "I thought you were overseeing the search of the Owens residence. Your guys finished already?" To CiCi, it looked as if they were daring the other to look away first.

"I've got it covered."

Logan let out a perturbed sigh before turning his attention back to CiCi. "Where was I? Okay, let's start with the basics. Tell me about your relationship with Mr. Owens."

"He was my boss," she replied. "He maintained a physical presence in the office more than the other two owners because he oversaw the day to day operations."

"What was he like?"

She gnawed on her lower lip. "Well, let's just say Bruce had a very charismatic personality and fancied himself as a ladies' man. There wasn't a female in the office he hadn't hit on at least once. We jokingly called him King Leer behind his back because he had a habit of leering. It was a well-earned title."

"Did he ever make a pass at you?" Logan raised a bushy eyebrow.

She shifted in her seat and shot a quick glance at Mark. "Several times, but I made it clear I wasn't interested."

"He was successful, financially well-off, and a good looking guy. Most women would consider him a pretty good catch."

"I'm not most women. Besides, I'm in a serious relationship."

Logan looked at her skeptically. "If you didn't have that kind of relationship with Mr. Owens, why did he call your phone number twice on Friday? You just said you hadn't been at work for two weeks."

"He called to ask if I'd found a document Julie Reynolds had given me. When I told him I had, he said he would swing by to pick it up." Out of the corner of her eye, Mark leaned forward and frowned. "He called the second time to let me know he had been detained."

"What did you talk about after he arrived?"

She took a deep breath and thought back over their conversation. "Well, he seemed genuinely upset over Julie's murder, and felt guilty for not addressing a problem after she asked for his help."

"Is that all?"

"He asked if I would meet him at Five Star on Sunday to look over the books with him. He had a potential buyer for his share of the company and an auditor scheduled for the following week. I was supposed to let him know if I would join him or not, but I never did."

Logan's interest peaked at the mention of Sunday. He wrote furiously on his notepad. "What time did he want to meet?"

"He didn't say."

"Are you sure?" He wiped his brow and downed the rest of his soda in one gulp.

"I'm positive. You can check with my handyman, Pete Mason. He heard most of the conversation. I can give you his cell number if you like."

Detective Logan sputtered and choked. Liquid dribbled down his chin and onto his shirt. Mark chuckled softly and shook his head, which earned him an angry look. CiCi hurried to the kitchen and returned with a damp hand towel to mop his shirt.

"Miss Winslow, are you positive that you didn't meet Bruce Owens Sunday morning at Five Star?" The disbelief was evident in Logan's voice.

"I told you I didn't!"

"Is there anyone else who might have met with him that morning?"

"No, the only people familiar with the books are Norma, Ashley Morgan, and me. I doubt he would ask Norma for help, and Ashley was fired earlier in the week."

Logan jotted down a few more notes and moved on. "Can you think of anyone who might've been angry with Mr. Owens? Did anyone ever threaten him?"

CiCi frowned. "Why would that matter if he committed suicide?"

"We're required to check every possible angle in a case like this."

"I've never heard anyone threaten Bruce." She sighed impatiently as Logan flipped to a clean page in his little book. "Detective, are you almost finished? There's really nothing more I can add." She stood, indicating he had worn out his welcome.

"Almost. I have one more question. Your home was vandalized a few weeks ago." He licked a thumb and flipped through his notes, "It says here you reported that two of your guns were stolen."

She stopped, confused by the sudden shift in the conversation. A chill crept down her spine. "What would that have to do with Bruce?"

Mark's eyes narrowed and his jaw muscles twitched as he leaned toward Logan. "How'd you find out?" he whispered.

CiCi's gaze bounced between the two men as the tension in the air ballooned.

"I have my sources."

"Leave it be, Logan."

Logan stood and pushed ahead, despite the warning. "I'm not a big fan of coincidence, Miss Winslow. It seems that Bruce Owens—"

"Logan, that's enough!" Mark ordered, but his attempt to stop Logan failed. Logan continued, refusing to let a younger man tell him how to conduct an interview.

"—blew his brains out using one of your *supposedly* stolen guns. That's quite a coincidence, don't you think?"

Mark jumped to his feet. "Back off, Logan. Now!"

She gasped. Her lungs clamored for air. The room swayed and shifted beneath her feet. Mark helped her to the sofa while Logan grudgingly fetched a glass of water. She took a welcome drink and struggled to find her voice. "Bruce killed himself with *my* gun? How...how can that be?" Her mind tried to make sense of the horrifying news. "Wait. Are you saying he's the one who broke into my place and stole my guns?"

"I didn't say that, but we have two dead Five Star employees, a vandalized townhome, and two missing guns. You seem to be the common link, Miss Winslow." Logan looked at her accusingly. "Where were you Saturday night and early Sunday morning?"

"You think *I* killed him? Are you crazy?" Her eyes flared with anger. His lame effort to connect her with the recent mayhem made her blood boil.

Logan waited for an answer, his pen and note pad ready. She stood and snatched the pen from his hand. His eyes narrowed. She returned the glare and angrily pointed the pen at him as she recited her whereabouts on Saturday night and Sunday morning.

Mark reached out and pried the pen from CiCi's vise-like grip. "Let me have this before you decide to stab him with it." His attention then turned to Logan. "I can vouch for her. She and Chad were both asleep when I stopped by on my way to the crime scene."

"I hope you're satisfied, Detective Logan," she said as she showed both men to the door, "because I've had enough of your nonsense. If you want to talk again, it'll be with my lawyer present. Understood?"

Logan handed her a business card. "Call me if you think of anything."

"Don't hold your breath," she muttered as he turned and left. Mark hesitated.

"I'm sorry. It wasn't my intention for you to find out about the gun like this." He pressed the pen into her hand and followed Logan outside.

FORTY-ONE

I t was close to eight o'clock when she heard Chad's truck rumble to a stop in front of her townhouse. Moments later, the front door opened, then closed. As she stood facing the kitchen sink, the sound of his boots on the hardwood floor drew near. He tossed a deli sack on the kitchen counter, slid his arms around her waist, and kissed the tender spot on the side of her neck. She turned to face him. A hug and a couple of kisses were exactly what she needed after such a rough afternoon.

"I heard what happened today. You okay?" he asked, as he looked deep into her eyes.

She nodded solemnly. "Did you know about the gun?"

He sighed. "I did. Mark told me this morning, but was firm about keeping the information under wraps. Apparently someone didn't follow orders."

"I understand why you couldn't tell me. Still, the news came as quite a shock."

"I can imagine. When Mark heard where Logan was headed, he dropped everything and rushed over. He was livid about the way Logan handled the interview and is looking into how he got ahold of the information."

"I hope Logan's not RGPD's poster boy." She plated the sandwich and chips while Chad poured something to drink. She took a seat next to him at the table.

"Definitely not. If it makes you feel better, I gave Logan an earful this afternoon. It's no wonder he hasn't been promoted. He's not exactly known for his finesse or sensitivity."

"You know how my afternoon went. How about yours?"

"Busy as usual." He held out part of his sandwich to share, but she declined. "Did you and Tasha have a good time at the picnic?"

"We did. After she dropped me off, I tidied up the spare bedroom and then called Pete to see if he was in the neighborhood and had time to move a few boxes to the basement. To sweeten the request, I offered to make a pot of coffee and thaw a few slices of banana bread. He drove by as I opened the door for Detective Logan, but for some reason kept on going."

Chad shifted uneasily in his seat, then put down his sandwich and leaned forward. "I have a confession to make, and you're not going to like it."

"Um...okay?" CiCi leaned back and gave him her full attention.

"Pete Mason is not the handyman you think he is."

"Why would you say that? He's a hard worker and did everything I asked, and then some. I wouldn't hesitate to hire him again or give a referral."

"That's not what I meant. Pete isn't a handyman, he's a retired detective."

As the words sank in, she frowned and crossed her arms over her chest. "He said he retired from the Public Works Department. So, you both lied to me?"

"Technically, we didn't. Pete said he kept the streets of Ripley Grove free of trash and rubbish, and that was true. *You* assumed he worked for the Public Works Department. We just didn't see the need to correct you."

"You hired him to babysit me, even after I told you no?" she said, her tone sharp.

He scowled and tossed his napkin on the table. "What was I supposed to do? Mark and I suspected you might've been the intended target of Julie's killer, and Jack posed a serious threat. And let's not forget the fact you were attacked in your own home. So, yes, I hired Pete to keep an eye on you despite your objections."

"Still, if you had mentioned—"

"You're only kidding yourself if you think you would have agreed to my plan."

She sighed. "You're right, I wouldn't have."

"Look at it this way. We both came out ahead in the long run. Your townhouse got restored to a livable condition, and I was able to focus on catching a killer without constantly worrying about you."

"You're lucky it worked out so well."

"I know." His brief smile of satisfaction disappeared, and his gaze turned serious, pinning her in place. "In the future, we'll need to find a common ground between your stubborn independence and my need to protect you. I love you, Cecilia. You're the most precious thing in the world to me, and I'll do whatever it takes to keep you safe—with no regrets, no apologies."

"I understand." To some, his actions would speak of control. To her, the overwhelming depth of his love was almost tangible.

He reached across the table and took her hand in his. "Are we okay?"

"Yes. Your heart was in the right place." She leaned over and gave him a lingering kiss, then pulled back. "Now my curiosity is piqued. How does Pete occupy his time when he's not pretending to be a handyman?"

"He owns PM Security and Surveillance Company. His experience on the police force paved the way for his business, which he opened a few years before he retired. He and his crew install and monitor security systems, provide security personnel for different venues and concerts, and do surveillance. I think this is the first time he's posed as a handyman."

"Maybe he should add undercover work to his list of services. Now I understand why Brian and the deputy who delivered the copy of the restraining order knew him."

"Pete said the hours spent helping you was the most enjoyable job he's had for quite some time. And, the two of you have some-thing in common."

"What's that?"

"A love of sweets."

"I suspected as much. By the way, did you talk with Mrs. Harmon?" she asked.

"Yes, I did. Her observations were helpful to a point, but things are still up in the air. It's not like she could guarantee Ivan and Izzy were home all night. That's all I'm going to say. Let's finish eating. I have an apartment to look at this evening."

CiCi nodded and reluctantly pushed the investigation to the back of her mind—for the time being.

FORTY-TWO

Leaving Doctor Cunningham's office on Tuesday morning, CiCi realized, in hindsight, she clearly misjudged the seriousness of her injury. Her favorite sunglasses hid her red-rimmed eyes as she briskly walked through the waiting room. Chad stood at her approach, glanced at the short brace immobilizing her wrist and hand, and frowned with concern. She brushed past him without speaking, determined to hold herself together. By the time she reached his truck, a tear, then two, trickled from beneath her sunglasses. She pressed her lips together, but a tiny sob bubbled to the surface.

Chad gently turned her to face him. "What's wrong, honey?"

She glanced down at her arm, then quickly looked away. "I didn't expect it to look so…"

He tenderly cupped her chin and tilted her head back. "Look at me, Cecilia. I don't give a damn what your arm looks like, now or later. Those scars remind me of what I almost lost that night. I'm thankful every day that you didn't bleed to death."

"You're right, it's just that…" A few more tears trickled down her cheeks.

He pulled her into his arms and stroked her hair as she buried her face against his chest. "Don't cry, Sugar. Now, tell me what else Doc had to say. I suspect there's something else going on for you to be this upset."

"I...I need to see a hand specialist. Even with therapy, I may not regain full use of my hand for months. What if I *never* get the full use of my hand back? How will I work, or bake, or take care of business?"

He ran a hand up and down her back as though he could erase all her fears. If life were only that simple. "I know that's not what you expected to hear, but don't dwell on the worst-case scenario. Think positive. I'll help you with whatever you need. At least you have a cushion to fall back on until you can go back to work."

"The inheritance is not the issue! I'd never be content to sit around and do nothing. I need to be productive, useful, connected."

"Consider this a temporary pass, or an unplanned vacation." He kissed her forehead, then unlocked the door to the truck.

Chad drove in silence as she wrestled with her emotions. When he pulled in front of her townhouse, she decided to take back the one thing that would put her in control and make her feel halfway normal again. "Keys. Where are the keys to my Jeep?"

"Doc say you could drive?"

"Yes, as long as I understand my limitations. His words."

"Think you can safely drive a stick shift with that brace on your wrist?"

"We'll see."

Reluctantly, he unlocked the glove compartment, retrieved the keys, and placed the jingling mass in her hand. They quickly disappeared into her purse. "Why don't we go for a test drive tonight? That way if there's a problem, I'll be able to help. Afterward, we can celebrate at the Sugar Shanty."

"Okay, but I shouldn't have to prove anything. I'm a good driver."

"True, but until I see with my own two eyes that you can manage driving with that brace, I'll worry about you behind the wheel. That kind of distraction might interfere with my ability to protect and serve the good citizens of Ripley Grove. You wouldn't want to put the public's safety at risk and have that on your conscience, would you?" He flashed a smile that put his dimple on full display.

She lowered her sunglasses and peered over the rim. "Seriously? Don't you think that's laying it on a little thick?"

"Maybe. Did it work?"

She shook her head and gave a half-hearted grin. "Okay, but be forewarned, I'm going to order the biggest dessert on the menu."

"I wouldn't expect otherwise." He gave her a kiss goodbye and promised to stop by after work.

An hour later, the Tech Trio van arrived. CiCi watched from the window as the technician unloaded a bag of gear from his vehicle. She met him at the door and led him to the second floor. He took a quick inventory of the stacked boxes in the corner and nodded with approval. He worked methodically to set up the new system and barely made eye contact. After updating and making the appropriate adjustments, he gave a short tutorial covering all the new features. The entire process took longer than expected, but the time and money were worth it.

At the RGPD, Chad sank into the chair behind his desk. It wasn't long before Mark entered the room and took an empty seat.

"We found Ashley Morgan living with a friend in Iowa. With a little persuasion, she's agreed to come back. So far, she's not saying much." He rubbed a hand across his eyes as though he could erase his mounting fatigue. "I'm beginning to think either Floyd or Rex wasn't happy about Bruce bringing in an auditor. To err on the side of caution, I've put them both under surveillance until we hear something definite from the forensic accountant. On a happier note, did CiCi get rid of her splint this morning?"

"The splint, yes; the brace, no." Chad leaned back in his chair and summarized her appointment. When he mentioned the test drive scheduled for that evening and the celebratory dessert afterward, Mark shook his head.

"You must have one hell of a velvet tongue to get her to go along with that."

Chad propped his black leather boots on the edge of the desk, clasped his hands behind his head, and grinned like a Cheshire cat. "I know the magic words—Sugar Shanty."

Despite CiCi's best intentions, Julie's murder lurked behind every thought. With nothing else on her agenda that afternoon, she curled up on the sofa, annoyed that she hadn't been able to find Julie's flash drive. The police hadn't found it during their search, and as far as she knew, Keenan hadn't found it either. *It couldn't disappear into thin air. Where could it be? Think, CiCi, think. Julie said she'd bring it to Stella's, and she apparently hadn't given it to Bruce, or he wouldn't have come by to pick up the copy.*

She replayed her last evening with Julie, minute by minute. An old expression sprang to mind that said if you need to hide something, hide it in plain sight. Her eyes grew wide and her pulse raced as she envisioned a far-fetched possibility. *Have I gone crazy? Maybe, but there's only one way to find out.*

She jumped from the couch and took the stairs two at a time to the master bedroom. She went straight for her purse and carried it to the bed. Sitting cross-legged on the mattress, she turned the bag upside down, spilling the contents onto the quilt. Her hand trembled as she picked through the mishmash of stuff. She brushed aside a paperback book, an empty tube of lip-gloss, a half of a bottle of water, a smashed candy bar, and a few fuzzy cough drops (*eww!*), her cell phone, a package of tissues, four pens, a roll of breath mints, her prized sunglasses, a small tape measure, her wallet, and key rings. There were now *two* key rings, where yesterday she had one.

Her breathing hitched as her eyes locked onto the smaller key ring. Nestled among the keys and novelty flash drives hung a little pink pig. *Julie must have slipped it onto my key ring at Stella's when I went to the ladies' room.* She struggled to contain her excitement as she jumped from the bed and powered on her laptop.

The pig's head popped off with ease and the body plugged straightaway into an empty USB port. Her heart raced when several folders materialized on the screen. Her eyes widened in shock. CICI —in bold, capital letters—appeared on the first folder. With an eerie sense of foreboding, she double-clicked on the icon and began to read.

Dear CiCi,

By looking through the attached folders, you'll discover a significant amount of money has been embezzled from Five Star. When I first asked for your help with the accounts, I honestly had no idea what I'd stumbled upon. With a little more digging, I put two and two together before the day was over. I know a golden opportunity when I see one, so I offered Rex my silence in exchange for a hefty fee that would enable me to leave town and start a new life elsewhere.

Rex—he's such an arrogant, demanding jerk! Does he really believe he's so much smarter, so much better than everyone else? I told you karma would come back and bite him in the butt, and I aim to make that happen by giving you the evidence. Considering your strict moral code and how much you love your job, I have no doubt you will turn the information over to the authorities in order to protect the company.

Thanks for being my friend. We enjoyed some fun times together, didn't we? But as they say, all good things must come to an end. By the time you find this flash drive, I hope to be hundreds of miles away, ideally on a flight to…well, that really doesn't matter, does it?

Take care,

Julie

PS: You'd better stake a permanent claim to that handsome cop before someone else does.

Stunned by the information divulged in the letter, CiCi leaned back in the chair to take it all in—but not for long. The letter's claims needed to be verified. By cross-referencing the data in the other folders, she discovered Julie had been right. Someone had embezzled a substantial amount of money from Five Star. Julie's knowledge of the crime may have led to her death, but what about Bruce's?

CiCi's nerves were stretched to their limit. When her cell phone rang, she nearly fell off the chair. She answered and couldn't have been more surprised.

"CiCi, are you still looking for Julie's flash drive?" Keenan said.

"No, I found it. Why? Did you—" A dial tone signaled the end of their conversation. With the phone still in hand, she pulled up the first number on her speed dial list.

"Chad, you're not going to believe this, but I found Julie's flash drive. It was on my key ring—the one you had locked in your glove compartment. This little pig holds the mother of all motives for murder." She barely took a breath and neared the point of hyperventilating.

"We've issued two arrest warrants. If that flash drive contains what I think it does, it'll cement our case," Chad said. "I'll be over in fifteen or twenty minutes."

A commotion erupted in the background on Chad's end and he disconnected before any further details were given. She returned to the laptop, intent on delving further into the files. Ten minutes later, the doorbell rang. She flew down the stairs, cracked open the door, and peered over the safety chain, expecting to see Chad's smiling face. The hardened eyes that stared back were anything but friendly.

FORTY-THREE

Warning bells clanged inside her head. She slammed the door closed, turned the lock and ran for the kitchen phone. After two strong kicks, the door crashed inward. Rex quickly caught up, jerked her backward with a viselike grip, and ripped the phone from the wall.

"You know what I came for," he snarled, "and I'm not leaving without it."

"What are you talking about?"

He whipped her around to face him. "Don't mess with me. I know you have it."

She stomped down hard on the top of his foot and wrenched free, dashing for the door. Having a longer stride, he closed the distance between them. Their feet tangled and sheer momentum pitched them both forward. Her head slammed against the doorframe. Pain exploded behind her eyes. Stunned and nauseous, her heart pounded with fear as blood ran down the side of her face. *He's going to kill me. I've got to fight, and fight hard.*

He pulled her up and pinned her against the wall. When the opportunity presented itself, she gave a hard thrust upward with her knee. Writhing in southern discomfort, he released his grip, doubled over, and fell to the floor. She stumbled toward the exit, determined to make it outside, but his hand wrapped around her ankle and brought her down. He threw his body on top of hers. She struggled and hit him in the head relentlessly with the edge of the metal hand splint. She screamed as loud as her lungs would allow, earning a hard fist to the mouth. Blood trickled down her throat as she fought to stay conscious.

"Where. Is. It?" he snapped.

She feebly pointed to the stairway, hoping he would leave her there on the floor. But no, he grabbed her by the arm and pushed her up the steps and into the master bedroom, where he shoved her onto the bed. After checking the nightstand for a weapon, he made his demand again. Impatient, he drew back his fist and hit her again. Dazed, she pointed to the open laptop.

The relief on his face was visible as he took a seat and tapped his fingers over the keyboard. She watched as he hurriedly scanned through the information on the monitor, and systematically checked to determine if any of it had been copied to her hard drive. She shifted to the edge of the bed. He pulled a gun from his pocket and motioned for her to stay put. It became clear to her he didn't plan to leave any evidence, or witnesses, behind.

———

Chad pulled into the lot of CiCi's complex and parked. As he passed her Jeep, he stopped. His body went rigid as he took notice of the car parked next to hers. Adrenaline pumped through his veins as he pulled out his cell phone and raced toward the entrance. "Mark! I've found Rex Hoyt. I need backup at CiCi's, now!"

He paused at the open door before entering. His jaw clenched when he spotted the blonde hairs tangled in the splintered frame, and the blood smeared on the casing and floor. He withdrew his firearm and called CiCi's name. A muffled noise drifted from the second floor.

"Ripley Grove police!" he bellowed. "Rex, I know you're here. I have a warrant for your arrest. Come out with your hands up!" His demands were met with silence.

He stepped around the blood in the hallway and past the reddish handprint that trailed along one wall. A floorboard creaked overhead. He cautiously climbed the stairs that led to the upper level, his gaze darting back and forth. Every muscle in his body tensed. Beads of perspiration formed on his brow. Once he ascended to eye level with the second floor, he saw CiCi, beaten and bloodied, sitting on the bed. She glanced to her right, where he supposed Rex lie in wait. Chad motioned her to lie down, hoping to keep her out of the line of fire.

As he advanced, his ears picked up the slightest whisper of movement. An arm swung out from the bedroom doorway and fired. A framed picture on the stairwell wall behind him exploded, raining glass upon his head. He returned fire, as did the shooter. A searing pain tore into Chad's left bicep. A deep groan from the bedroom suggested Rex had been hit. Chad regained focus and kept his sight trained on the doorway to the bedroom. There was silence. He quickly repositioned himself on the top landing behind a tall, decorative plant. *Could Rex have slipped through the bathroom and into the spare bedroom?*

A rustle and muffled whimper of resistance answered his question. Rex appeared in the doorway with his arm wrapped around CiCi's neck. Blood from a deep gash on her forehead trailed down the side of her face and onto her shirt, and one eye had swollen shut. Rex himself looked like a crazed madman with his normally perfect hair sticking out at all angles. Several cuts on his face and hands were bleeding, and the blood on his forearm indicated he had been, at the very least, grazed by a bullet.

Rex held the advantage, and he knew it. Not only did he have a hostage, he had a gun pressed to her head—one that looked like the weapon stolen from her townhouse. Chad's heart lodged in his throat at the terrified look on her face.

"Get in here, and drop the weapon."

Chad kept his aim steady and stepped into the bedroom. "Reinforcements will be here any minute. Look at her. She can barely stand. You won't make it far with her in that condition. Let her stay, and take me." CiCi shook her head no, but Chad had no intention of giving her a say in the matter. This was one of those times he spoke of—that he would do whatever necessary to keep her safe.

Sirens wailed in the distance as Rex weighed his options. "Put the gun down and turn around."

Chad maintained eye contact as he held one hand up, slowly laid the gun on the floor and kicked it to the side. As Rex pushed CiCi to the floor, Chad whipped around and knocked the gun from Rex's hand. Rex fought back with a strong right hook, knocking Chad into the desk. Chad plowed into Rex's midsection, leading with his good shoulder, pinning Rex against a wall. Brutal blows were exchanged as the fight continued.

With her limited vision, CiCi couldn't tell who had the upper hand in the battle. She struggled to stay conscious despite the crippling pain in her head. The sirens outside were close, but not close enough. *I need to stay awake. I need to help Chad, if it's the last thing I do.*

Inching over to the bedside caddie that hung from the side of the bed, she slid her hand behind the library book and wrapped her fingers around the only help available. Her vision blurred, and the room swayed as she struggled to her feet. Chad lay on the floor, wounded and bleeding, his fingers mere inches from his weapon. Rex stood a couple of feet away, smirking and holding a gun pointed at Chad's chest.

She raised her arm, not knowing for certain if she could manage to fire the weapon left-handed. The movement caused Rex to turn. She pulled the trigger without hesitation, and a crimson stain blossomed on his shirt. As he faltered, Chad reached for his weapon. His hand wrapped around the gun as Rex fired, hitting her in the side just above the waist. Chad fired twice, hitting Rex in the chest and shoulder. Rex fell with a heavy thud. Chad struggled to his feet, kicked the gun from Rex's hand, and rushed to her side as she crumpled to the floor.

The sirens fell silent outside the building as Chad knelt beside her, his face etched with fear and worry. "CiCi, stay with me, hon. Help is here."

She gave a slight nod but found it impossible to stay awake. "Love you," she mumbled, her last words barely a whisper. Her hand went limp in his as she passed into a world that made her pain a distant memory.

FORTY-FOUR

Five days later, Chad sat on a wooden bench that overlooked a small pond and raked a hand through his hair. He thought about moving to a seat under a nearby shade tree, but lacked the energy to get up and move. He had gotten little sleep since Tuesday, and each day blurred into the next. Mark and Pete appeared and took a seat on either side of him. Mark patted him on the back and Pete handed over a hot cup of coffee. Chad thanked him and took a few sips. He sat for a time in complete silence, enjoying the strength of their presence.

He glanced at his watch, impatiently counting off the minutes until ten o'clock, and spoke to no one in particular. "She missed her court date for the restraining order."

Mark nodded. "I know."

Pete pulled a pack of smokes from his pocket and tapped out single cigarette. He held it between his fingers and stared at it as though it might light itself. After a minute, he shook his head and slipped it back into the pack.

Chad set his cup on the bench and gently rubbed his arm where the bullet had been removed. He hoped to be rid of the sling in a few days. His arm throbbed, but he was lucky—no bones were broken, no arteries severed. The RGPD had placed him on medical leave and, beyond giving his report, suspended his involvement with the case until those in charge could determine if he had followed protocol and had been justified in firing his weapon. Without looking up, he asked Mark how the interrogation played out.

Mark sighed and ran a rugged hand over his face. "The doctors transferred Rex out of ICU yesterday morning. After hearing about Norma's arrest, he was more than willing to tell his side of the story. By late last night, with his lawyer present, we had a videotaped confession."

"So he killed Julie Reynolds?"

"He did. Rex and Norma were romantically involved and embezzled a substantial sum from the company. When the temp agency sent Julie to fill in after Norma's accident, they assumed they had nothing to worry about. However, Julie wasn't as inexperienced as they thought. She discovered their secret, copied proof of their embezzlement to a flash drive, then blackmailed Rex. Julie expected to be long gone by the time CiCi discovered the flash drive on her key chain and brought the theft to the attention of the authorities."

Chad mulled the information over. "So, when Julie said the word *key*, she wasn't trying to say Keenan. She was trying to tell CiCi to look on her *key* chain. CiCi had the right idea all along. That flash drive was connected to Julie's murder. But why did Rex kill her?"

"Rex agreed to pay for Julie's silence, provided she leave town. When she doubled her asking price at the last minute, they argued. He went crazy and stabbed her in the heat of the moment."

"How did he link CiCi to the flash drive?"

"Something Julie said gave Rex the impression CiCi had proof of the embezzlement on a flash drive. Rex searched CiCi's cubicle at work, and later trashed her townhouse looking for it. Remember when someone snatched CiCi's purse at the restaurant?" Mark asked. "Rex had been after CiCi's key ring but didn't realize she had two. The one he needed was locked in the glove compartment of your truck."

"If I had only given those keys back earlier, she would have noticed the flash drive." Chad put his head in his hand and closed his eyes.

"You can't blame yourself. She wasn't allowed to drive and probably wouldn't have given the key ring a second glance."

"Where did Ashley, Rex's niece, fit into the picture?" Chad's leg bounced with impatience. He downed the last of his coffee and glanced at his watch again.

"Rex paid a visit to Ashley's apartment to find out what she knew about the flash drive. He lost his temper and scared her so bad, she decided to move in with a friend for the summer. Even now, she refuses to believe he had anything to do with either murder. After all, he was a trusted family member who supported her all through college after her parents died, and he promised her a lifetime position with the company after graduation."

"What about Bruce?"

"Bruce tried to do the right thing and it cost him his life. Bruce had been looking over the books when Rex showed up to remove some of his personal belongings. During a heated argument, Bruce realized what Rex had done and threatened to go to the authorities. Bruce went to his office to make the call, and Rex slipped in behind him, shot him in the head, and then tried to make it look like a suicide. He thought he would be in the clear with Bruce taking the blame for Julie's murder."

"Money can certainly bring out the worst in people," Chad said. "Everyone wants to live a life of luxury at someone else's expense."

"Unfortunately, Rex slipped Logan's surveillance detail. After we obtained the warrant for his arrest, we couldn't locate him quickly enough to save CiCi from…"

Chad nodded as he repositioned the sling's strap around his neck. "I don't understand. If Rex didn't find the flash drive when he trashed CiCi's place, why did he go back?"

"Rex paid a visit to Keenan to see if the flash drive had found among Julie's belongings. After he learned CiCi had also been looking for it, he offered Keenan a hundred bucks to call and ask if she'd found it. When she confirmed she had, Rex left and headed straight to her place."

270

"I kept her safe, but not safe enough," Chad said. He leaned back and rubbed a hand over his eyes. "And the gun CiCi used?"

Pete cleared his throat. "That was one of CiCi's recent purchases, and I'm the one who tucked it behind a book in that caddy thing on the side of her mattress." Pete nervously stroked his mustache as he explained how CiCi had conned him into helping her shop for a new gun. "I'm sorry, Chad. I should've told you about it."

"No need to be sorry." Impatiently, Chad checked his watch again. He stood, threw the empty cup into a nearby trash receptacle, and headed inside. Mark and Pete followed as he walked down the hallway. Megan and Tasha stood outside the closed door, their heads together in muffled conversation. Megan turned, teary-eyed, and gave him a hug.

A young woman scooted by with a vase of burgundy-red roses. They were nearly dead, and so dark in color they appeared to be black. The unusual arrangement immediately caught Chad's attention. He intercepted her before she reached the door.

"Are those for Winslow?" She nodded. "If you don't mind, I'd like to know who sent them." He pulled the gift tag from the floral pick and slid the small card from the envelope. "You reap what you sow" it said; the initials J. P. were scrawled below the message. He looked away while trying to contain his anger. He passed the card to Mark, then turned back to the girl. "Toss them in the trash, take them home—I don't care. Just get them out of here."

When she recovered from her shock, she scurried off with the flowers.

Mark stopped her. "It might be best if I get a picture first." He snapped a photo with his cell phone, and then slipped the sender's card into his pocket. "I'll look into this later."

Chad nodded, then checked his watch again. Nine forty-five. He turned his attention to the room. His heart raced. He reached for the door's handle, but pulled back, hesitant to enter.

Mark laid a reassuring hand on Chad's shoulder. "Go on. You'll need some time alone. I need to pay Rex a visit. While I do that, Pete can hunt us down a cup of coffee."

Chad nodded. Almost reverently, he opened the door and entered the room. A peaceful calm permeated the very air he breathed. He walked over to where his better half lay. Standing at her side, every detail seemed magnified. The soft waves of her hair spilled across the pillow. Long lashes rested against her cheeks like fine fringe. Make-up couldn't begin to hide the bruises on her face and arms. The stitches in her lip had turned black. Above her swollen left eye, a row of neat stitches closed the three-inch gash. The very sight of her in that condition broke his heart.

Tears fell as he slowly turned his attention to the flowers spread around the room. He pulled a card from each arrangement, read the sender's name, and smiled at their thoughtfulness. It looked as though everyone who knew and loved her had sent flowers.

FORTY-FIVE

CiCi opened her eyes at the sound of a muffled sneeze. Chad stood with his back to her, reading a card from one of the many flower arrangements on the window ledge. She studied him for a moment. He seemed thinner somehow. His broad shoulders sagged, and a sling cradled his left arm. The ordeal had taken its toll on him, and her heart ached for what he'd been through. She glanced at the clock on the wall and shifted to a more comfortable position. "I didn't expect you until ten."

Smiling, he turned and came to her bedside. "I couldn't wait. I didn't mean to wake you."

"My first shower felt wonderful, but it wore me out." She looked away, then self-consciously pulled a lock of hair to cover the stitches in her forehead. "I wasn't quite ready for you to see me like this."

"You'll always look beautiful to me." His eyes were filled with love as he gently took her hand and pressed it to his lips.

"Is that the best you can do?"

"I don't want to hurt you."

She cupped the side of his face with her hand. "Kiss me like you mean it."

He bent his head and kissed her softly. Each kiss grew more

intense than the last, until he pulled back and rested his forehead against hers. "I love you so much. I thought I would lose you after—"

She placed a finger over his lips. "But you didn't."

They kissed again, but were interrupted by Nurse Hattie, a middle-aged five-foot bundle of energy wearing scrubs. She entered the room, shook her head and chuckled as she set a bundle of gauze and a roll of tape on a bedside tray. "This may be a private room, but it's not *that* private. Mr. Cooper, I hope you remember she needs to rest. Don't go getting her excited or upset, or you'll have me to deal with." She smiled, then marched over to the bed and patted her patient's hand. "Let's get these fresh bandages on your head before the respiratory therapist gets here. The doctor has also ordered another CT scan."

"Maybe I should go with—"

She fixed Chad with a look of someone in charge. "Like I told the two gentlemen waiting outside, she'll be ready for visitors in about an hour. I'll call your cell when she's back."

He sighed. "Fine." Leaning down, he gave CiCi a parting kiss. "I'll grab Mark and Pete and head to the cafeteria for a snack."

Ninety minutes later, Chad returned. "There's someone waiting outside. Are you feeling up for a visit?" She nodded, and Chad raised a hand and beckoned to someone in the doorway.

Pete entered with a cup of coffee in one hand, and a cookie in the other. "I can't tell you how happy I am to see you, missy. And by the way, the cookies here don't hold a candle to the ones you make."

A small smile played across her lips as she raised the head of her bed to a sitting position. "Thank you, and thanks for the beautiful flowers, *Detective Mason.*"

Pete choked on his coffee and turned his gaze on Chad. "Well, *boss,* I guess you decided to come clean."

Chad chuckled. "She would've found out sooner or later."

Pete faced CiCi with a wary look on his face. "We still friends?"

"Of course. Although, it's disappointing to know you're not a handyman. Now I'll have to find someone else to..."

"Don't worry about your place, missy. I've taken care of it. Of course, you might notice a loaf of banana bread missing from your freezer." He grinned sheepishly.

"Thank you, and speaking of that, I'll be expecting you to stop by every now and then. I have a few new recipes I want to try as soon as I'm able."

"With pleasure." He took a seat on the small couch next to Chad and entertained her with a lighthearted tale or two. A short time later, he left, assuring her there would be plenty of opportunities to talk in the future.

She thanked him for coming, then settled in for a short nap. When she awoke, she picked up the TV remote and pressed a button. The screen remained blank. "Chad, the TV is broken."

"It's not broken. The doc had the signal disconnected to this room. He doesn't want your mind over-stimulated right now."

Unhappy with the answer, she frowned. "So, what am I supposed to do?"

"Rest and let your body heal."

She ate a bland lunch while Chad read her an interesting article from the newspaper. Hattie returned to check her vitals, and an aide brought a stack of get-well cards, which Chad also read to her. Then, from out of nowhere, the tears began to flow.

"Sugar, what's wrong?" Chad asked, jumping to his feet in a panic. "Are you hurting? Do you need the nurse?" She shook her head after each question. He fetched a cool, damp washcloth from her bathroom and wiped her face and neck with slow, gentle strokes. "Close your eyes and try to steady your breathing. It's not unusual to have emotional ups and downs after a head injury. It'll pass."

Late that afternoon, Mark poked his head in the doorway and motioned for Chad to step outside. When Chad returned, he asked, "You up to having another visitor?"

She nodded, and Mark entered the room.

"How are you feeling?" he asked.

"Other than a persistent headache, I'm feeling a little better every day."

"It's always a positive sign when they kick you out of ICU."

After a bit of small talk, she looked at Mark. "Have you seen Rex?"

His gaze swept the room. "Looks like a flower shop in here. You have a lot of people who care for you."

"You didn't answer my question."

He stiffened, then looked at Chad, who shrugged ever so slightly. CiCi had never understood their mysterious, silent way of communicating. Mark turned and looked out the window, while Chad studied his boots.

"Well?"

Mark stared at her for a moment, as though weighing his options. He breathed out a heavy sigh. "You'll find out soon enough. Rex died of his injuries an hour ago."

"Did I…?" Her question hung in the air.

"No, but no one would blame you if you did. You shot him in self-defense."

She nodded, but her emotions teetered on the edge. The knowledge that another co-worker was dead was too much to bear. She broke down into deep, heart-wrenching sobs. Chad rushed to her side and rang for the nurse. Hattie hurried into the room, shooed the men into the hall, and shut the door. Ten minutes later, Hattie left and Chad returned to her bedside.

"Where's Mark?" CiCi asked when he entered the room alone.

"He got a call and had to leave. Besides, Hattie said you need to rest. She's restricted you to one visitor at a time for the remainder of the day, and that visitor will be me."

"But…I had questions." Her eyelids suddenly felt heavy, and she could barely keep them open.

"They can wait." Chad reached over and tenderly stroked her cheek as she drifted into a peaceful sleep.

FORTY-SIX

Ci slipped the blue dress over her head, then reached behind her back and tugged the zipper up as far as she was able. She inspected her reflection in the full-length mirror, first turning one way, then another. It didn't hug her body as well as it had in the past. She'd lost weight since the attack but decided to wear it anyway. The dress had always been Chad's favorite.

Butterflies fluttered in her stomach. Tonight would be her first big outing with Chad since her release from the hospital two months ago. Her recovery had been slow, but the doctors were pleased with her progress. She still tired easily, but the frequency of her headaches had tapered off substantially and she hadn't had a dizzy spell for several weeks.

She slipped on her shoes, then went to the bathroom to do a final check of her makeup. She glanced in the mirror and smiled at the image that stared back. As time passed, she had begun to accept her "new" look. Gone were the deep bruises, the swollen eye, and the stitches. She touched a finger to the side of her forehead and traced along the raised scar. It served as a reminder of just how lucky she was to be alive. With the right lighting tonight, it would barely be noticeable. She dusted the shine from her nose and added another layer of mascara before heading downstairs.

As she entered the kitchen, the doorbell rang. She paused to adjust the strap on her shoe, expecting Chad to enter, but he didn't. Curious, she went to the door and peeked through the peephole. She opened the door and her heart skipped a beat at the very sight of him. Chad wore a tailored suit, checkered dress shirt with a coordinating tie, and a polished pair of black boots she'd never seen before. "Wow. You look especially handsome tonight. New boots?"

"Thank you. And yes, they're new. Genuine Raleigh lizard."

"I think your boot collection might rival my trove of sunglasses."

He chuckled. "You might be right, but I couldn't resist. The salesman said they would be perfect for a special occasion. I believe tonight qualifies." With a glint in his eyes, he bowed slightly and produced a stunning bouquet of red roses from behind his back. "For you."

"How pretty. Thank you." She gave him a kiss, then took the flowers and walked toward the kitchen. "Let me put these in water."

He followed. "I certainly like the view from here."

She turned on the tap and raised an eyebrow. "What do you— oh! I nearly forgot. I'll need help with my zipper." After she arranged the flowers to her satisfaction, she turned her back to him and lifted her hair off her neck. He slowly pulled up the zipper, then rested his hands on her shoulders. His simple touch sent a shiver down her body. He tilted his head and placed a tender kiss on the side of her neck, then worked his way up to her ear lobe.

"You look beautiful," he whispered.

She closed her eyes and enjoyed the moment, until the alarm on his watch sounded. They both laughed and broke apart. "Is that our cue to leave?" she asked.

"I have a table reserved at The Angus Steakhouse." He extended his arm. "Shall we?"

A short time later, they sat at a table for two on the portion of the terrace that overlooked the twinkling lights of the city. With the overhead awning retracted, they had a perfect view of the night sky.

They talked over a wedge salad, filet medallions, grilled asparagus, and mashed potatoes. About halfway through her meal, she pushed her plate aside.

"I'm so full, I don't know if I'll have room for dessert."

"What?" A look of panic flickered across his face, but it disappeared as quickly as it had surfaced. "Perhaps you would like to dance, and have dessert a bit later?"

Not wanting to disappoint, she said, "That sounds wonderful. I'd love to try their white chocolate cheesecake drizzled with dark chocolate. Would you order while I freshen up?"

When she returned, they walked hand in hand to the large outdoor patio. Music filtered from the outdoor speaker. He slipped an arm around her waist and pulled her close. Their bodies fit as though they were made for each other. She rested her head against his shoulder and sighed with contentment as they swayed to the music. Several nearby couples followed their lead and began to dance under the stars.

He whispered, "Do you know how much I love you?"

She lifted her head and gazed into his eyes. "Yes, and I love you. I never thought it was possible to love someone as much as I love you."

A couple of songs later, the waiter motioned to Chad, who tucked her hand in the crook of his elbow and escorted her back to their table. "I think you'll be glad you stayed for dessert."

The waiter brought a cup of coffee for Chad, then promised to return shortly with her cheesecake. Chad's hand shook slightly as he raised the cup to his lips. He straightened, then reached across the table and took her hand in his, and looked upward.

"There's not a cloud in sight. How many stars do you think there are?"

She tilted her head and became mesmerized by the sea of twinkling lights in the sky. "It *is* beautiful, isn't it? I'd be at a loss to guess how many. Oh, look—a shooting star."

"The brightest star in my universe, CiCi, is *you*. Your smile and infectious laugh light up my world. Every moment with you is an adventure, and I want to spend the rest of my life with you. I want to make a home with you, have children with you, and grow old with you."

Their eyes met and her pulse quickened. Suddenly, the waiter appeared and placed a small covered tray in front of her on the table. Chad dropped her hand. With a sly grin on his face, he nodded toward the tray. "That looks promising."

The waiter removed the lid with a flourish, then stepped aside. She smiled as her gaze feasted on the beautiful presentation. She lifted her fork, but stopped when something caught her eye. Her heart thumped with a nervous excitement as she gave the plate a 180 degree turn. Her fork fell to the table and her eyes widened. The words "Will You Marry Me?" were artfully written in chocolate around the perimeter of the plate. She looked up, only to find Chad's chair empty. Around the terrace, heads turned. To her left, Chad knelt on one knee, a ring box in his hand. He gave her a dimpled grin as he slowly opened the lid.

"Will you marry me, Cecilia Marie Winslow, and make me the happiest man on earth?"

Her smile turned to shock. "Wait!"

A hush fell on the onlookers.

"Is that…?"

"Yes, it is." His grin widened as he removed her grandmother's wedding ring from the box and slipped it on her finger. The center diamond, flanked on either side by a deep blue sapphire, sparkled like the stars overhead.

"How…where did you get it?"

"Your mother gave it to me a month before she died. She asked what my intentions were, and I promised to give it to you, one way or another. I added a custom wedding band. The set now represents the perfect blend of the past and the future—our future."

Her eyes brimmed with tears of happiness. Audible sighs echoed across the patio and cell phone cameras flashed. She held her hand out and stared at the symbol of his unconditional love. "It's perfect," she whispered.

Chad beamed, then stood and pulled her to her feet. "Is that a 'yes'?"

Without any hesitation, CiCi wrapped her arms around Chad's neck and gave him a kiss guaranteed to dull the shine on his fancy new boots.

DOUBLE VISION IN RIPLEY GROVE

A RIPLEY GROVE MYSTERY, BOOK 2

CiCi's face beamed with happiness as she emerged from the dressing room and stepped onto the raised platform. She turned one way, then another to view the one-of-a-kind wedding dress from different angles. *This is the feeling I wanted to have. The dress is perfect... well, almost perfect.*

Rebecca, the consultant, noticed the slight hesitation. "Let me bring in the owner. With a few changes, I'm certain she can give you the dress of your dreams."

As Tasha and Megan, the maid of honor and bridesmaid, oohed over the latest selection, the sound of footsteps drew CiCi's eyes to the mirror's reflection of the doorway behind her. Rebecca entered first, followed by a petite woman in her mid-fifties who wore a bold yellow tape measure underneath the collar of her silk blouse. The floral print skirt fluttered when she walked, and her hair, the color of golden wheat, fell in a soft bob just below her jawline. A captivating smile highlighted her flawless skin and clear blue eyes sparkled behind a pair of chic eyeglasses.

Rebecca moved aside. "Miss Winslow, I'd like you to meet Katherine Bliss, owner of Blissful Creations."

When the owner's gaze caught first sight of the dress, she sucked in a sharp breath and clutched a hand to her chest. Her smile faded as she turned an icy glare on her employee. "Get her out of that dress and bring it to my office. Now!"

CiCi tensed and Tasha's and Megan's eyes grew wide at the outburst.

Turning a deaf ear on the consultant's apology, Katherine Bliss composed herself and shifted her attention to the bride-to-be. Suddenly, her face drained of color. Her eyes filled with tears as she lifted a trembling hand toward CiCi's cheek. "Jenna? Jenna, darling, is that you?"

CiCi shook her head. "I'm sorry, but you've mistaken me for someone else."

Mrs. Bliss stared as if frozen in time. Without saying a word, she turned and disappeared down the hall, leaving everyone in shock. CiCi followed Rebecca back to the dressing room, where her trembling fingers unzipped the dress and carefully returned it to its hanger. Overcome with emotion, the consultant fled the room in tears.

CiCi's stomach tightened in a knot as a million questions raced through her mind while she dressed. *What just happened out there? How could this beautiful dress bring such joy to one person, and distress to another?* While bent to adjust the strap on her shoe, she noticed a small tag attached to a thin silver cord lying on the floor. She picked it up and threaded the tag around the neck of the padded hanger. She turned the tag over, expecting to see the price. Instead, she saw the name "Jenna Bliss" written in calligraphy. That's when she realized there had to be more to the story.

CiCi carefully tucked the dress inside the clear plastic garment bag and zipped it shut. With the bag draped over her arm, she made her way down the back hallway. She rapped on a door with the owner's name painted across the upper panel. A muffled voice from within told her to enter. "Mrs. Bliss? Rebecca left, so I thought I'd bring the dress to you myself. I'm sorry if my trying it on caused a problem."

CiCi stepped over and hung the bag on one of the coat rack's brass hooks. As she did, Mrs. Bliss turned. The charming smile and flawless face from earlier were gone. The woman who stared back now had puffy, red-rimmed eyes, mascara streaked cheeks, and a runny nose. Her shoulders sagged with a heavy sadness.

CiCi stepped forward and took the box of tissues from the corner of the desk and placed them in front of the distraught woman. Taking the hint, she plucked out several tissues and blew her nose as delicately as possible. Once she regained her composure, she squared her shoulders and met CiCi's gaze.

"I apologize for my behavior today. I strive to make every bride-to-be feel special, and their shopping experience unforgettable. I failed you in that regard. If you'll give me another chance, I'll personally see that you find exactly the dress you're looking for. But that particular dress is not for sale. Not now, not ever."

Available From Your Favorite Bookstore or Online Retailer

ALSO BY SHIRLEY WORLEY

Double Threat in Ripley Grove

Double Vision in Ripley Grove

ABOUT THE AUTHOR

Shirley Worley and her husband Bert have been married since 1969 and reside in Merriam, Kansas. They have two adult children and love spending time with them and their families. She retired from the U. S. Postal Service in 2009 with 39+ years of service. She enjoys bowling, working puzzles, playing Farkle, and having lunch with her sister every Saturday. Shirley is an avid reader, always in search of the next mystery that will keep her awake far into the night. Some days, you may find her sneaking in a nap after her husband goes to Panera for his afternoon cup of coffee.

Readers can reach Shirley through her publisher:
ShirleyWorley@epublishingworks.com

Photo by: Joseph Keehn